T.M. CROMER

To Kate Bateman & Sara Whitney:
Thanks for always coming through for me.
I'm thrilled you're part of my tribe.

CHAPTER 1

*B*eing dead wasn't so bad. Preston Thorne was enjoying the experience—for the most part. Mainly he missed his family. His daughters. His siblings. And now, with the addition of grandbabies in the mix, he missed them, too. Or rather, the idea of spoiling them. He'd yet to meet or cuddle one.

But dead was dead, and the Goddess liked to constantly remind him of this. Especially whenever he borrowed her scrying mirror or escaped the Otherworld to watch over the Thornes without her permission.

All in all, it wasn't a horrible existence. Mainly because he was able to spend time with the woman he loved. The only problem was that the love of his life was, in fact, the love of his *afterlife*, and she wouldn't give him the time of day or... er, well, any time... period.

Current case in point, the lovely Selene Barringer was going about her day, feeding the ducks at Isis's favorite lake and refusing to acknowledge his existence. She was naturally reserved and kept to herself, but Preston also suspected she wanted nothing to do with a Thorne witch. His family had caused her enough problems when she was alive and was the direct reason for her death. On the day she died, she'd attempted to help them escape the evil clutches of her asshat half brother, Victor. For her disloyalty to him, she'd received a bullet to the head.

Preston intended to find a way to rectify the situation. Perhaps convince Isis to restore all Selene had lost. The only reason he hadn't done it yet was because all the color in his life would bleed dry when she left, and he'd truly be dead.

"Stop following me, Mr. Thorne."

Her cool, cultured English accent reminded him of his widow, Aurora—now the fiancée of his brother, Alastair. Both women had that same smooth way of putting a man in his place with the lift of a well-groomed eyebrow.

"I'm simply enjoying the morning, Ms. Barringer." He worked hard to keep the grin off his face. Annoying her had become the best part of his day. "The view is spectacular from here."

She straightened from her bent position, flicked back her long, glossy black hair, and glared over her shoulder.

Preston was male chauvinist pig enough to admit he loved the fire lighting her chocolate-colored eyes and the way her irritation increased her breathing, thereby making her breasts heave.

"Go view some other spectacular sight. This lake is mine for the moment."

"I wasn't talking about the lake," he said with a chuckle.

Really, she'd set herself up for that one.

"As if I didn't already recognize your sly innuendo for what it was," she scoffed.

As she stalked to where he sat on the stone bench, she reminded Preston of a twitchy feline. If she had a tail, it would be flicking a warning. Standing before him with her graceful and delicate hands fisted on her hips, she was magnificent. When she was annoyed by his very existence, like right now, her fiery passion would simmer beneath the surface and she stole the air from his lungs.

He wanted nothing more than to sweep her into his lap and show her what she was missing with her stubbornness. But he wouldn't. He wasn't a damned caveman. Also, she'd likely bloody his nose if he tried. Despite being dead, pain was still pain when someone decided to plant a fist in your face.

When Preston rose to his full height, he assumed she'd retreat a step or two. Instead, she held her ground, tempting him—no, *daring* him—to make a move. Although her lips were pressed together in her pique, they were infinitely kissable. If he allowed himself to go there in his mind, he could almost imagine their pillowy softness as they opened to allow him entry.

Selene was tall for a woman. At nearly five feet ten, she could almost look him in the eye. Her body was willowy, like a dancer's, yet oh so sultry. If she ever decided she wanted him in return and took him up on his millionth request to go on a date, Preston would drop to his knees and kiss the hem of her skirt. Or any other part of her she desired him to kiss.

"Have dinner with me tonight." He already anticipated her denial, and when it came, his disappointment was keen.

"Bugger off," she said just before stomping away.

"Was it something I said?" he called after her, grinning as she gave him the finger.

"Her continued refusal is a mystery."

Preston didn't bother to turn around. He'd sensed the Goddess's presence the moment she appeared. "She's warming to me. I can tell." With a deep, regretful sigh, he faced Isis.

Today, she wore a dress the color of pale pistachios, belted with a gold filigree chain draped loosely around her waist. The hem of her dress swept the ground, hiding what he knew would be perfect bare feet with bright-red toenail polish. The woman loved her cosmetics. She'd once told him it was the one thing—besides mini lemon cakes—she loved most about the human world.

With her upswept black hair and her bold but feminine features, she reminded him a lot of Selene.

"I could influence her," she offered.

"*No.* Her mind should be her own. Anything else is tantamount to rape, my beloved queen. You, of all people, would hate having your will removed."

"It wouldn't be like that. I would just convince her to have dinner with you. Maybe add the suggestion that she would enjoy herself."

Preston's lips twitched. "I appreciate your offer, but I'm enjoying the chase. Oddly, I believe she is, too. In the end, I'm certain my antiquated way of wooing her will win her over." Although he was from a bygone era when flirting could dance on the edge of risqué, he felt it was important to remain a gentleman in dealing with women. He believed they deserved respect and the right to make their own decisions. "Besides, where's the fun in having you make her fall for me?"

"You sound exactly like your brother. He has to do things the hard way, too."

Her dry tone made Preston laugh. Nine times out of ten, Alastair deferred to Isis. But when he didn't, the Goddess was fit to be tied. "What's he done now?"

She waved a hand as if to reject the idea his brother was caught up in a new problem. Still, she couldn't hide her concern.

"Exalted One, what can I do to help?"

"I've a mission for you, and I expect you to carry it out without delay." She gave him a stern look.

"Of course." *Don't I always?*

"Not always. There's been a time or two when you've gone off on your own for the sake of your family."

He shrugged. It wasn't as if he could deny it. And although she'd get in a barb here or there, Isis never truly reprimanded him for his side trips to deliver a message under the guise of it coming from the Goddess herself.

With a mock scowl, he said, "Stop reading my mind. It's creepy."

She smiled, and the sun shone a little brighter in the Otherworld. Even the ducks turned their faces to the light. As quickly as it appeared, it was gone. "I'm going to miss you when you leave."

"I'm never gone for long."

Frowning, she crossed to stand at the shoreline.

He followed at a slower pace. No amount of prodding would get her to tell him what was on her mind. The Goddess kept her cards close to her chest at all times. If, or when, she decided to show them, she would. Otherwise, Preston would be left in the dark—as he'd been on so many occasions before—until she dropped her four aces on the table and left him scratching his head over his two pair.

"You might as well tell me," he urged. "Whatever it is, we'll deal with it together, my queen."

With a heavy sigh and a heavier frown, she faced him. "Evil has invaded the Otherworld, and I know not the source."

Mentally, Preston reeled from the news. As calmly as he could, he asked, "What sort of evil, and how do we eradicate it?"

"It happened recently. I believe it was attached to the Enchantress when she crossed over."

Isolde de Thorne had died after an intense battle with her son, Damian. After years as the Aether—the one responsible for the balance of good and evil in the magical world—she'd given in to the Darkness. When she became infected by its poison, the deterioration of her mind began, and she'd morphed into one of the most deadly creatures imaginable. As an Enchantress Aether, she'd been able to seduce other witches and warlocks into sacrificing themselves so she might gain their magic. The first time she was entombed, it had taken a god, a goddess, and the most powerful beings from both sides of the veil to subdue her. When she'd awakened almost two hundred years later, she'd gone completely mad and had taken on Damian as well as Preston's family before she was finally stopped.

"Is there no way to tell?" He rubbed a hand along the back of his neck. Evil on this plane should be nonexistent. If it leached into their world, the situation was dire.

She gave a tight-lipped shake of her head. "If you weren't so enamored with Selene, you might have noticed it on your own."

"I don't understand. What does my flirtation—"

Isis waved a hand, effectively cutting him off. Without answering his half-spoken question, or what was left of it flitting about in his head, the Goddess began to pace.

In all his time in the Otherworld, he'd never seen her worked up to this degree. "Tell me, Exalted One. How may I assist you?"

"You and your blood relations are the only ones it doesn't seem to affect. You, Nathanial, your father… the entire Thorne male line, in fact. Yet the women are not exempt." She rubbed her arms and gazed up at him. "I feel it. It's trying to attach itself to my power."

"Perhaps it's why I've been blind to it before now." Preston looked at his surroundings with new eyes. On the far side of the lake, a couple argued, and the sound of the woman's palm cracking against the man's cheek was as loud as a gunshot in the otherwise quiet, peaceful park.

"You see?"

"I do." Perhaps it was why Isolde, a distant cousin, had been infected in the first place. A sense of dread settled in his chest. "Where is Isolde? Can she shed light on this?"

"Doing her penance as my handmaiden."

Preston barked out a surprised laugh. "You made her a servant? For how long?"

"Until I deem her reformed," she snapped. Once again, she frowned, as did he. They knew her temper was an oddity. "I haven't alerted her to the problem. Should she become infected a second time, and should she find a way to regain her powers, she'll be unstoppable."

"If this Evil is here, my queen, shouldn't we find a safe place for you until I rip out the source?"

"I cannot leave until it's time to destroy it. I risk bringing it with me to another plane." Unease rested in her kohl-lined amber eyes.

His heart rate picked up, and he looked over his shoulder in the direction Selene had gone. "Is she…?"

"Not yet. But it won't be long." Isis touched a hand to his cheek. "Take her and go with my blessing, Beloved One."

"What are you saying?"

"If you stay here to fight this, you risk losing your one true love. I promised you a happily ever after, Preston Thorne."

CHAPTER 2

Selene stopped walking about halfway to her destination. The crack of a palm on a cheek jerked her from her musings, and she spun back toward the lake, curious to see what or who had caused the sound. She half feared Preston Thorne had irritated another woman with his ridiculous flirting. Despite his ungodly good looks, he was a nuisance, and he had a tendency to appear anywhere Selene was.

Insufferable man!

Her lips curled.

Okay, yes, he could be annoying, but he was also a charming rogue. With his rumpled auburn hair and those twinkling eyes of his, he woke butterflies in her lower belly whenever he looked her way. She'd never let on how much she enjoyed their dance. Not for a good long while anyway. They had time. It wasn't as if they were going anywhere. They were dead.

Her mouth tightened as she remembered the circumstances that had brought her here. Thankfully, she didn't remember the pain of the bullet wound.

But the slap she'd heard couldn't be attributed to Preston. Across the distance, he stood deep in conversation with Isis. With a suddenness that halted Selene's lung function, his head whipped up and he looked in her direction as if he sensed her regard. His troubled expression sent her heart into overdrive. The man was never serious. If something was upsetting him now, it couldn't be good.

With fresh eyes, she turned in a circle. All around her people had begun to argue over the most inconsequential things. A shiver of awareness swept through her. Without a doubt, the balance of the Otherworld was off. To what degree, she couldn't say, but perhaps it was why Isis and her favorite consort were holding such a bone-chillingly serious discussion for anyone to see.

Selene started back the way she'd come, stumbling momentarily when she realized Preston was running for her as if his life depended on it. She met him halfway.

"What is it?"

"We have to go. *Now*."

When he reached for her hand, she allowed it for a second until her mind caught up with her body's disturbingly eager desire to touch him. Only then did she pull away. "I don't understand. What's happening?"

"Selene, I don't have time to explain. I need you to trust me when I say we have to get the hell out of Dodge."

She looked over his shoulder and noticed Isis watching them intently. When the Goddess nodded, Selene understood this wasn't another of Preston's flirty games. She gave a single incline of her head in return and allowed Preston to lead her away.

"Where are we going, Mr. Thorne?"

"Back to the earthly plane."

Due to the endless years of showing no emotion when her psychotic half-brother had made her life a living nightmare, she was able to keep the shock from her expression.

Preston led her to the sorting area of the Otherworld. The place where time stood still as a deity determined where a soul would end up after their life was over: the beauty of this plane or the hell of another.

"Wait here, Selene. Please."

Cautioned by the solemness in his cognac-colored eyes, she could only nod. His brand of charm lent to teasing and fun. This serious side disturbed her.

"Where are you going? Is it safe?" She was showing too much concern for a man she professed to dislike and whom she continually brushed off, but she wasn't going to be coy at a time like this.

He flashed a cheeky grin, squeezed her hand, and darted off, leaving her to begin the worrying process.

She remembered the day she'd first seen him. Not here in the Otherworld, as one would assume, but at an estate auction to bid on one of her mother's favorite art pieces. Everything they'd owned that wasn't destroyed in a house fire had been sold off after her mother's death, leaving Selene a pauper as well as homeless. She'd been a mere girl, and yet Preston had stood out among the sea of eager-faced adults who were there to scavenge through the wreckage of her life. In her gray, lifeless world, he'd been a wave of bold color. When he'd entered the room, he commanded attention.

Other than initially to squat down in front of her and express his condolences regarding her loss, he'd paid her no mind. Or so she'd believed at the time. Years later she'd learned the "small bequest" she'd inherited from a unknown distant relative was, in fact, an account he'd set up for her to live off while she pursued an education. Why a stranger would do that for a child related to his brother's greatest enemy, she'd never know. But it bespoke a kindness she'd not encountered to that point in her life. She'd only known pain and abuse, especially at her brother's hands.

She supposed she should have a conversation with Preston someday and thank him for securing her future. He'd never mentioned it—almost as if he'd forgotten the kindness that meant the world to her—and he acted as if he had no expectations of repayment. The man was an enigma.

She wondered whatever had happened to the antique artwork. Had he turned around and sold it to another? Made a tidy profit? For sure, he'd acquired it for a steal.

As she strolled around the garden of the sorting area, she

became nervous. Although it was true all time was suspended here, the same couldn't be said of the world outside this garden. Preston could be gone mere minutes or for countless hours, maybe even days, while she waited.

The curtain surrounding the garden was of a mystical nature. Not a true cloth material, but an invisible barrier that didn't allow one to see beyond what the Goddess decided to project. So anywhere Selene looked, there was no life other than a handful of deer and the occasional rabbit in the distance.

When the curtain shimmered and a golden light formed the outline of two people—a man and woman—Selene held her breath, praying Preston was returning to her.

He stepped through the magical wall with his great-grand-mother, Evelyn. The haggard expression on his face tugged at Selene's heart, and she rushed to his side. "What's happening, Preston?"

Surprise lit his eyes as he stared down at her. She knew the reason; she'd never called him by his given name in all the time they'd known each other. She saved it for those long, lonely nights by herself, when no one was around to lecture her on the impropriety of her amorous thoughts about him.

"Selene, this is Evie. She's going to accompany us on our journey. She's a Guardian. Or was, at least." He smiled down at the petite blonde woman with great affection. "Although, I suppose your powers have been returned to you once more for this particular problem, haven't they?"

Evelyn looked harried and upset. Preston's teasing manner did nothing to relieve the tension around the other woman's eyes. "For now," she said briskly. "Let's get this done. I don't want Nathanial facing this threat alone."

"Isis has assured me he's immune to the Evil. It's why he needs to be here to try to temper its impact." His words were meant to soothe, but Selene suspected Preston, too, was having a hard time believing Nathanial would be safe. "But I agree, we need to stop this in its tracks."

"Why am I here?" Selene asked, curious what she could do.

"You're the brains of this operation, my dear." Some of his standard charm returned, and it made her stupidly happy.

Shoving down her ridiculous giddiness, she looked at Evelyn for confirmation.

Preston's great-grandmother wasn't like a normal elderly person. In fact, she appeared no older than forty. Her skin was unlined, and her golden hair was shiny, falling in long wavy layers around her shoulders. She had a body to cause envy. Even after children, she didn't possess an ounce of extra weight. Of course, this might be due to her Guardian status. They needed to be in top shape to fight, if ever the need arose. Ordained by the gods, Guardians were the badasses of the magical universe, second only to the all-powerful Aether.

"He's partially correct," Evelyn said with an affectionate smile for Preston. "We can use any input you might have to find a way out of this. But primarily, he's taking you to safety."

Selene glanced between them, a frown tugging her brows down. "Why me? Why not pull your other family members out?"

His impatient scowl was her answer. "We don't have time for this, Selene. We have to get to the Aether and make a plan of attack."

"Damian Dethridge?" Selene had heard of the man, but she'd never had the opportunity to meet him in person. The dastardly Victor had feared incurring the wrath of so formidable a being.

"Yes. We hope he has some insight." Evelyn must've heard the unease in her voice because she smiled. "He's actually a lovely young man." She shot Preston a side glance then looked back at Selene. "Maybe I'll introduce the two of you. He seems like your type of fella."

"Over my dead body," Preston growled.

Selene was hard-pressed not to point out he *was* dead.

Evelyn caught her eye, and the two women shared a smile.

"I saw that." He gave them both a warning look. "Now come. Every minute we spend in here is an hour we've lost in the Otherworld."

They followed him to a large oak tree, where he drew a knotted birch wand from the cross-body bag he sported. He reached for Selene and gestured for Evelyn to hold her opposite hand. Then he traced a symbol visible only to him and wordlessly cast his spell. Fire flared to life, burning away the invisible shield covering the tree's opening. One moment, they were inside the holding area; the next, they were stepping out of the tree into an exquisite English garden next to an enormous old manor house.

"Where are we?" Selene whispered, unsure exactly why she was being quiet other than it felt like she should.

PRESTON SQUEEZED SELENE'S HAND, REALIZING THIS WAS ONLY THE second time she'd ever let him touch her. It seemed like he'd been chasing her for a millennium in the Otherworld, but it took the downfall of their home for her to give him pay any attention to him. And still, she questioned why he chose to save her. The woman was completely oblivious to his deep feelings for her.

"We are on the Drake estate," Evie answered for him. A sad expression tightened her features as she looked up at the house she'd lived in for over half a century.

"Are you all right, Evie?"

She released a heavy sigh and nodded. "It's surreal being back here after all this time."

Evelyn had followed Nathanial shortly after his death. Although by earth's standard she'd been deceased a year, time wasn't the same across the dimensions, and to her, it would feel as if she'd been gone a good ten or more.

"I know you'd like to visit with Mackenzie and Sebastian as much as I would, but we don't have a spare minute to lose."

"I know, darling boy. Let's go find Damian and figure out what's contributing to this mess."

Before they could set off toward the neighboring estate, the terrace doors were flung open and a small sprite of a child tore down the stone steps. A beaming smile graced her perfect little face, and her black hair flew behind her as she raced toward them.

"Grandma Evie! Grandma Evie!"

Evelyn met her halfway and swept the girl up in her arms. "Sabrina!"

"I knew you were coming. I told Papa, but I'm not sure he believed me."

The Aether appeared at the top of the stairs. Tall, dark, and dangerous, he moved like a jungle cat, ready to pounce should someone threaten his child. "I always believe you, beastie."

Damian's dark hawk-eyed gaze zeroed in on Selene, and Preston heard her sharp intake of breath.

"Wow," Selene murmured.

Her reaction was no different than that of thousands of women who'd entered Damian Dethridge's orbit. Still, a tiny jab of jealousy punched Preston, and he had to fight the overwhelming urge to remove her from the Aether's presence. Instead, he released her hand and stepped forward to greet his long-time friend and distant cousin.

"Preston. It's good to see you again." Damian pulled him into a hug and heartily pounded on his back. "Not that I'm not thrilled you're here, but I'd like to know why. Especially with so powerful a Guardian by your side." He hugged Evie tightly and kissed her forehead. The affection they shared was that of mother and child. Understandable, since she'd raised him after Nathanial stole him away to safety, protecting him from Isolde, who'd craved his unlimited power.

"Evil has invaded the Otherworld," Preston stated grimly. "It's poisoning the place, and Isis is worried it will decimate her plane. Not to mention, obliterate the existing souls."

Damian stiffened and gave him a sharp look. "That's what she said? Obliterate the souls?"

"Yes. Do you know what it means?"

"It sounds like my mother is back to her wicked ways."

"No. I don't think she had anything to do with it this time."

Preston met his contemplative gaze. "I'm not saying it didn't piggy-back a ride, but it's not controlling her. Isis was sure of it."

"Lovely. So where the bloody hell do we start?"

"Your guess is as good as mine, Dethridge. But I suggest we call Alastair. If anyone can find trouble without trying, it's my brother."

CHAPTER 3

$\mathcal{A}$t precisely 2:37 in the morning, Alastair's phone rang. He wasn't one prone to nerves, but to be awakened in the early hours wasn't normal, and his heart beat faster at the disturbance.

Lifting the receiver of the house phone, he growled, "What is it?"

"Is that any way to greet your brother, Al?"

Preston's amused voice registered, and a wave of happiness washed over him. "*Pres?* Is it really you?"

"It is. Isis has allowed me to come play for a while."

Alastair snapped his fingers, illuminating the room with soft glowing candlelight. "Why didn't you teleport directly here?"

"And be murdered by your henchmen on my first day as a living, breathing human being again? I think not."

Scrubbing a hand over his face, he glanced to his right. His wife, Aurora, eased into a sitting position as she rubbed the sleep from her beautiful sky-blue eyes. She looked delightfully rumpled with her delectable body wrapped in only the ivory sheet and her short, mussed hair. The cobalt spikes shot out in every direction and made her appear like a startled—but extremely sexy—faerie queen.

Alastair clasped her hand and placed her palm flat on his chest, over his heart. "Where are you, Preston?"

Rorie's fingers spasmed, and her eyes rounded. It wasn't every day you learned your deceased husband was alive. Alastair's mouth curled in wry amusement at her reaction.

"I'm at the Drake estate. Damian and Evie are with me."

"Evie?" His great-grandmother had passed last year, breaking the hearts of all who had known and loved her. "She's back, too? What about Nate?"

"I'm afraid not. It's a long story, but we need your help."

"Right." Alastair shoved aside the weight of disappointment. "Can you spare me ten minutes?"

"Yes, but only that."

The seriousness in Preston's tone sent a sizzle of awareness dancing along Alastair's spine. Whatever was going on was dire, indeed. "I'll be there in five."

"Thank you, Al."

"It's so good to hear your voice, little brother."

"I've missed you, too."

After hanging up, he tried to get his wayward emotions under control. Preston's return harbored bad news, but despite the threat, Alastair was thrilled. Shoving aside his euphoria, he shifted to face Rorie.

Love shimmered in her incredible eyes, and he couldn't resist the urge to drop a soft, lingering kiss on her mouth. Satisfaction unfurled inside him when her lips clung to his and her amorous energy caressed him. This was the part of being an empath he enjoyed the most—feeling her honest emotions. She never needed to put on an act, and should she try, he would see right through it.

Alastair ran tender fingertips along her jawline. "Preston needs us, my love."

"You say 'us' as if he specifically asked for me to join in your upcoming adventure," she said dryly. Her crisp English accent added to her witty comeback.

"Are you telling me you want to stay behind?" Alastair knew full-well she'd never let him go on his own. Not because she didn't trust him, but because after nearly twenty years apart, it was difficult to face even a few hours of separation.

Her answer was to stand in all her naked glory and snap her fingers.

Alastair sighed his disappointment when she covered up her beautiful trim body. "I hate when you do that."

"Answer you by getting dressed?"

"Dress in general."

Rorie laughed and reached for her cellphone. "Should I call the others?"

By 'the others' she meant his sister, GiGi, and her husband, Ryker, knowing Alastair had his brilliant son, Nash, on speed dial if it came to a crisis.

"Not yet. Let's see what Preston's about first. If he decides we need to involve the entire family, we will."

PRESTON WAITED ON THE EXPANSIVE TERRACE FOR ALASTAIR AND Aurora, knowing she'd show up with his brother come hell or high water. In this case, the former. He didn't have long to wait.

Around him, the air crackled, and seconds later, the curtain of space was folded back to allow them through the rift between Alastair's home and the Drakes' estate. His older brother created static in the atmosphere whenever he teleported. Alastair was a formidable warlock with the power to seriously wound using only an elegant flick of his wrist. Preston, although similarly gifted, never had the temerity to pit his abilities against his older brother's.

Preston grinned in welcome.

Alastair wore a matching smile.

They embraced for the first time in over a year.

"It's good to see you, Pres," Alastair said gruffly. "Goddess, how I've missed you."

"I'll admit I spy on you from time to time. It makes me feel better, knowing you're all safe." He shrugged. "I'd leave the Otherworld in a New York minute if it meant protecting any of you. But never tell Isis, or she might remove my magic."

"She's aware." His brother's tone radiated his certainty on the matter.

"I've no doubt."

They shared a laugh.

Next, Preston greeted Aurora. After giving her a tight hug, he held her hands out to her sides to visually inspect her person. She'd gained a few pounds in the interim and appeared to be in good health. He was happy to see her looking hale after the extended stasis. "You are still as stunning as ever, Rorie."

"And you're still very much a flatterer, Preston, dear." She unclasped their hands and pressed hers to his shoulders as she kissed his cheek. "Welcome back."

"I'm not sure for how long, but come on. We have a lot to discuss, and there's someone I want you to meet."

One of her dark brows lifted. "She's important to you. I can tell by your tone."

"Yes." He grimaced. "Apparently, I had to die to find my one true love."

"I'm crushed." A smile teased her lips, and she leaned her head on his shoulder as she wrapped her arm through his. "Here I thought I was your one true love."

"You have the honor of being my first love," he assured her gallantly.

Aurora and Alastair had been enamored with one another from the time they were young teens. They'd separated for a few years when her family returned to England, but the two of them found ways to sneak and meet in private. But when Alastair had disappeared during the witches' war and was later presumed dead, Preston and Aurora had grown close in their mutual grief. After a time, they'd married and began a family.

Alastair's sudden return had shocked them all. There was never any real contest between the brothers. Although Preston's feelings for Aurora were those of a man for his wife, she'd never loved him in return, or perhaps she had, but not with the all-consuming passion she held for Alastair. And when his brother had come for her, she'd run away with him.

Alastair stepped forward and slapped him on the back. "Stop all this drivel, or I'll lose what's left of my dinner."

Preston gave him a light elbow to the ribs. "Shut it, Al. I'm flirting with my wife."

"Ex-wife. And not to put too fine a point on it, but you're dead, so technically, she's your widow."

With a snort of laughter, Preston led them into the house.

Selene was perched on the settee, taking tea with the Drakes and Evie. Her exotic eyes widened when she saw Alastair.

"Ms. Barringer." His brother inclined his regal blond head. "A pleasure to see you again." A look of profound sadness passed across his face. "I never had the opportunity to thank you for your sacrifice. My children are my world, and your selflessness saved them. I cannot tell you how sorry I am you had to pay such a great price."

"Water under the bridge, and all that." Selene waved a hand. "How is Holly? I imagine her child must be a toddler by now, no?" She frowned slightly, a mere ripple of her brows. "It's so difficult to tell time between our worlds."

"Holly is doing well. Young Francesca is a handful and the apple of her father's eye," Alastair assured her with a warm smile. "Quentin calls her Frankie, and I'm sure it's to spite me. My granddaughter turned out to be as mischievous as he is."

"More so," Aurora added.

The warmth of Selene's smile struck Preston right in the chest, and he sucked in a sharp breath. He didn't miss Alastair's amused side glance.

Damian stepped forward to greet Alastair and Aurora, as did Sebastian and Mackenzie Drake.

Alastair took the spare moments to hug their hostess and slap their host on the back.

Preston suspected that whenever his brother witnessed the couple's interactions, he felt the euphoria of a well-made match.

Mackenzie and Sebastian were his latest success story. To first encounter them—the flamboyant American model with the shockingly bright red hair and the intensely driven English laird—one wouldn't think the two would mesh well. But they'd be wrong. The two were a match made in heaven, and the loving looks they sent one another proved it. Of course, their romance had been helped along by his busybody brother, Alastair. The man couldn't resist matchmaking.

Sabrina beamed at the group from her place beside the hearth, where she was holding the Drakes' infant daughter, Delaney. And Alastair—skilled at making everyone feel important—approached Sabrina's chair. He accepted the baby from her to cradle close to his chest.

"You've got the touch, child." He smiled down into her pixie-ish face. "She's radiating happiness. Mackenzie couldn't have chosen a better person to help care for Delaney."

Sabrina basked in his praise, and her joy filled the room, making all the adults smile.

Alastair kissed the baby's brow and handed her back to Damian's daughter. "I'll leave her in your capable hands."

"Mama's going to have a baby next, you know," she said without looking at her father. "I'm going to take good care of him, too."

Preston glanced at Damian in time to see his pained expression. He'd heard the Aether and his wife were estranged, but Sabrina seemed positive there would be a reconciliation.

With sardonic resignation, Damian shrugged. "I've learned not to question the beastie's premonitions, no matter how fantastical they seem."

"Maybe we should pull her into our planning meeting," Alastair quipped.

While Sabrina appeared interested, Damian quickly vetoed the idea. He ushered everyone to the sitting area on the far side of the room, away from his daughter.

"Preston tells us there's trouble in paradise... or rather the Otherworld. What can we do to help?" Rorie accepted a cup of tea from Mackenzie and perched beside Selene on the settee. Two English roses. Each holding a special place in Preston's heart. A portrait should be painted of them just so.

As if she sensed his stare, Selene turned her head and meet his admiring gaze. Her expression was unreadable, and Preston had the pressing desire to ask Alastair if he could channel her emotions. Anything to give him a hint as to her feelings for him. But he'd never invade her private thoughts. She deserved better than that, and Preston wanted her to open up to him all on her own.

Color crept into her cheeks, and she shifted to focus on the conversation around them.

He decided he should tune in, too, if he wanted to do what he was sent here for.

"Preston said Isis doesn't believe the threat is from my mother," Damian was saying. "I'm not sure I agree."

"The Evil wants everyone, Papa," Sabrina called out. "You have to eat it, like Grandma did to save the witches."

They all whipped around and stared at her.

"Excuse me?" Damian's face was startlingly pale.

"You have to eat the Evil," she said matter-of-factly.

Silence reigned for an entire minute. No one removed their focus from her.

"Does anyone know what the devil she's talking about?" Alastair kept his voice low enough that only those closest to him could hear.

Sebastian cast him a sharp look. "Not the foggiest notion. We are talking about the convoluted ramblings of a seven-year-old child." His comment earned him an irate look from Damian. Sebastian simply grinned and shrugged. "Have *you* been able to decipher everything she's predicted?"

"I've never known the baby Aether to be wrong," Mackenzie said, expression thoughtful.

"Sabrina's a Seer, or what is known in our world as an Oracle. There is only one. After the one dies, another is reborn to take their place. The last Oracle I knew was killed during an uprising at the turn of the previous century. So, if my daughter is forewarning of an event, you can pretty much take it to the bank." Damian crossed the room and squatted beside her. "It looks like you're going to be included in the planning meeting after all, beastie. But I don't want you to be afraid. I'll be with you."

"I know, Papa." Sabrina stroked a finger down her charge's cheek, then carefully rose to her feet.

Mackenzie met her halfway and accepted her daughter. She smoothed a hand down Sabrina's shiny hair and kissed the crown of her head. "You're the best babysitter."

"It's true," the child said. "Del doesn't cry for me."

"Cute nickname, kid. I think I'll keep it."

"You can't, Mack. It's Nate's name for her." Sabrina shrugged. "But he doesn't mind if I use it, too."

Mackenzie and the others looked as confused as Preston felt.

Damian was clued in to what was going on. "She doesn't mean Nathanial. She means her future brother."

"Nate and Del will be best friends. They'll sav—"

"Sabrina!" Damian scooped her up in his arms and placed a finger lightly over her lips. "We talked about this. You cannot go around regurgitating future events to everyone. It has the potential to alter timelines."

She pulled his hand away with a frown. "But Nate and Del will always be together, Papa. They always are, and they—"

"I think you're purposely missing my point, you gremlin. So let me put this in a way you'll understand. Stop telling people what you know. It simply isn't done." With a shake of his head, he touched his nose to hers. "You will be the Aether one day, my love. What you say and do has importance. You must only feed people the information relevant to the moment, or you can influence an outcome."

"But Del is now," she said stubbornly.

"But Nate isn't," he retorted.

A twinkle entered her dark eyes, and she grinned. "But he will be after tonight."

Damian tossed her over his shoulder so she hung upside down.

"That's it. I'm shipping her off to boarding school. Who knows of a good one? A place where they serve kale and broccoli."

"No, Papa! Not broccoli!" Sabrina squealed her displeasure. "You said I'd never have to eat broccoli. Ever!"

"That was before." He shot the group a wink. "Now, you have to suffer the consequences."

"I'll be good. I promise!" she shouted against his back.

"I don't know." Damian's voice sounded unconvinced, and he battled a revealing smile.

Mackenzie handed Delaney off to Sebastian and reached for Sabrina. "Give her to me. You've tortured my favorite baby Aether long enough. I'll have to soothe her with ice cream now."

"Oh, thank you, Mack! Thank you!" Sabrina wrapped her skinny arms around Mackenzie's neck.

"Don't thank her too quickly, my darling beastie." Damian pasted on a gleeful grin and flared his eyes wide. "The ice cream is broccoli flavored."

"Nooooooo! You promised, Papa."

"Fine, fine. But if you are going to have ice cream, you must conjure enough dessert for everyone."

A devilish look crossed her tiny face. "For everyone? And they have to eat it?"

"I'm not eating anything that tastes like pickled pigs' feet. Do away with that thought immediately."

Sabrina laughed as Mackenzie led the way to the dining room. Their group followed, with Preston and Selene taking up the rear.

"You look a little sad, Mr. Thorne." Her voice was soft, with a hint of concern.

"Sabrina reminds me of my daughters when they were her age."

Selene nodded her understanding. "It's lovely to see such closeness in a family. I never had anything remotely similar."

"Not with your mother before she passed?"

She gave him a sharp look. "So you *do* remember? I had my doubts you did."

"I do now. I hadn't prior to my demise." He grimaced. "However, as Isis's consort, I was granted access to what she believed to be relevant knowledge."

"I see." She seemed to be weighing something and finally gathered the courage to ask. "Why did you create a trust for a child you didn't know?"

"Had you had a representative and had there been more time, you might've sold the painting I purchased for ten times the amount I paid." He shrugged lightly. "It bothered me to think you'd been cheated out of your inheritance due to your desperate straits."

"You arranged for me to be paid what the piece was actually worth." She nodded as if she understood. "The school and the elderly woman who raised me? Those were from the trust you set up?"

"They were. As was the cost of the papers to forge your new identity."

"You knew my mother's death wasn't an accident, didn't you?"

"I scryed for the events of that night, *after* our initial meeting."

"And you made it look like I died in the fire to protect me?"

"Guilty as charged."

"Then I'm in your debt."

"No." He stopped her with a hand on her arm. "You owe me nothing, Selene. What I did for you that day, I'd have done for anyone in need. Until recently, I'd honestly forgotten about the incident. I paid Agnes a good sum of money to hide you from Victor and see to your care. She was hired to keep you cloaked and to send reports to my assistant." He felt a hint of embarrassment for not following up to make sure she, as a child, was safe. But thirty-plus years was a lifetime, and many other things in his life had gone belly up back then. Not the least was his marriage to Aurora. "I had no idea you were that girl until Isis told me, *long* after you and I met in the Otherworld. I never made the connection to your name."

"I find that difficult to believe."

"Believe it, my dear," Alastair said from where he leaned against the doorjamb. "My brother is a bit like an absentminded professor.

His plight was made worse by the arrival of a baby girl he was left to raise on his own."

She whipped back to face Preston. "It really is true?"

"Yes. By the time I gave it a second thought, many years had passed." He shrugged. "Apparently, you'd changed your name again after Agnes died, and since I assumed you were in hiding, I left you to your fate. I'm sorry."

A small smile played upon her lips as she leaned in and kissed his cheek. "You are nicer than I imagined."

CHAPTER 4

Selene didn't want to make Preston feel worse by telling him Victor had eventually found her. No one else needed to share her miserable memories. It was bad enough that she lived with the horrors dealt to her. Time and time again, her brother had pulled her into his vile schemes and made her life a living hell. Every chance she got, she'd circumvented his unscrupulous plans, but more often than not, she was forced to go along or suffer the consequences of her refusal.

Yet the moment she'd met Holly Thorne, Selene had felt compelled to help her. Perhaps it was the fierce, unwavering love the woman bore her husband, or maybe it was Holly's never-say-die attitude, but the admiration Selene had felt for her was strong.

In the end, she'd paid with her life for siding with the Thornes instead of Victor. Her half brother deserved no loyalty, and when news of Victor's demise reached Selene in the Otherworld, she'd lifted her wineglass to toast Karma. And when she'd learned it was at the hand of Alastair's future daughter-in-law, Selene had laughed and downed the rest of the bottle, sending blessings to each and every Thorne in existence as well as all their future babies.

She found it telling that Preston would care for a child he had no attachment to with no agenda or expectations. She'd meant what she said; he was a kind man. He seemed startled she'd noticed, and he stared down at her with something akin to confusion.

Tucking her arm through Preston's, she looked at Alastair and smiled. "Please, lead the way so we might join the others. I'm sure we all want this mess resolved sooner rather than later."

A blinding smile curled Alastair's mouth, and Selene had the distinct impression she'd passed a test of sorts. Wordlessly, he dipped his head in acknowledgment and moved away.

"I'm not quite certain what that's all about, but apparently, my brother likes you," Preston murmured. "It's always a good thing to be on the right side of Alastair Thorne."

"I'll keep it in mind for our future interactions." She gave his bicep a light squeeze. "Do you think we can conjure some lemon cakes with sugar drizzle? I've missed those most of all."

"My dear Ms. Barringer, you can conjure anything your heart should desire."

"You say the sweetest things."

"Oh, I'm happy to say bawdy things as well." He shot her a wicked glance. "If you'd ever let your guard down long enough, I'd go overboard with all the naughty suggestions."

"The one time I let my guard down, I ended up in the Otherworld," she said softly, hoping he'd understand it wasn't him she was rejecting. "My life wasn't conducive to allowing anyone in."

"And that carried over after death," he concluded, all teasing gone.

She tightened her fingers in response.

He covered her hand with his. "Perhaps you'll come to trust me."

"I'm trying."

"That's all I ask." He halted outside the large dining hall. "If you find you can't, I'll understand, Selene. It won't be easy for me to walk away, because of who I am and how I'm programmed, but I won't push you into a relationship you find abhorrent."

How did she tell him she wasn't repelled by him in the slightest, when the words seemed to stick in her throat? Instead, she did the only thing she could think to do—she kissed him. A single light, clinging kiss, applying just enough teeth to his lower lip to show she was serious with her love bite.

When he opened his eyes to stare down at her, they had lightened to a golden hue. The changing irises were a barometer of a witch's deeper feelings. The darker they were, the stormier the emotions within. To see Preston's this clear and bright was a beautiful sight to behold.

"It's mean, you know," he murmured huskily.

"What is?"

"Kissing me right before we're needed in there." He gestured to the double doors with his thumb. "I'm fighting the urge to teleport with you to the Drakes' maze."

Selene lowered her eyes and suppressed a laugh. When she could speak without a hint of her amusement, she asked, "What would you do when we got there?"

His eyes slowly ran the length of her body, and on the return trip, he lifted his hand. Fire flared from his fingertips as his gaze held hers. "What do you think?"

Shifting so her back was to him, she allowed her grin. "A bonfire?"

"Oh, something would be burning, all right."

She did laugh then. "Come on, you charming rogue. We have evil to conquer."

Inside the dining room, everyone was gathered at one end of the table. A ten-foot sideboard was littered with countless dishes ranging from appetizers to desserts. As Selene lifted a serving spoon to fill a plate, Preston presented her with a small tray of the lemon cakes she craved.

"They aren't as tasty as you," he whispered.

"But you barely got a taste," she whispered back.

"One was enough."

Before she could reply, Alastair joined them and stole one of the mini cakes for himself. "I don't mean to be insensitive here, but the sexual vibes the two of you are putting off are killing my concentration. Can you dial it back a bit for the sake of saving the world?" With a wink, he popped the lemony goodness into his mouth and strolled off, casual as you please.

Selene sputtered in her embarrassment as Preston laughed. "How did he… how could he…?"

"My brother's an empath."

"Ohdeargod!"

"Personally, I'm glad the 'sexual vibes' aren't all one-sided." As he walked away, he whistled. A jaunty off-key tune.

She didn't know whether to laugh or be irritated by his cavalier attitude. Glancing down at the lemon cakes, she giggled. The man was impossible, but she fancied him all the same.

Preston held out a chair for Selene, then took the seat next to hers. With her attention focused firmly on Damian, who was currently calling their meeting to order, she placed one of her beloved lemon cakes on Preston's plate.

He couldn't prevent his smile of satisfaction even if his life depended on it. Across the table, Aurora pressed her lips together, and he suspected it was to hide her own amusement. When she met his eyes, he knew it was true. Her approving gaze darted between the two of them before she flared her eyes slightly as if to say, "You're making progress, darling."

Aurora would forever be in his corner, just as he would be in hers. During their married years, they'd developed an unbreakable bond of friendship. Neither her seventeen-year stasis nor his death had destroyed it.

She suddenly became serious. "Thank you," she mouthed.

He frowned his question.

She formed the words, "For everything."

"You're welcome," he said soundlessly. He didn't know whether she referred to the last day of his life, when he'd saved her from drinking poison, or whether she meant the uncontested resolution of their relationship so she could be with Alastair, but it didn't matter. Whatever it took to make her life better, he would do. He owed her for their beautiful children and all the years she'd made his home a happy one.

"Preston."

He looked up in question when Damian called his name.

"For the sake of everyone, why don't you repeat your conversation with Isis? We all need to know exactly what we're dealing with here."

After Preston relayed everything verbatim, he paused to let his words sink in. The idea of lost loved ones on either side of the veil was terrifying, and they all needed to come to grips with the horror of the situation before moving forward.

"Why did Nathanial stay behind?" Alastair hadn't bothered to dress in his standard suit, but he instinctively reached to straighten his tie before he purposefully stopped his nervous habit. Anyone close to him would recognize the gesture for what it was—Alastair working through a problem.

Evie replied for Preston. "People were becoming aggressive toward one another. He hoped to keep the peace for as long as possible."

"And Mother?" His brother's eyes darkened to the deepest sapphire.

"I don't know, Al." Preston's continued guilt at leaving behind their remaining family was a cancer in his gut. "The rest decided to stay behind when I offered to bring them back. Days have passed for them since I've been here."

Aurora set down her fork and clasped Alastair's hand in hers. "When I returned to my body from my stasis, part of my soul was lost to the Otherworld. Are you suffering the same? Alastair has a way to help."

"No, Rorie, but thank you." Preston gave the group a cursory glance as he explained. "When a body is left behind on the earthly plane and the soul crosses from one side to the other then back again, it fractures. Our return..." He indicated Evie and Selene with his nod. "... wasn't the standard run of the mill. We were essentially resurrected by the Goddess with one of her spells. It's not the same as returning to a comatose body or a body that has been recently departed. We are soul whole."

"Excellent." Aurora cleared her throat. "That's excellent."

A pang of sadness struck him. It had taken Alastair four attempts to heal her spirit, and there would always be a piece missing. Preston hated her discomfort with the subject, but appreciated she was the first to want to help them should they be experiencing the same.

"Nathanial relayed to me the conversation he had with Sabrina in the holding area after the showdown with Isolde." Preston gave the girl a soft smile. "Was Isolde's necklace destroyed?"

"I made sure of it," Damian said with a nod.

Using her fork, Sabrina began to viciously stab her pastry. "I brought the Evil."

"No." Her father moved the plate and tipped her chin up to meet her gaze. "No, you didn't. The Evil was here long before you, my love. You will not take this on your shoulders."

"But if Grandma didn't die and if I didn't tell you to smash the stone, it wouldn't be free." A single tear trailed down her pale cheek, and Preston thought it the most tragic sight he'd ever seen. This small girl was shouldering the blame for a circumstance that was no fault of her own.

"Sabrina."

She looked Preston's way, and her lip trembled.

"You must understand this isn't on you, child. Promise me you won't take on such a heavy burden of guilt from something not of your own making."

"But if I hadn't gone with her—"

Mackenzie jumped up and hugged Sabrina. "No, kid. I was there. It was my body your grandmother possessed. You lured her away to save Baz, Evie, and Ryker. You were a hero that day, darling." She gave the young girl a stern look. "The Evil is a centuries-old darkness. I felt its malevolent tentacles trying to feed on my magic. You stopped it, Sabrina. *You* did," she insisted when the girl looked like she would argue the point.

"But it's going to hurt Papa," she cried.

Damian looked pale and shaken but resolute. He lifted his daughter into his arms and strode with her from the room. Amid her harsh sobs, his low rumble could be heard, although not the exact words. Preston assumed he was trying to soothe and reassure her, as a father was wont to do.

Alastair met Preston's gaze across the table. If Damian could be hurt by the Evil, they had a bigger problem on their hands than they'd imagined, and they both knew it.

Sebastian scrubbed his hands over his face and let out a weary sigh. "The peace was fun while it lasted."

Mackenzie snorted and crossed to the swinging chair holding Delaney. "I think it's time to call the family. We're going to need all the brainpower we can get to stop this thing. I've felt it, and it's relentless."

CHAPTER 5

Sabrina had Damian's neck in a death grip. Whatever she'd seen with her random visions had traumatized her to the point of hysteria. Her hot tears seared the skin. Not because they were toxic, but because each one represented her terror and he didn't know how to ease her fears in a way she'd believe.

All he could do was continue to walk the garden and rub her back, talking soothing nonsense as he went. Finally, when her sobs tapered off to the occasional hiccup, he eased down on a stone bench and hugged her close.

"There, there, my sweet beastie," he murmured. "It's going to be all right. I promise."

"You can't promise, Papa," she cried raggedly. Sabrina drew back and ducked her head, playing with the top button of his shirt. "You have to eat the Evil to save them all."

"You said that's what my mother did. Was that before she went crazy?" Although he needed to know the truth, he didn't want it. One hundred and ninety-three years after he'd written off his mother as a horrible bitch for giving in to her desire for more power, he was forced to question what had really happened to her.

If he hadn't been filled with resentment, might he have helped her find a way to be free of the demons possessing her sooner?

"Do you want to see?" Sabrina's large rounded eyes held trepidation, and Damian hated the misgivings he saw there.

"I suppose I need to, don't I?"

She simply watched him.

A child her age should never be forced to carry this kind of weight on her shoulders. She should be laughing and playing with her friends whenever possible. If he could've given her that gift, he would've, but their cursed bloodline made them grow up much too soon.

As he geared himself for the vision she would share, another thought occurred to him. "Beastie, how far back do you see as the Oracle? Is it just our family's history?"

"I can see back to when the Goddess was in her temple."

"That far, huh?" He forced a teasing grin.

His daughter didn't smile.

"Do you know when the Evil came to be, Sabrina? Was it as Mack said, and it's been here forever?"

"It's been here since magic."

"Since magic? As in, when Isis granted power to humans, or before, when the gods and goddesses were born?"

"The first witches. There were..." She paused and looked at her hands as if they held her answer. "...seven."

Seven? He knew of five: Air, Earth, Fire, Metal, and Water. "What are the other two?"

"Electricity and Aether."

"Of course." He nodded and looked toward the secret garden where his mother had previously been entombed. He'd never considered himself as an Elemental witch, but he supposed he should've. His bloodline manipulated all the elements and had been originally known as the Force. "Electricity isn't a common elemental today. I can't think of any witches or warlocks who have that power."

"There is still one, Papa."

"Who?"

"The Traveler."

The only remaining Traveler was Alastair's son-in-law Quentin Buchanan. Was he an electricity elemental? Damian had never heard that he was. Like Oracles, Travelers were rare, and they didn't all share the same ability. The last one he'd known had been killed in the war between their kind and the anti-witch faction known as the Désorcelers.

Castor.

Damian hadn't thought of his best friend for years. The pain of his loss was too great.

"Who was Castor, Papa?"

"I can't have a private thought with you around, can I, beastie?" He laughed at her sheepish expression. Until she was older, she'd have a hard time controlling the impulse to eavesdrop on another person's internal dialogue. Most times he could block her from his own, but he'd let down his guard when she broke down earlier and never put it back up.

"Alexander Castor. He was a great man and my dear friend. He died about a quarter century ago or more. It's hard to remember exact dates at my age."

She patted his cheek. "He's not dead."

"What?" An icy wave of shock crashed over him.

"He lives in the trees by Alastair's house."

It wasn't often Damian was overcome by fury. He couldn't afford to be. If he let his temper reign supreme, he could decimate an entire city within minutes. But the itchy, bubbling sensation growing inside him was the telltale sign he was about to "lose his shit" as Mack would say. That bloody bastard Castor had let Damian believe he was dead. *Who does that?* They'd been best friends for over fifty years!

The wind around them picked up, and the branches of the mighty oaks standing vigil over the estate began to sway. The green leached from the lush grass lawn as the blades flattened against the earth, and the water in a nearby fountain began to steam.

When he found Castor again, he was going to beat him bloody!

"Don't be cross, Papa."

Damian was startled from his tumultuous thoughts by the hand Sabrina placed at the center of his chest. The tendrils of her healing magic wrapped around his heart, stroking and soothing the inferno raging inside him. It took an effort, but he shoved aside his hurt and the awful sense of betrayal. He still might plant Castor a facer when he saw him again, but Sabrina didn't need to know that.

"Thank you, beastie." He grimaced when he saw the state of the gardens. "I suppose I need to clean this mess up, huh?"

She nodded. A second later, she grinned. "Or go to your room without supper. That's what happens to naughty little witches when they misbehave."

He squinted his eyes in warning. "Or baby Aethers who think it's funny to sass their fathers."

Jumping to the ground, Sabrina clasped his hand. "Come. I'll help you."

Damian couldn't contain his laugh. Many times, after she'd made a proper mess of her room, he'd do the very thing she just did and offer to help her.

"You see? I'm going to be a good big sister to Nate."

"You *really* want that brother, don't you?"

"He sav—"

"Nope!" He held up his free hand to stop her from revealing future events. "No spoilers."

"It's not a film, Papa."

"I suspect, in your mind, it plays like one." He surveyed the damage to the fountain. A crack ran from the base to the curls on top of the cupid's head. Water sputtered and spewed from the opening, indicating Damian had ruined the mechanics of the statue. "I'll take care of that monstrosity while you give the greenery around us a boost of life."

"Maybe Cousin Baz won't miss it," she said with a skeptical look at the chubby cherub.

Damian choked back another laugh. Her humor was a perfect

blend of his and Vivian's. "Go on and take care of the grass and trees. I'll repair this. Then you can show me what I need to know about my mother."

They worked in silent harmony until the garden was back in perfect order.

When Sabrina joined him at the fountain, he crossed his arms over his chest and tilted his head as he contemplated the ugly design of the piece. "I feel as if he needs a mustache."

She giggled and flattened her hand over her mouth.

"No?" He heaved a heavy sigh. The time for frivolity was over. "I need to know what happened to my mother now, beastie."

They crossed to the bench, and Sabrina wordlessly touched his temple.

A kaleidoscope of reverse images took him back to his infancy. Although she looked fresh-faced and innocent as she gazed down at the baby in her arms, Isolde was hundreds of years old at that point. Her sweet, soft voice crooned a lullaby, and she brushed the downy hair from his temple. The glow of the firelight reflected off the strands of her shiny black locks. Love shone from her dark eyes, and she was, in a word, exquisite.

Damian felt his breath hitch. Emotions he thought long buried tried to surface.

His infant self let out a faint mewl and flailed his fist. Damarius Dethridge stepped from the shadows and joined Isolde by the hearth. The firelight caught off his golden hair as he squatted beside her and took Damian's tiny hand in his.

"Our boy," he said softly. "He's fierce."

Isolde's face softened as she looked at her husband. "Yes. A true warrior."

"Like his mother."

She laughed and readily accepted his kiss. Temple pressed to temple, they returned their attention back to Damian. "Is it possible to love a child too much?" A hint of fear had entered Isolde's voice. "I worry we won't be able to protect him from all the evils of our world."

"Did you not just claim him to be a true warrior?" his father teased.

"He shall be the strongest Aether to exist. I feel it here." She placed a fist against her heart.

"If you feel it, then so it shall be, my love." He cradled Damian's fragile head in one large scarred hand. "Our son will be the best of men. With our combined power and wisdom, he cannot be anything less."

"I pray to the Goddess your words are true."

Damian was so deep in the past, he jerked when Sabrina tapped his temple a second time. His mind took a leap and ended up two years after the first scene.

This time, he was a toddler. His arms were extended upward, his hands held within his father's, and his feet were atop Damarius's as they stomped across the lawn toward Isolde. About ten feet from her, Damian squealed, and his father released him to run to his mother. She laughingly scooped him up in one arm as she tickled him with the other.

The scene was stunning in its entirety. A perfect family unit.

Sabrina's finger tapped his temple once again.

The next vision showed five-year-old Damian hiding in the corner of the salon as his father yelled obscenities at his mother. Pain and confusion were on her face, as if she didn't understand where the ugliness was coming from. Damian's younger self charged across the room. Anger screwed up his tiny visage, and his fists were balled.

"Leave her alone!" he yelled at his father. He'd been ill-prepared for the hand cracking across his cheek, and he stumbled backward. The fullness of his mother's skirts was the only cushion for his fall.

Isolde rose, a fierce lioness ready to defend her cub. The atmosphere of the room became thick with intent, and a crackling sound filled the air around them. "You *dare* strike my son?"

Damarius paled.

She flung her arms wide, and he flew across the room. The

sound of his skull hitting the scenic mural wall behind him was sickening, and Damian cried out.

"Never touch my child again, or I will smite you from existence." She stood protectively over him, her fury causing the candle flames to flicker and dance. Furniture rocked back and forth as the window sashes rose up and down, slamming harder with each closing. *Do I make myself clear?*

Damarius's wary gaze darted to Damian, who knelt on the floor behind her, before flicking back to her. "I swear by the Goddess, I don't know what came over me, Isolde." Deep regret was etched on his father's face. "Forgive me, my love."

The room settled around them as she crossed to him. "I will forgive you this once, but should you ever hurt him again—in any way—I *will* kill you."

A sob from young Damian drew their notice, and Isolde rushed to console him.

"There, there, beastie," she whispered. "You're all right." She hugged him tightly to her breast. "You were a brave boy, defending your mama. Thank you, my darling."

Damian met his father's eyes across the room. Even as he watched, a look of hatred flashed across Damarius's hard face.

The Evil had infected his father first!

"Now you see why she did it, Papa?" Sabrina asked. "She ate the Evil to save the witches."

CHAPTER 6

*D*amian wore a sickly look when he returned to the house, and Preston worried what could have possibly upset the Aether to such a degree.

"Where's Sabrina?" Mackenzie asked.

"I brought her home to Vivian. The subject matter is a bit heavy for a child. Even a baby Aether, as you call her." Damian gave her a half-hearted smile.

Sebastian poured two fingers of scotch into a tumbler and handed it off to Damian, who accepted it with a single nod of his head and downed it in one shot.

Damian held out the glass to his host. "Thank you, Baz."

"Need another?"

"No. I fear I'll get lost in the bottom of the bottle if I start."

"That bad?" Preston asked before taking a sip of his own drink.

"Worse."

"Do you want to tell us now or wait until the others arrive?" Alastair shoved away from the mantle and crossed to join their group.

Preston noticed his brother often distanced himself when an emotionally fraught situation was happening. He frequently needed to separate from the group so he wouldn't be overwhelmed.

Alastair paused about three feet away and rubbed his neck. A sure sign he was picking up on the Aether's deeper, more intense feelings. "I suspect it's not a pretty tale."

"The Evil had infected a third of the witch community by the time the Witches' Council approached my mother with the problem. She and my father were isolated out here on their estate, away from the happenings in the magical world." Damian scrubbed his face with his hands. "When word came, my father went to discover what the problem was, leaving Mother to care for me. He became infected, too."

"Am I to understand Isolde didn't seek the Evil out?" Preston leaned forward. "How did she end up with all of it inside of her?"

"Sabrina was able to show me. It happened when I was approximately five or so. Father was becoming worse in his behavior, more violent in his dealings with Mother and me. I believe she consumed it to protect us both." He used his thumb and forefinger to rub his eyes. Looking more soul-weary than Preston had ever seen him, Damian gave a small, sad smile. "She loved us. Who knew? She paid for it in unspeakable ways, not the least of which was madness."

Evie touched his arm. "But she wasn't innocent. She murdered countless people, my dear boy."

He lifted her hand to kiss her knuckles, then held it to his cheek. "No. The Evil inside her did that. It destroyed her sanity until she had no choice but to feed it. Nate saved me, Evie. We suspected it, but not to the extent I now know." Sadness weighed his shoulders down. "Mother would've killed me had Nate not stepped in when he had. She had the presence of mind to send me away. To warn me against trusting her. But eventually, she'd have found me to syphon off the power that darkness craved."

Preston rose and crossed to the French doors as the others peppered Damian with questions. Alastair joined him on the terrace.

"Sabrina said Damian needs to 'eat the evil.' The idea of him trying to contain it makes me nervous as hell," he told his brother. Turning to face him, Preston ran a hand through his hair. "I'm worried, Al. Damian is naturally more powerful than Isolde was. As rumor had it, she was nearly unstoppable when she was possessed. If Damian consumes this darkness, he may be harder to defeat should he go off the rails."

"I know. The questions rolling about in my brain will keep me up tonight."

"They're probably the same ones I'm asking myself. Does he go to the Otherworld to fight this? Should we let the Otherworld be decimated by the Evil? What happens if there is no afterlife for our kind?"

"All the souls scheduled to reincarnate would simply cease to exist," Alastair said heavily. "But my true fear is this: if some manage to escape and be reborn, will they bring the darkness with them?"

"Christ! I hadn't thought that far ahead." He moved to the stone railing and rested his elbows on top. He'd been in this garden a time or two. The last was with Isis as recently as past year to oversee the restoration of Mackenzie's broken mind. He'd forever associate this beautiful landscape with strife. "How do we defeat this enemy, brother?"

"It'll be a challenge, for sure."

Preston chuckled at Alastair's droll tone. Glancing over his shoulder, he had to ask, "Does nothing truly faze you? I swear you sound as if you're looking forward to the fight."

"It eases the tediousness of life."

"Tediousness? You have your one true love back after nearly two decades. You should enjoy the peace for a change."

"The truth?"

Preston nodded.

Alastair grimaced. "The quiet makes me nervous. I become twitchy when things are going smoothly."

The knowledge struck Preston as the words sunk in. His brother's life had been fraught with danger from the onset. He knew nothing else, and when he wasn't gearing up to battle a new threat, he was at a loss as to what to do with himself.

"This might be more than any of us can handle, Al. It's bigger than our combined power. You know that, right?"

"Yes. I fear I do." Alastair copied Preston's pose with the exception of the tumbler of Glenfiddich in his hand. His brother sipped his drink before he spoke again. "It took the most powerful—the Goddess, a god, and witches from both sides of the veil—to put Isolde in her tomb. When she tried to use Mackenzie as her meat suit, Damian was able to defeat her all on his own." He turned slightly to meet Preston's worried gaze. "You're right to be concerned. We won't be able to stop him after he consumes the Evil."

"What's the solution?"

"Damned if I know." Alastair sneezed, and Preston curled his hand, throwing out a pulse of magic to stave off the wave of locusts that usually accompanied his brother's swearing. The fact his brother forgot himself enough to use harsher language was a cause for concern. "You'd think Isis would've removed your ability to summon a plague of insects with a simple sentence enhancer."

Alastair chuckled. "It keeps life interesting."

"You never told me why you and your offspring were cursed."

"Why is anyone cursed by the gods or goddesses? I displeased the wrong person."

"Isis?"

"Ra."

"I'm going to need that story, brother."

"Maybe someday." Alastair took a long pull of his scotch.

Preston grunted. "You're still putting people off with that damned vague response."

Before his brother could reply, the atmosphere around them grew thick, and they both straightened. The weight of the air indicated multiple incoming witches.

When the newcomers appeared, joy infused Preston's entire being. Standing at the base of the terrace steps were his daughters,

Autumn, Winnie, Spring, and Alastair's daughter Summer. They frequently arrived as a unit.

Summer had grown up believing she was Preston's daughter, a full sibling to the others. When she'd found out his brother was actually her father, she was fit to be tied. He'd never forget the betrayal on her face. But being the forgiving soul she was, she saw her way past it, and she still called him "Dad." Preston experienced a warm pleasure that she'd turned up to greet him.

Autumn, Preston's firstborn and a snarky female version of him, stood tall and proud, with one brow lifted as if in challenge. When she saw him, a wide grin split her face and she put her hands on her hips. "I suppose it only took the apocalypse to bring you back, Pops."

"I don't know why you didn't think of it before now," he quipped. He rushed down the stairs and gave her a fierce hug. "As my favorite troublemaker, you could've whipped one up sooner."

She laughed and hugged him again. "Please tell me you're back forever."

"I honestly don't know. We need to get through this next week first." He caressed her cheek before turning to Winnie. She was the spitting image of Aurora with the exception of her hair length. She wore her thick black locks long and wavy. The cobalt highlights were a recent addition, and he liked the touch of whimsy.

"Winter Rose, my beautiful girl. If what you're holding are those delicious cinnamon rolls you usually make, I'll declare here and now that you're my favorite. Hang the others."

She handed off the container to Summer and ran into his embrace. "Then consider me your favorite. Welcome home, Dad."

He felt tears burn behind his lids as he held her tight. "Thank you, child."

Releasing her, he shifted his attention to his youngest. The Thorne Jewel, they liked to call her. Spring was stunningly beautiful in all her many facets. Face, figure, spirit, but most importantly, her brilliant mind. "Hello, baby girl."

Although twenty-eight, she didn't object to his "baby girl" endearment. They both knew he would continually view her as such despite the fact she'd grown into an independent, intelligent woman who everyone turned to when the chips were down.

"Hi, Daddy." Her blinding smile chased the clouds from his sky and made him forget the terrible tragedy taking place inside the Otherworld. Spring's magic was her genuine love of people. Of him —the absentee father. She ran to him and jumped. He caught her with no effort and swung her around as he'd done when she was a child. This had been their ritual any time he returned home from a business trip. "I'm so glad you're back. I missed you."

"I missed you, too," he said gruffly. He kissed her forehead, finding it difficult to let her go.

Eventually, he did, and he turned to Summer, who was on the verge of laughter. She'd been in the process of slapping Alastair's hand away from the container when Preston caught her notice. Passing the plastic tub off to Spring, she gave stern instructions to keep it away from her "hog-face" father. Finally, she turned to Preston.

"Hey, Dad." Her large blue eyes shimmered with happiness, and she wrapped her arms around his neck as he lifted her off the ground. Summer was the tiniest of the sisters, but she was the one with the biggest heart and the greatest magical power—although she often had a difficult time controlling it. She was getting better with Alastair's guidance.

"How's your zoo?" Preston asked after setting her back on her feet.

She snorted a laugh. "You mean my animal sanctuary and veterinary practice?"

He grinned. "Yes, that."

"Great, actually. Coop is in charge of security now that he's retired from his sheriffy duties. And by security, I mean wrangling wayward animals, but Morty and Eddie seem to be toeing the line."

Preston shuddered when he thought of her child-like chimpanzee and that damned perverted elephant. He opened his mouth to reply when a chattering from her jacket pocket distracted him.

Without looking down, she pulled out her familiar, Saul, and propped him on her shoulder. "I forgot he was there when I hugged you. I'll hear it now!" She grimaced as she shot a side glance at the squirrel. "Coop hates when I leave this one behind."

"Is Saul still threatening to castrate the elephant?" Alastair asked around a mouthful of the cinnamon roll he'd managed to steal.

Summer laughed and nuzzled her head against her pet. "Daily."

"Can't say as I blame him." Preston accepted the treat Winnie handed him and sunk his teeth into the pastry. His eyes rolled back in his head as he savored the rich, sweet taste of doughy goodness combined with the cream cheese sweetness. "You know, you missed your calling, Winnie, my dear. These would make you a fortune if you decided to sell them globally."

"But to do that, they'd have to be manufactured at a plant and wouldn't be made with love." Winnie smiled and pinched off a piece of Alastair's roll, ignoring her uncle's scowl. She winked and popped it into her mouth.

"You raised a bunch of heathens, Pres. These girls have no manners. See how she steals food from a starving man?" Al's words held no heat. "I told you time and again they should've gone to boarding school for refinement."

Husky laughter brought everyone's attention to the terrace. Aurora and Selene stood side by side, watching them all. Both women were roughly the same height, but it was Selene who attracted Preston's notice. She seemed bemused by the playful banter and deep affection.

Of their own volition, his feet started up the stairs. Coming back to himself, he stopped and half turned to address his daughters. "Girls, there's someone special I'd like you to meet." Four sets of curious eyes turned toward Selene. "This is my new partner in crime, Selene Barringer."

"Victor's sister?" There was no mistaking the hardness in Autumn's voice.

"Half sister," Selene returned coolly. "And there is no love lost between us, I assure you."

"I'll have to take your word for it." Preston's eldest crossed her arms over her chest, her ever-present suspicious attitude alive and well.

Winnie slapped her on the arm. "Tums, be nice." She was the first to climb the stairs. "It's a pleasure to meet you, Selene. Holly sang your praises when she returned from Greece. We owe you for saving her life."

The reserve eased from Selene's stiff features, and her mouth curled up on one side. "You own me nothing. Your sister deserved every chance at happiness, and I was honored I could help toward that end."

Summer, who had joined their small group, impulsively hugged Selene, surprising a squeak from her. "Holly's my twin, and I'm doubly grateful. Thank you."

"My pleasure."

"Where's Gigi?" Aurora asked as she shifted sideways to make room for Mackenzie to join them. "I'd have thought she'd be the first to arrive."

"She's instructing my cousins on proper babysitting procedure." The smooth, deep voice came from beside Spring mere seconds before the cloaking spell concealing Knox Carlyle dropped.

"Way to make an entrance!" Mackenzie laughingly applauded. "Tell me you weren't hiding to get out of baby duty."

"I can neither confirm nor deny."

"Not without incriminating yourself, anyway." She rolled her eyes. "Never a dull moment in this family."

"Good to see you again, Mack." Knox gave her a one-armed hug. With a reserved smile, he held out a hand to Selene. "Ms. Barringer, it's a pleasure to finally meet you."

Selene looked stupefied as she stared up at him. It wasn't hard to understand why. Knox Carlyle was hands down the most attractive man in existence. His golden hair brushed a pair of wide, well-defined shoulders, and his azure eyes were set in a perfectly symmetrical face with sculpted cheekbones, a Grecian nose, and full winsome smile. Added to his unbearably good looks was his keen intelligence and challenging stare. He was uniquely flawless in appearance, and Spring's match in every way. It was difficult to say which of the two was more jaw-droppingly gorgeous.

Amusement lit Spring's eyes, and she placed her arm around Knox's waist. "He's a sight, isn't he? He stuns women stupid when he smiles."

A sweep of color tinged Knox's cheeks at his wife's praise. "Knock it off," he growled.

"Darling, you really should drop the glamour and let your pirate scar show so women don't throw their panties at your head." Spring teased.

Selene's laugh was unexpected. "A pirate scar would only make him more irresistible, I'm afraid." A sparkle lightened her chocolate-colored eyes to dark honey, and Preston was completely entranced.

He didn't miss Autumn's narrowed-eyed stare or Winnie's mischievous grin, but he didn't acknowledge their reactions, either.

Preston shook hands with his son-in-law. "I see you still aren't letting Spring out of your sight. It's good to know some things will never change."

"You charged me with taking care of her, sir. I don't take my promises lightly," Knox said with a wide smile for his mate.

Preston heard Selene's sharp intake of breath. Leaning close, he murmured, "My daughter tried to warn you. But please, if there's going to be any panty throwing, let them be at my head, my love."

She compressed her mouth in a straight line, but the humor lurking in her eyes betrayed her.

After five minutes and a few more hugs, Gigi arrived with Alastair's remaining children and Quentin Buchanan.

Holly clapped her hands in one loud, echoing slap. "Well, now that the gang is all here, whose ass are we kicking?"

CHAPTER 7

Selene wasn't sure she was comfortable being in the midst of so many Thornes. They had every reason to despise her based on Victor's past sins, and yet they all treated her to a welcoming smile—with the exception of Autumn, but Selene figured she was a hard sell.

Holly and her husband, Quentin, were especially thrilled to see her and took her aside to thank her once again for helping them.

"I don't know how we can ever repay you, Ms. Barringer, but you have my undying gratitude for saving Holly and Frankie," Quentin said.

"Nonsense. There is no need for repayment. I'm thrilled you're all living your best lives."

It was rumored Quentin was a descendent of Zeus, and Selene found it easy to believe. He was taller than the average man, standing around six-and-a-half feet tall. In a style similar to Knox, he wore his hair long. The thick brown waves begged a woman to run her hands through them. Quentin had a flirty way about him, and he never seemed serious. But his easy charm was a front for the deeper passion lurking beneath. A passion reserved only for his small dark-haired wife.

Selene had been drawn to him from the first. He was a yummy treat—not unlike old Agnes's baklava. No matter how bad it was for her, she'd gladly eat an entire tray. However, it had only taken one quick glance to see the unbreakable bond between the pair of them. Selene had been envious then, as she was envious now. Not enough to wish them ill, but enough to be saddened she'd never found her mate while she was alive.

Her gaze drifted to Preston, where he stood in deep discussion with his sister and his daughters. As if he sensed her regard, he looked her way. He halted mid-sentence, drawing the attention of the group to her. Selene couldn't hear what Autumn said, but it made her father flush and grin.

Without a doubt, Preston Thorne was a handsome devil. Not as stunning as Knox Carlyle or as seductive as Quentin, but definitely attractive. His easy confidence made him even more so.

As he continued his conversation, his gaze continually darted to her, making Selene inwardly preen. When this mess was resolved—if it *could* be resolved—she'd put him out of his misery and tell him how she felt about him. Until then, she would try to keep her secrets to herself.

Holly inched closer to Selene. "I see you're having a difficult time keeping your eyes off Uncle Preston," she teased.

"He's a compelling man," Selene replied. "I'd have to be dead not to notice him."

Quentin laughed as Holly winced.

Selene realized what she'd said, and she chuckled. "That didn't come out as intended."

"Uh huh." Holly's lips quirked, and she turned on her heel, saying over her shoulder, "I need to conjure some coffee and find a bathroom, not necessarily in that order. Tell the others to get it in gear. I'm not comfortable leaving Frankie alone too long."

Quentin caught up with Holly and scooped her into his arms. "Liz and Rafe will not allow anyone to harm our child, my prickly pear. We should treat this as a vacation and take advantage of our alone time." He shot a wink at Selene and only grunted slightly when his wife tweaked his nipple.

"Put me down, you tool. We don't have time for flirting."

"Hol, don't be ridiculous. There's always time for flirting." He dropped a kiss on her mouth and swept her through the terrace doors.

Selene sighed at Quentin's romantic response. She wanted someone exactly like him. Someone outrageous who would temper her seriousness. A man willing to steal a kiss regardless of the fact there were ten other people mingling about.

She felt Preston's presence at her back before he spoke. "They are the most romantic couple I know. Mainly due to Quentin's fun-loving nature."

Facing him, she smiled. "Oh, I think Holly would surprise you. That young woman has a wild side she doesn't let many people see."

He smiled in return. "I believe my brother can attest to that fact. She drove him to distraction as a teenager, constantly sneaking out to meet Quentin. Alastair once said he'd have bound her powers and locked her in a convent if he thought it would've done any good."

"I also said she'd have the nuns dancing to her tune in nothing flat," Alastair added. He'd joined them in the middle of Preston's explanation. "If we weren't pagan already, we'd all be excommunicated because of it."

Selene laughed. "I suspect you're correct, Mr. Thorne."

"Call me Alastair. I insist." His sapphire eyes locked on her for a moment, then he said, "You're family now, Selene."

Unexpectedly, she became emotional, wanting to weep at his kind words. She'd never truly belonged anywhere after her mother died. Forming attachments had been pointless. Victor would've found and used anyone she cared about against her.

With an understanding expression, Alastair patted her arm. "No need to thank me, my dear. But be careful. Even honorary Thornes tend to attract unsavory attention."

"More unsavory than Preston?" She shot the man in question a quick side glance, not bothering to hide her smirk.

"Probably not." Alastair's quip earned him a light punch from his brother. "Okay, fine. Maybe a slight bit more unsavory than Pres, but not much." He surprised her when he wrapped his arm around his younger brother's neck and gave him a noogie.

"I swear to the Goddess, I will end you if you ever do that again, Al," Preston grumbled as he broke the hold and smoothed back his hair. "You're lucky I don't set your Armani suit on fire—with you in it."

Alastair laughed and hugged him. "I truly missed you, little brother. Let's go save the world."

AN HOUR AND COUNTLESS IDEAS LATER, NONE OF THEM WERE ANY closer to discovering what might be the Evil's original source or how to divest the Otherworld of the problem. Preston found himself growing tired of the discussion as the urgency to act gripped him.

"This is insane. We're in the dark and likely to stay that way. After all this time, I'd be surprised if anyone was left on the other plane." He stood to pace, his irritation growing with every step he took across the Safavid silk Persian carpet under his feet. Even the beauty of the antique he trod upon couldn't drag him from his pique. It was a rare day when pieces like that didn't distract him.

He'd often wondered who Autumn had put in charge of his business after he died. Had she sold it? The small antiques shop had been his pride and joy, and he hadn't been able to bring himself to scry to find out its fate.

"Let's go over what we know," Selene suggested. "The Evil arrived in the Otherworld roughly around or shortly after Isolde and Nathanial crossed over. Isolde gave instructions to smash the jewel she'd been entombed with. Damian carried out the order." Everyone nodded. "Is it possible, when the necklace was smashed, it released the Evil instead of destroying it? Perhaps she didn't know or had been tricked into believing the only way to stop it was to crush the stone, but in fact, the opposite was true."

"Terrifying thought," Damian muttered. "I'd like to think I'd have felt something if or when it escaped. And if it *was* in the stone and I released it, why is it infecting the Otherworld and not this plane?"

"Great question," Selene said with an elegant shrug.

Preston joined her on the settee and stretched his arm along the back of the sofa. Her hair brushed against his arm, and he wanted to curl the silky mass around his hand and draw her into his lap. But he couldn't tuck her against him with everyone around. She'd hate any display of affection.

He smothered a sigh and brought his mind back to the conversation. "Was anyone else in the vicinity when you opened the tomb?"

"Me." Everyone looked at Evie after she spoke and waited for her to elaborate. "I was with Damian then and also a short while later when he smashed the piece. Within a day, I passed on to join Nathanial." She wore a troubled expression. "What if it didn't attach itself to Isolde or Nathanial at all but instead latched onto me?"

Alastair narrowed his eyes, and Preston could practically see the wheels turning in his head. "It would make sense," his brother said with a nod. "Whatever this darkness is, it wouldn't have known Isis was about to call you to the other side. Perhaps for reasons unknown to us, it couldn't attach itself to Damian, and as the next most powerful being, it wanted your magic."

Damian perked up. "That had to be it. Evie, you're a genius." He gave her a kiss on her temple. "Now, we need to find a way to reverse engineer the problem and return it to earth for me to consume."

Preston noted the Aether looked ill at ease. "Do you fear turning into your mother?" he asked quietly.

"How can I not?" There was a raw, vulnerable quality to Damian's reply. "How much worse will it be if I give into the madness? How many more people need to die to feed the monster's hunger?"

In all the time Preston had known Damian, he'd never seen him display any uncertainty. For a human to live over two hundred years, they would've seen and survived practically everything. With their experience came a matter-of-factness and a lack of alarm for everyday happenings. Yet Damian's fear was present and well-founded. He'd been through this once before with his mother. And the truly disconcerting question was: who could stop *him*? The simple answer—no one.

"What if we bring down all magic?" Spring's suggestion caused a chorus of gasps. While she waited for everyone to wrap their brain around the idea, she calmly sipped her tea.

Damian sat down opposite her and, bending forward to rest his elbows on his knees, gave her his undivided attention. "How would it help?"

"We know the Evil craves magical powers. What if it has none to steal? Will it starve and weaken? Possibly die out?"

A smile kicked up the corners of Knox's mouth. "Brilliant as usual, sweetheart."

"Thank you," she said primly, but there was a twinkle in her eye as she reached for a scone and smothered it with cream. "I do my best."

"You may be onto something, child." Alastair nodded his approval. "We'll have to confer with Isis and have everyone hit their family archives to search for any available information on this cursed darkness, but I believe we now have a starting point."

"I can take the Weird Season Sisters with me," Nash volunteered with a smirk toward Preston's daughters. "We can sort through what's in the vault at Thorne Industries."

Autumn snapped her fingers and flames sparked from the tips. "I've got your Weird Season Sister right here, you asshat."

Nash blew her a kiss and grinned when she did.

In the time Preston had been gone, the cousins—once unknown to each other—had become close. It saddened him he'd missed the bonding, but he was thrilled they'd all come together. Family was important. Never more so than right now.

Ryker refilled his brandy with a swirl of his finger and nodded. "I can meet with the Witches' Council. Perhaps their librarians might have knowledge on how to create a magical blackout or can reference something in their files."

"I'll pair up with Mack." GiGi sent a look of inquiry toward Mackenzie. When the other woman nodded, she said, "We can get a list of covens and visit each to see what they might know or what stories have been passed down to them."

"My sister and aunt can work with Evie to see what secrets are left here at the estate. For years, the Drakes were tasked with being the Keepers of the Gate, and logic tells me there must be something." Sebastian rose and kissed his wife. "But you and GiGi aren't going off on your own. I'll accompany you."

Mack laughed. "Darling Baz, you'll only be a distraction. With you around, none of our female friends will be able to form a coherent sentence."

Autumn snorted when his skin reddened. "I can see it now. Women will throw whatever's handy on the floor. Each of them scrambling in an effort to see what he's wearing underneath that sexy-ass kilt." When he glared, she giggled. "I think you're confined to baby duty, studly."

"Hey! That's your nickname for me, Tums," Knox growled out with mock indignation.

"That's her nickname for every hot male." Summer gracefully rose to her feet and crossed to the large floor-to-ceiling windows. She tilted her head to the side, then drew the curtains back and opened a window. "Hol, I need you to swear."

"Excuse me?" Holly, like her siblings and father, was cursed. If she became angry enough to swear, she would be overloaded with power and sneeze. The pulse called to the avian population and brought them flocking to her. Only a magical intervention could prevent a real-life reenactment of Hitchcock's movie, The Birds.

"I need you to swear, but not emphatically. There are ravens close by, and I want to talk to them."

"You can't simply call one with your magic?" Holly asked dryly.

"Where's the fun in that?" Summer and Alastair locked gazes as they said the words in stereo.

They'd never resembled each other more, and Preston had to laugh. "You're a chip off the old block, Summer, my dear."

Holly threw her hands up and moved to stand next to her twin. Taking a deep breath, she said, "Hell." A sneeze followed, and no one tried to stem the magical blast that followed. Within a minute, three ravens perched on the outside ledge, cawing for all they were worth.

"Hello, my feathered friends." Summer's greeting soothed them, and their gleaming blue-black heads bobbed as they took turns speaking in a language few witches could understand. She happened to be gifted with the ability to talk to animals, which made her an outstanding veterinarian. When a patient could say exactly where they hurt, it was easier to treat them.

Selene watched the whole proceeding with wide-eyed wonder.

Unable to resist, Preston stroked his fingers along the exposed line of her graceful neck. "Fascinating, isn't it?"

She leaned into him and smiled—effectively shocking him. "I knew your family was powerful, but I had no idea you all held such a variety of talents. Empaths, zoo linguists, Aethers. It's incredible, really."

"We also have a psychic." Preston nodded at Mackenzie. Why he felt the need to confess was a mystery. "No one outside our family and the Drakes know."

"For obvious reasons," Selene murmured.

Psychic witches tended toward madness, as most were unable to maintain magic and visions without the two merging and creating untold problems. Both abilities took a toll on the one cursed to experience them both together. They were feared by the witch community because they were unpredictable, and the Thornes didn't need one more thing to incite terror in lesser witches. His family was reviled enough by the more petty ones.

Selene placed her hand on his thigh and shifted closer. Keeping her voice low, for his ears only, she said, "Have you thought about what might happen if magic is removed? How long would it have to be down, and how vulnerable would it make you?"

He met her worried eyes. "All factors will need to be weighed before we jump in. Most of our enemies are gone, but I'm sure there are still a few stragglers."

"Serqet has never gone away." She squeezed his knee. "I fear she's waiting for her moment to strike."

The Goddess Serqet, sister to Isis, had held a grudge against Spring and Knox since before witches came into being. It was known that Knox, in a previous incarnation, had been gifted with god-like abilities and was the first true warlock in existence. Isis, in an effort to protect him and his lover against Serqet's jealous rage, had infused his very soul with unimaginable power. The spiteful Goddess had maintained a grudge against anyone descended from Isis's line ever since. The Thornes had been a particular favorite to target.

"Thank you for the reminder. I hadn't given her much thought in recent years."

"Your family should be protected, Preston. They are a treasure. So perfect and beautiful in their love for one another." Selene dropped her eyes and swallowed.

It didn't take a brain surgeon to understand. Her life had been isolated and vastly different from his own. There had been no loving parents to see her to adulthood or protect her from the horrors of twisted fuckers like Victor.

Preston wrapped an arm around her shoulders and pulled her close. After placing a tender kiss on her temple, he said, "You're one of us now, love. Just as Alastair said. We'll do whatever is necessary to protect you from harm and to make you secure in that knowledge."

Her hand tightened on his thigh, but she remained quiet as she turned her attention back to Summer and the ravens.

"In case you're in any doubt, I love you," he whispered into the shell of her delicate ear. "We value our mates and protect them at all costs. A Thorne only truly loves once."

"What about your wife?" Selene returned with an arch look.

Preston smiled at the undeniable jealousy in her tone. "My *widow*, and she was only marking time with me, waiting until she could be with Alastair again. I did love her as one would love a dear friend." He rubbed a lock of Selene's silky hair between his fingers, admiring the way the light reflected off the blue-black strands. "Nothing like what I feel for you. Nothing at all."

The tension left her body, but she kept her haughty expression firmly in place. "Let's shelve this discussion until a more appropriate time, shall we?"

He grinned at her formal tone and couldn't resist a bit of teasing. "The world is ending, Selene. Who's to say what's appropriate or not? I say we find a room and make love until we can no longer stand."

"All right."

He sat up straighter. "What?"

"I'm calling your bluff. Let's go—what is it you Americans say?— boink? Bang one out?"

His shout of laughter turned heads their way. With a wave of his hand, he dismissed gawkers. "Don't mind us. We're just talking about boinking." He grunted when Selene's solid elbow nailed him underneath his rib cage. "You started it," he muttered.

"No, I don't believe I did, *agápi mou*. But I certainly know how to finish it."

Under the pretense of scratching his jaw, Preston smothered another laugh behind his hand. "You do realize I know the Greek language, don't you, *my love*? And however we finish, I'm all for banging one out."

"Be serious," she admonished.

"Oh, I most certainly am."

CHAPTER 8

The heat of embarrassment burned Selene's cheeks as Preston's family not-so-subtly watched them. They were all comfortable with the playfulness of a large close-knit group, but she wasn't. Not that she couldn't get used to it if exposed to such a wonderful thing, but she felt gauche at the present.

Although she and Preston had been teasing one another, there was an element of seriousness in their flirty game. And oh yes, she'd love to boink, bang, make love, or do any one of the thousands of euphemisms for sex with him. He'd been driving her to distraction from the moment he sat down next to her. Her senses became heightened when she'd come back to life, and she needed to discover if this was normal or if it was simply the spellbinding man next to her. This need to touch him, to have him touch her, was overwhelming in its intensity. Even now, she couldn't seem to remove her hand from his thigh. If she shifted her fingers a few inches, she'd be able to feel the divot between those defined muscles.

His scent was clean, sharp, and addictive. His breath was a mix of peppermint and coffee. It reminded her of the holiday lattes she was fond of and had missed so dreadfully. Of course, the thought of delicious flavored coffee brought her around to taste, and Selene wanted nothing more than to kiss him. To explore the inside of his mouth with her tongue and sample all he had to offer. She'd nibble on his lips and lave the hardened nipples of his chest. She'd trail her mouth down to—

"Excuse me?" She'd missed what was being said, and for the second time in as many minutes, her cheeks flamed.

Alastair sent her a knowing look, and Selene felt exposed. How did one hide their feelings around an empath?

"Summer said the animals in the area are restless," he said without giving away a hint of what he had to be picking up from Selene. "They all sense the oncoming threat."

"I see." She forced herself to inhale a calming breath and *not* clear her throat like a guilty child. "I suppose I'm not surprised. The balance must be off here as it is in the Otherworld. Especially if the gods and goddesses are ill at ease by this threat."

Spring nodded. "It's a good observation. The earth will be similarly affected. More earthquakes. Stranger weather patterns. Plants losing some of their healing properties as they become stressed by the conditions." Sadness touched her eyes and disappeared as quickly as it came. "Non-magical humans will feel off and not understand why. Their tempers will be close to the surface."

"Balance is the key," Winnie said. She looked at Damian. "It's why I don't think you should consume the Evil when it comes down to it. You're too valuable as that balance."

"Our future Oracle has predicted it." The skin around his eyes grew taut, and his mouth tightened. "Although she hasn't told me what happens after. For reasons unknown to me, I can't see the immediate future anymore. It's a concerning development."

Tension radiated from the arm wrapped across Selene's shoulder. Whatever Damian's issue, it couldn't be good. Especially if it caused Preston to stiffen beside her. "What does it mean?" she asked with a side glance at him.

Damian gave her a tired smile. "I've always been able to see upcoming events to a small degree. Similar to my daughter, but she has better clarity and an ability to see long-term. I get near-future visions, and on occasion, I catch long-term glimpses." His expression grew thoughtful. "However, I can't see anything at all. Not today. Not tomorrow. Nothing. I wonder if it's by design."

Quentin sat rubbing his wife's shoulders, but at the Aether's statement, he paused and looked at Damian. "How so?"

"The Goddess gives or takes away certain perks of my job. Perhaps if she sees I'm hesitant to do what she wants based on future events, she'll make sure I can't see them." Damian shrugged and sighed. "It's a mystery. However, earlier in the garden, Sabrina mentioned the seven original elementals. Between us, there are six. I need only to find the seventh for an idea I want to try."

"Seven? I've never heard of seven elementals." Selene had worked for the Greek branch of the Witches' Council for many years. She'd had access to all sorts of information about the magical community, and only thirty or forty percent of what she learned had been fed to Victor to appease him. She'd kept the most important stuff to herself. "I imagine you are the sixth. But what could the seventh be?"

A slight frown puckered Alastair's forehead as he nodded. "Electricity, if I'm not mistaken."

"How do you know these things, Al?" Ryker shook his head and shot his brother-in-law a rueful smile. "I've been a spy for the Council for the majority of my life and never heard of a seventh elemental."

"At least I don't feel as uninformed as I did a moment ago," Selene said with a soft snort.

Preston rubbed his fingertips along her shoulder. "I worked for the Council on occasion and never knew. Al is a cagey beast and possesses more knowledge than the average bear."

"I like to keep my finger on the pulse of the magical world. You never know what you'll discover if you watch and listen." Alastair's grin bordered on wicked. "Besides, I knew Castor, too."

Quentin stilled, and his face paled. "Alexander Castor?"

"What is it, son?"

"Is that who you're talking about? Alexander Castor?" Quentin demanded, rising to his full height and glowering.

Damian's gaze turned thoughtful as he watched him. "Yes. What do you know of Castor?"

"From the family grimoire Athena handed off to me in Greece, I know a great deal. Like the fact he was my father, and also an electricity elemental."

"Jesus!" Alastair and Damian jumped to their feet at the same time, their expressions showing pure shock.

The Aether recovered first and approached Quentin. "May I have your hand?"

With a wary look at the rest of them, Quentin gave in to Damian's request. The Aether placed his palm over the top of Quentin's, leaving only a half inch of space between them. A soft, glowing red light pulsed between them, growing stronger and more golden as the seconds passed. Finally, like a dying star, the flash momentarily blinded them all.

When Selene opened her eyes again, Damian was sweating and Quentin looked pale. His wife clasped his hand and urged him to sit on the rounded arm of her chair.

"What did you see?" Alastair asked. There was concern in his tone. For Quentin or Damian, Selene couldn't be sure.

"Castor is indeed his father." Damian gave Quentin a half smile and shook his head. "I don't know why I didn't recognize it right off. Your coloring is the opposite of his, but your features, your build, even the way you carry yourself is all the same."

"I never registered the similarities, either," Alastair said. "But maybe it's why I liked him from day one."

For the first time since Castor's name was mentioned, Quentin looked more like his playful self. "You never liked me, or if you did, it certainly wasn't from day one."

"Hush, son. You're not privy to my thoughts." Alastair winked at Holly and resumed his seat. "Castor. What a carefree devil he was! Very much similar to how you are, my boy."

"Wait. You said *is* my father. Does that mean he's not dead?" Quentin asked Damian.

With a shrug, Damian said, "Based on something my daughter said, I believe he's still around."

"If he's alive, why did he not claim me? Why let me grow up an orphan?" Although Quentin tried to keep a moderate tone, Selene could hear the underlying hurt behind the question.

"I don't know," Alastair admitted. He locked gazes with Damian. "Do you?"

"No. Until Sabrina told me, I had no idea he was still alive. Rumor has it Castor died twenty-five or thirty years ago."

"You mentioned our opposite coloring. Did he have white hair and ice-blue eyes?" Quentin watched Damian carefully.

"He did."

Quentin sagged as if the knowledge deflated him. "He came to see me when I was a small boy. He told me he was a friend of the family and he'd do what he could to protect me. Castor encouraged me to be a good boy, no matter what. He said if I was fair and kind, I'd grow to be someone he'd be proud to call son."

"Definitely a father's parting words," Alastair said grimly. "But why would he walk away? Dethridge?"

"I don't know, Al. But I certainly intend to find out." Damian faced Quentin again. "What of your mother? You said you were an orphan."

"She died right before Castor came to see me." Quentin rose and crossed to the blazing fire. Staring down, he seemed transported to another time. "Maybe that's why he visited. I was to be placed with a family the next week. A year later, the paperwork was finalized and I was adopted by the Buchanans."

Holly remained quiet but sent a beseeching look toward her father as she rubbed the area over her heart. She appeared tormented on her husband's behalf, and Selene felt sorry for her. The inability to ease the suffering of someone you loved exacted a heavy toll.

"Why wouldn't he take me in?" Quentin asked, and the ragged question tore at her heart, making her want to comfort him.

"Maybe he didn't feel he had anything to offer you," Selene said gently. "Maybe he believed you were better off with a loving couple to raise you."

He lifted his head and met her eyes across the distance. Angst had replaced his normal twinkle, and he stared at her almost unseeingly. "Perhaps."

"You're a traveler, Quentin."

"So?"

"Can you not go back and ask?" Everyone looked at Selene as if she'd suggested the moon was purple. "None of you thought of it?"

Spring laughed. "No, but it's the perfect solution." She crossed to Quentin and touched his arm. "You can tell him to meet us here tonight."

Although he didn't seem particularly happy about the idea, he shifted his attention to Damian. "Is this what you want?"

"Yes."

"And you're sure he's still alive?"

"Sabrina said it was so."

Quentin grimaced and glanced toward the snapping fire. "Then I'll go back. What is it you'd like me to tell him?"

QUENTIN RESTED AGAINST THE BASE OF A RED MAPLE TREE AS HE watched the playground where his younger self sat, mourning the loss of his mother from days earlier. This childhood version of him had hunched shoulders, and pain was etched on his tiny face. From here, Quentin could see tears cutting a trail through the dirt on the boy's cheeks, and he was immediately reminded of Frankie when she was upset. The desire to console was so strong, he had to fight the urge.

"You were a tragic figure."

Quentin jerked and spun around. There, before him, stood Alexander Castor in the flesh. "How did you know I'd be here?"

"I spoke to adult-you the last time I visited you as a boy. It was only after I left that I realized who you were."

"So our conversation wasn't the same?"

"No." Castor cocked his head, and a twinkle lit his ice-blue eyes. Quentin could see Damian had called it right when he said their mannerisms were the same. "Did you grow up to be the kind of man a father would be proud of, son?"

"Why would you give a shit now, Castor? You didn't then."

The other man flinched, and though his eyes grew more serious, he didn't lose his smile. "I did. Then and now, Quentin. But circumstances aren't always what they seem. You've led a good life, if I'm not mistaken?"

If he was being fair, Quentin couldn't say he hadn't. But he wasn't sure he wanted to be fair. He'd missed out on knowing his real father, and it hurt like hell to learn Castor had been alive all this time and never sought him out. "Why didn't you ever contact me?"

Castor looked beyond him to the tragic figure on the bench. "I was protecting you, son."

"From what?"

"From those who would enslave you for your ability."

A cold sensation washed through Quentin, and he acknowledged it as the truth. "Did they enslave you?"

"Yes. Until I faked my death."

"Is that why the Castor grimoire disappeared, along with any knowledge I had of our history? So no one would know I was your son?"

His father grinned, and approval lit his eyes. "How long did it take you to work that out?"

"I just did. So either longer than it should've, or I'm a damned genius."

"I suspect the latter because you're of my blood." Castor turned serious and grew restless. "I can't be here long, dear boy. Tell me what it is you need to say, so I can comfort your younger incarnation."

"The Aether knows you're alive and wants you to come meet with us at this location. The date and time are there, too." Quentin handed him a paper with the details. "Come or don't," he said flatly. He didn't bother to tell his father not to talk to young Quentin. He supposed it was necessary so he'd remember the moment and be able to inform Damian and Alastair in the present day. But oh, how he wanted to yell at Castor to fuck off. Who left their son? Why not *stay* to protect him? Teach him what he was and what he could do, instead of leaving him to flounder?

As he started to walk away, his father called his name.

He stopped but didn't turn. "What?"

"You are my son, and I love you, Quentin. I did what I thought was best."

"You are descended from a God with the ability to time travel, Castor. You could've protected me if you chose to remain." He took a step and halted long enough to say, "Don't let Damian and Alastair down."

As Alexander Castor observed his grown son disappear into a fold of space, he felt a surge of pride. Quentin had no way of knowing he'd watched over him. Only once had Alex failed to get to him in time, but Quentin's Traveler daughter had helped resolve the issue and altered her family's timeline.

Castor read the paper in his hand and promptly burned it with a simple touch of his finger. His son wouldn't have agreed to seek him out if it weren't important. Alex grimaced at the thought of facing his former friends. They certainly wouldn't be happy with him. Severing ties by creating the illusion of your own death wasn't the best for a relationship. Damian was likely to be salty as hell, and Alastair would fillet Castor alive with his acerbic words.

Alex grinned. They'd eventually forgive him, and it would be wonderful to see them both again after all this time. With a careless shrug, he strode across the field toward his five-year-old son. Perhaps this time, he'd tell young Quentin the truth about who he was and how much he was loved. It would go a long way toward quelling Quentin's animosity when next they met.

CHAPTER 9

*R*oughly thirty minutes after Quentin returned to the Drake estate, Alastair heard a knock on the door. He smiled in anticipation and followed Sebastian as he went to welcome their caller. The second Alexander Castor stepped into the foyer, Alastair was impacted by the excitement the other man was feeling, along with the mild trepidation.

"Castor. Back in the land of the living, I see."

A wide grin took up half of Alex's face. "Hello, Thorne. Good to see you again, my friend."

"Am I? Your friend, that is?" Alastair made it a point to keep his eyes cool and his tone frosty. Inasmuch as he used to consider Castor one of his closest companions, he felt betrayed by the deception. Not as much as Damian likely did, but enough to not welcome the man back with open arms.

"I thought Damian would be the saltier of the two of you."

Damian spoke from behind Alastair. "Salty? I'm more than salty, you bastard!" With a flick of his wrist, the Aether had Castor suspended five feet above them. "Tell me right now why I shouldn't snap your worthless neck."

"I lied to protect my son."

The wind died from Damian's sails, and he lowered his palm. There wasn't a damned thing any one of them wouldn't do to protect their children. Betraying a friend was on that list.

Once Castor had his feet planted firmly on the marble floor, he stepped forward. "I'm sorry, Dethridge. Truly."

"You think we wouldn't have helped you protect Quentin?" Alastair asked archly. "Did you forget who and what we are?"

"Ah, so he's told you I'm his father."

"Only just. Also, *he's* the 'salty' one at the moment." Alastair uncrossed his arms and gestured with a thumb over his shoulder. "You changed the timeline, and he's dealing with the hangover of new memories merging with old."

"Come, Castor. We need your input." Damian turned on his heel and stalked back toward Sebastian's study, never doubting they would all follow.

"You'd think twenty-seven years would mellow a guy out," Castor muttered.

Damian turned on a dime and was toe-to-toe with him in a second. "You're a heartless prick. We mourned for you, you sonofabitch."

Alastair felt the air shift and tighten around them. Priceless works of art clapped against the wall as antique vases wobbled on their perches. Damian's anger prickled his skin, and he found it difficult to breathe under the weight of the Aether's fury. "Dethridge, please."

With a concerted effort, Damian shoved down his rage. "Apologies, Al."

"I'd watch the snark if I were you, Castor. None of us are in the mood." Alastair led the way to the study. "Ladies and Gentlemen, may I present the infamous Alexander Castor."

"Holy shit! He's as gorgeous as Quentin. I wonder if he does dishes without his shirt, too."

"Try to remember you're married, my dear." Alastair gave Autumn a quelling look, but she simply shrugged, unrepentant.

Castor grinned and shot her a wink. He did a slow turn, taking in every face around him before he abruptly faced Holly. They studied one another for a long minute. "Hello, my dear. Or should I say, prickly pear?" he said softly.

"Mrs. Buchanan or Holly is preferred." She looked none too happy with his familiarity. Stepping backward, she clasped Quentin's hand. "I see you know how to scry. If that's the case, you've already figured out I don't tolerate pricks like you. Also, you should know only my husband is allowed to call me prickly. I'll cut anyone else." Holly was basically telling Castor that until Quentin was ready to forgive and forget, she wouldn't be charmed. Alastair had never been prouder of his daughter.

After a choked laugh, Castor said, "You're very much like your father." Admiration lit his pale eyes, and he gave her a quick nod of understanding. "The perfect match for my son."

From behind her, Quentin enfolded her in his embrace. "We don't need your approval, Castor."

"I would've thought the new timeline changed how you felt about me," his father said softly.

"You honestly believe a few well-chosen words and a surprise visit once a year would soften me up? It was a nice try, but the one thing you seemed to forget is how impossible it is to forget the old memories."

Castor sobered and gave him a nod. "Of course. I only wanted you to know you were cared for, my boy. I meant no harm."

"The slightest change in my past could've altered my relationship with Holly and, as a result, my daughter's entire existence. Perhaps if you were less reckless and more *caring*, you'd have taken that into consideration." Quentin's tone was harsh and unforgiving.

Alastair understood his reasoning. The young man lived for his family. They were Quentin's whole world, and he wouldn't take kindly to anyone risking their safety or happiness.

Evie stepped around Holly to stand directly in front of Castor. "You were a reckless rogue, Alexander. It looks like nothing's changed. You were missed by us all." She opened her arms in welcome, and with what Alastair interpreted as relief on his friend's part, Castor embraced her.

"I missed you, too, Miss Evie."

Unexpected emotion clogged Alastair's throat as he watched them hug. Castor had been a fixture in his family's life when they were all much younger. The day he disappeared and was presumed dead had been painful for them all.

Alastair met Damian's dark, brooding stare. Knowing the Aether could read his mind, he mentally telegraphed, *"Let's get through this first. Then I'll hold him while you plant a fist in his smug face."*

From Damian's ghost of a smirk, Alastair knew the message was received loud and clear.

OFF TO THE SIDE, SELENE WATCHED THE DRAMA UNFOLDING. SHE'D forgotten Knox stood next to her until he spoke. "You'll get used to it."

Surprised, she lifted her head to meet his compassionate eyes. "Will I?"

"They are a bit much in a large group, but it isn't always like this. The quiet times are worth the chaos."

"You believe you have me figured out, Mr. Carlyle."

"I'd never be so bold as to claim a working knowledge of a woman's mind, ma'am, but I've been in your shoes. I'm happiest in the quiet of Spring's garden or spending time in a barn with my horses. This…" He gestured to the small crowd in the center of the room. "…well, it's an introvert's nightmare."

Selene bit back a smile. "Thank you for trying to ease my way into the family. But as a figurehead for the Greek Witches' Council, I'm quite accustomed to crowds. My guarded nature is what sets me apart."

"Fair enough. But when they drive you crazy, don't say I didn't warn you."

She allowed a small smile as he strolled off.

Leaving the Thornes to bring Alexander Castor up to speed,

Selene began exploring her surroundings. In the gallery, she admired the family portraits and pieced together what she knew of Sebastian Drake. They'd met once at a Council function. He'd been debonair and reminded her of a James Bond character. She supposed the comparison was apt because she'd never had a clue he protected the Enchantress's tomb. It was all so cloak-and-dagger-like.

In the distance, she heard a fussy mewl and went to investigate. She found a massive modernized kitchen and Mackenzie Thorne nursing her daughter at the center of it. "Oh, I beg your pardon. I—"

"No worries, Selene. I'd enjoy the company if it's not going to make you uncomfortable to see me feed Delaney."

"Not at all. She's a beautiful baby," she felt compelled to say as she sat down.

"Thank you. She has her moments when I'm convinced she's a demon spawn from hell, but for the most part, I adore her."

"Preston told me you're psychic." Why in the world she felt the need to say it aloud, Selene couldn't be certain. But she was fascinated with any abilities beyond those of a standard witch, and the Thornes seemed to be possessed of these extraordinary powers. "How does it work exactly?"

Mackenzie looked uncomfortable, and Selene opened her mouth to withdraw her question when the other woman spoke. "Mostly by touch. A simple brush of an object will allow me to see its history. This long English oak table, for example." She ran her hand along the length of the wood. "It was crafted by a local woodworker in the nineteenth century. Right here, in place. When Baz gave me free rein to renovate the kitchen last year, I insisted on keeping the table instead of adding an island."

"It's perfect for the space."

"I thought so, too." Mackenzie smiled at her. "As for visions of the future for family or friends, that's also done by touch. Although I rarely volunteer the information unless pressed."

"Is there ever a time you can't see ahead? Is your gift sporadic?"

"Is there something specific you'd like to know, Selene?"

Mackenzie's gentle voice held understanding. "Perhaps your future with Preston?"

Uncomfortable with the other woman's insight, Selene shifted in her seat and folded her hands together in her lap. "I don't like uncertainty."

"Ah." There was a wealth of compassion in the one word. "Well, if you love him half as much as he loves you, everything should work out."

"I don't know the extent of his feelings for me, although I'd like to," she confessed, mortified to her very soul that she had.

"His feelings run deeper than the Mariana Trench and will last for all eternity," Preston said from behind her.

Her heart sped up as she met Mackenzie's cheerful grin. "You set me up, Mrs. Drake."

"It's Mack, and yeah, I sort of did, but only so you could hear it from the horse's mouth." With a quick snap of her fingers, her clothing was back in place. She shifted Delaney to her shoulder and patted her back. "From the second you and Preston arrived on this plane, my visions went dark, Selene. I'm afraid no one knows the future but the baby Aether at this point."

"I see."

"If my ability returns, I'll be happy to relay anything that comes to me." Mackenzie rose, kissed Preston's cheek, and teleported away.

Selene didn't bother to look at him, instead studying the room around her.

"Have I scared you?" His deep voice held a curiously vulnerable note.

"I worry I can't live up to the legend of the Thornes' undying love stories." The truth was hard for her to speak. Her upbringing didn't allow for the openness Preston's intimate circle seemed to share, and she was used to keeping her feelings under lock and key out of necessity.

"No one expects anything, Selene. Hell, we might not live to see next week." He squatted beside her chair and stared into her eyes. "It's why I didn't want to wait to tell you how I feel about you."

She cupped his jaw and stroked the pad of her thumb over his lower lip. "When I first saw you in the Otherworld, I knew you were a danger to my heart." She stopped watching the motion of her thumb and met his steady gaze. "Isis said I was your one true love. That's a lot of responsibility to bear. Perhaps it's partly the reason I kept turning you down."

"You're not responsible for my happiness. I am." He gently bit her thumb and grinned when she scowled. "Do I want to share my life with you? Yes. But if you choose to go about free of me, so be it. In the end, you are responsible for your own happiness, too. If I can't add to that, then we both go on without the other."

"You sound blasé about the whole thing." And she wasn't sure she liked it.

"Nah." He straightened up and drew her to her feet. "Nothing is more important in this very moment, but I want you on *your* terms. Not mine."

"What's to become of us if we succeed in destroying the Evil?"

"I got the impression we return to this plane permanently to live out the remainder of our days." He sighed heavily. "But we have to survive the trial ahead, and I'm not quite confident of our chances."

Her heart dropped to her knees. When had a Thorne ever lacked confidence? "Is the Aether serious about bringing all magic down?"

"I believe it's why he's brought in the final elemental. Alastair told me Castor is descended from Zeus. He's powerful in his own right."

"Where do we go from here?"

His full lips curled and sent her into a tizzy. What was it about this man's wicked grin that made her want to drag him to the nearest bedroom and make him live up to its promise?

"You kiss me for good luck, darling."

"I don't believe in luck, *agápi mou.* You'll have to try another way to claim your kiss."

"I could simply steal one."

"It's not stealing if I freely give it."

Again with his wicked grin, and again with her trembling limbs.

"Pucker up, buttercup," he growled in a low tone.

The kiss was more than she'd imagined. Soft, loving, demanding, passionate. It was… *All. The. Things!* The taste of him was to be savored, yet she wanted to consume it all at once. And oh, his skill. Before she could form a coherent thought, her bottom was on the nineteenth-century table and Preston stood between her legs with one hand cupping her head as his other splayed along her lower back. He leaned over her, forcing her into a semi-dip. Her position was precarious in more than one way and more than in the physical form. If he let her go, she'd fall.

"Done inspecting her tonsils, Pop? If you are, we have a big baddie's ass to kick."

Preston took his time releasing Selene. When she peeked up into his handsome visage, his expression was an equal blend of amused and frustrated.

Without breaking eye contact with her, he said, "Tums, my darling daughter, if you don't leave immediately, I'll take my revenge out on your good-for-nothing husband."

"Now you're just being mean," Autumn muttered. "But if you want to spend your time playing tonsil hockey instead of saving the world, who am I to complain?"

A muscle ticked in Preston's rigid jaw, and Selene suppressed a laugh. She'd never had children, but she imagined, with four daughters, the man in front of her had dealt with interruptions of this nature many times in the past.

"She's right. We have to save the world." He sounded resigned and out of sorts, which made Selene ridiculously happy. "Let's go."

CHAPTER 10

"It's hopeless."

"No, Tums. You're just bored with the research." Spring shot her older sister an annoyed glance. "Really, just pop back home and check on the kids. You're much more suited to action than all of this, anyway." She returned her attention to the pages of the ginormous tome in front of her.

"Thanks for understanding." Autumn shot her a cheeky grin and teleported in the blink of an eye.

"Like we weren't aware of her game," Summer muttered.

Winnie rolled her eyes but said nothing.

Selene watched their interactions from where she sat at the end of the dining-room table with her own monstrous book. Those four women had grown up together, and although their personalities were vastly different, somehow they worked perfectly as a team. She'd never had that, and felt slightly envious.

Winnie blew out a breath, shoved a piece of folded paper between the pages of her book, and turned her bright, curious eyes toward Selene. "Ready for a coffee break?"

"Absolutely."

With an elegant swirl of her hands, Winnie conjured four mugs and a carafe. Then she poured and prepared a cup for Summer, Knox, and herself. She cast a quick look her way. "How do you take yours, Selene?"

"Black, please."

"Cinnamon roll?"

"You intend to send me into a diabetic coma, don't you?"

Winnie laughed and cut the dinner-plate-sized pastry into five portions. After dishing up a piece, she carried the coffee and dessert to Selene. "Here. Research is best done on a sugar high."

"Thank you, Mrs. Carlyle."

"Ugh! Call me Winnie. *Please.* There are far too many of us married to Carlyles now, and we won't know who you're talking to."

Selene laughed around a bite of cinnamon roll, then moaned. "I swear I could get used to this."

"*All* of Winnie's baked goodies are to die for," Summer said as she reached across the table to snag a plate for herself. "We fight like rabid dogs to get the last bite."

"Not to be a hard-ass here, but can you all focus for five minutes?" Spring cast them all an irritable look. She softened it with a smile solely for Selene. "Sorry. This crew would rather leave the reading to Knox and me, but this mess is rather dire."

"I quite agree." Selene shot a glance toward the study doors where Preston was closed up with the Aether, Alexander Castor, and Alastair Thorne. "I wonder what they're concocting?"

"Nothing good without Spring and Nash," Winnie quipped. Bending over Spring, she hugged her from behind and pressed her alabaster cheek to Spring's. "We all know to leave the genius ideas to this one."

"Stop buttering me up and park it, sister. We need all the brainpower we can get here."

"You forgot her tea, Winnie." Knox conjured a fresh pot and poured a cup for Spring. "She's cranky without her chamomile."

"Dirt," Spring said archly with a pointed look at his mouth.

Knox simply grinned and dropped a lingering kiss on her lips.

An inside joke, based on the light laughter of Spring's sisters.

Again, a pang of envy struck Selene. Always the outsider, she bent over her book and resumed reading again. It took her a second to process what she was seeing. She gasped. Four pairs of curious eyes turned in her direction.

"Maybe we don't need to bring magic down so much as we need to pull the Evil into another dimension," she said with dawning confidence for her idea.

Knox stilled. "What do you mean?"

"We know of the Otherworld, the Underworld—or Hell as some call it, and the earthly plane. What if we are limiting ourselves by thinking we have to bring it back here? Can we take it to the Underworld or some lesser-known dimension?"

Spring slowly began to nod, gaining momentum as she mentally worked through the problem. Finally, she grinned. "I think you may be on to something, Selene. Let's run this by Nash before we present it to the others." She tapped out a lengthy text.

Within minutes, Nash Thorne strolled through the doors. "Who do I need to kiss for their brilliance?"

Selene's hand shot up like a rocket, and they all laughed.

"There will be no kissing of my woman," Preston growled.

She jumped in her seat, having failed to notice his entrance. She didn't want him to assume too much at this point, so she said, "*Your* woman? I don't believe any commitments were made."

"I've committed to beating up any males who even *think* about touching you," he countered with a smug smile. Striding forward, he placed his hand on the chair back and one on the table in front of her, effectively boxing her in. "How about we compromise, and *I* kiss you for your brilliance? Afterward, you can tell me what triggered this discussion in the first place."

Her answer was to weave her fingers through the thick auburn hair at the back of his head and draw him close. His lips brushed hers and ignited white-hot need within her. They kept their kiss at a fairly PG rating due to their audience, but Selene would definitely be seeking more when they were in private.

"Mmm." She smiled as she drew back and gazed up into his

desire-laden eyes. "Okay. I suppose you can claim me as your woman." When he grinned, she held up her index finger. "However, I want it to be known that I'm free-thinking and independent. And I rely on *no* man. Understood?"

"Whatever you wish, my love."

"Great answer, Dad," Winnie said approvingly.

"I learned *some* things while raising a houseful of free-thinking, independent women," he said with a wink at her. He looked down at Selene. "Independent women are my specialty."

She snorted a laugh and pointed to the book. "Shall we discuss what I've found?"

"By all means."

Nash plopped into a nearby chair and crossed his arms, sporting a playful pout. "It's so not fair that I didn't get to kiss her."

"Consider the consequences, my darling brother." Summer thumped his bicep with the back of her hand. "Had you kissed her and Ryanne found out, you wouldn't have had to worry about my dad killing you."

Nash chuckled, and his jade eyes took on a warm glow. "Yes. And I've no doubt my darling love and our pesky cousin Liz are scrying and spying right now." His phone buzzed in his pocket, and he removed it to read the message. With a snort of laughter, he turned the screen toward Summer. "Can I call it, or what?"

Summer glanced around the room, not quite focusing on one particular spot. "You never have to worry, Ry. I've got your back. I can loan you Morty's baseball bat if Nash gets out of line."

The phone buzzed again.

Nash snorted and shook his head. "She said, 'thanks.'"

"Okay, let's get back to the subject at hand." Spring closed the book she was reading and rested her arms on top. "Nash, Selene's idea is to find another dimension and dump the Evil there. Is it a possibility?"

"Theoretically, yes."

"What would prevent us from doing so?" Selene asked.

"It would have to be a place without magic to feed on. It would also have to be a plane it can't leave. But I'm of the belief that magic exists everywhere, so…" He shrugged.

"Would Damian know?" Spring tapped her fingers on the leather-bound tome in front of her.

Preston straightened up. "We can ask."

A few minutes later, Damian—joined by Alastair and Castor—entered the dining room.

As Selene outlined the basics of her idea, Preston watched her closely. She was elegant in her movements, as minimal as they were. Sultry, without being overtly sexual. Her statements were an economy of words. Everything about her appealed to him. And when she caught his eye, he imagined those exotic peepers of hers had warmed.

He'd only been half serious earlier when he said no one else was going to kiss his woman. Mainly because he knew Nash was deeply in love with his girlfriend, and Preston hoped Selene held feelings for him. She might not be ready to tell him, but he preferred to believe he could sense them under the surface. Why else would she say she was prepared to be his?

"The only place that might work would be the Nether," Alastair was saying. "It's neither good nor bad, and magic can't be sustained there."

"It won't work." Damian appeared grim and frustrated.

"Why ever not?" Selene's back straightened, and her expression cooled. Preston laid his palm on her shoulder and gently squeezed to show his support.

Damian's gaze snapped to her, and he gave her a rueful smile. "I didn't intend to reject your idea outright, Ms. Barringer." He shot Alastair a mocking glance. "While Al is rarely wrong, he is in this case. The Nether represents Yin and Yang. You see, it's not only that magic can't be sustained there; it's that no human can without a counterpart."

"As in a mate?" Winnie asked.

"No. As in an enemy."

The occupants of the room all seemed in various stages of confusion or disbelief. Preston was no exception. "I don't understand, Damian. Are you trying to say that if Alastair was to go there, he'd need an evil Alastair to match him?"

"Close. Not necessarily an evil twin of himself, but yes, his greatest enemy. Of which, none survived to the best of my knowledge. Am I wrong, Al?"

"No. Not wrong. Those who would harm me or mine are indeed gone."

His brother didn't sound bothered in the least, and Preston couldn't say he was, either. Zhu Lin—the head of the Désorcelers during his time on earth—and Victor Salinger had targeted their family one too many times to be allowed to live.

"Great, so it's back to the drawing board," Knox muttered.

"Not necessarily."

Everyone's attention turned to Castor. The smile he turned on them was wide and engaging. "I'm a Traveler. So is Quentin. Between my son and me, we could bring forward everyone we need."

"No!"

The ground rumbled, and they all scrambled for purchase. Selene clung to Preston where he knelt beside her.

"Jesus, Knox! You're likely to kill us all with those bursts of temper!" Nash complained.

"We are not bringing back anyone who might harm Spring," Knox stated flatly. "I'll kill the first person who tries."

Spring touched his arm. "Babe. It's okay."

"I mean it. You've suffered enough." The hard-as-steel expression on Knox's face said he wouldn't be swayed by her softly spoken words, and Preston couldn't fault him for it. As a matter of fact, he admired the hell out of his son-in-law. The young man would do what was needed to protect Spring whether she agreed or not. But then again, they were two of the oldest soulmates in existence. Preston suspected Knox couldn't live without her. He'd seen the toll her disappearance had taken on the man a few years ago. Knox had nearly gone out of his mind, but had done whatever it took to find her and bring her back.

"That's why I said it wouldn't work," Damian said calmly, as if the mini earthquake hadn't happened. "The risk is too great to bring back enemies of that caliber."

"We have to try," Spring cried. "Our families could be facing annihilation in the Otherworld. It's ridiculous to sit on our hands and do nothing when we have it within our power to stop it."

"But is it? Within our power?" Summer came around the table and hugged Spring. "Yes. We are a mighty family, but we still have limitations. Not to mention I don't want to lose a single one of you. Everyone here is too important."

"Summ—"

"No, Spring. You always have your say, and ninety-nine-point-nine percent of the time we go along with your plans." Summer shook her head and blew out a breath. "The souls in the Otherworld have lived their lives. Shouldn't we be allowed to live ours?"

"You're missing the point, child." Alastair met Preston's steady stare, grimaced, and faced his daughter. "Those are our ancestors and loved ones on the other side of the veil. Should their souls be obliterated, they can never be reborn. That could mean your child or Spring's. Perhaps your future grandchild. If there are no souls to reincarnate, no lives can be born."

"So what's our option?"

"As Castor said. We bring our enemies to this time and place, to ruthlessly use them. Consider them decoys, if you will."

CHAPTER 11

As the evening wore on and everyone hammered out the solutions for the problems surrounding the retrieval of the Thornes' nemeses, Selene's anxiety grew. The conversation around her barely registered as she thought about Victor's resurrection. Could she face him again after what he'd done to her? A chill took her, and she absently rubbed her hands up and down her arms.

"Selene, are you all right?" Preston's soft question penetrated her fog, and she attempted a smile. It fell flat. Concern darkened his eyes, and he rose to his feet, drawing her up beside him. "We'll be right back," he told the others.

He guided her out the French doors and onto the terrace overlooking the shadowed garden. Twilight had come, and even the exquisitely landscaped backyard seemed threatening to her. She shuddered.

"What's wrong?"

Selene met his steady gaze and grimaced. "I'm being somewhat ridiculous, I'm afraid."

"I'll be the judge of that. Tell me."

"I can't help but feel that bringing back enemies—and such deadly ones as ours—is wrong. They'll do whatever it takes to remain here and most likely harm every one of us in the process." She touched his arm, half hoping he'd pull her into his embrace and chase away her demons. "Victor is vicious and not to be underestimated, Preston. Facing him after what he's done… well, I'm terrified, if the truth be known."

"I believe Victor should be Alastair's counterpart, not yours."

"You intend to leave me here while you go to another dimension?" Her voice rose with her fear. Rarely did things excite Selene, but the idea of Preston popping into an alternate dimension without her triggered all sorts of internal alarms.

"The short answer is yes. I won't put you in harm's way, my love."

His words thrilled and irritated at the same time. She adored him for his protective nature, but she meant what she'd said earlier. She was a strong, independent woman with no intention of being shoved to the background for her own safety. "Preston, no one knows my brother like I do. If anyone is going to face him down, it's me."

"As my daughter Autumn would say, that's a whole lotta not gonna happen, Selene."

She didn't appreciate his dismissive tone and said as much. "Isis sent us both back to fight this Evil," she reminded him.

His dark auburn brows slammed together, and the beginnings of temper showed on his face. "If I have to bind your powers and tie you to a chair, I will."

Her own anger took hold, and she took a threatening step forward. With a sharp poke to his chest, she snapped, "Try it."

They stood toe-to-toe, each glowering at the other, when a soft laugh broke their standoff.

Selene cast a sharp glance over her shoulder in time to see Ryker Gillespie step from the shadows. Clamped between his teeth was an unlit cigar. "If she's even half as stubborn as your sister, Pres, you might as well give in now," he said. "And it's a well-known fact you wouldn't dream of laying a finger on a woman, so this is all bluster. You're fighting a losing battle, my man."

Selene didn't know whether to thank him or tell him to bugger off.

"Thanks for pointing out I'm a marshmallow, Ryker. Anyway, it's a moot point until we can find a spell to transport us all to the Nether." Preston uncrossed his arms and sighed.

"Spring has the entire Book of Thoth stored in her brain box." Ryker tapped his temple. "If anyone can come up with the perfect solution, it's her."

An affectionate smile tugged at Preston's mouth, and Selene marveled at the sudden change in him.

"Will you try to prevent your daughters from going to the Nether, Preston?" she asked curiously.

"Yes. If I can, I will."

Again, Ryker chuckled. "This is going to be fun to watch."

"You've been hanging around my brother too long," Preston said dryly. "If there's humor to be found in a situation, Alastair will be the one to find it."

"Why do you think he's my best friend?" Ryker quipped.

"Your spying capabilities?"

"There is that."

As Selene listened to the two of them banter, she once again felt like an outsider. She'd lived an isolated life for so long she didn't know how to be anything but the ice queen she'd portrayed while she was alive. Yes, she'd had pleasant conversations, and she'd taken passionate lovers to her bed in an effort to feel something—anything, but she'd lived in a bubble of her own making since her mother died.

"We should go back inside," she said, pivoting on her heel to leave.

"Selene."

She paused in her escape. "It's as you've said, Preston. A moot point until the specifics of the spell have been worked out." With those parting words, she left the men on the terrace and fled into the main house.

· · ·

"When it comes down to it, will you trust her?"

Preston tore his frustrated gaze from Selene's retreating back and shot a glare at Ryker. "Of course I will. What type of foolish question is that?"

"A legitimate one. How well do you know her?"

"I'm not having this conversation with you." Preston stepped toward the house.

"Pres. I'm not trying to stir up trouble here. Don't forget, I worked for the same organization she did for many years. It didn't go unnoticed by the higher-ups that she fed her brother information when the occasion presented itself."

"She didn't have a choice, Ryker," he snapped.

"How do you know?"

"Isis showed me all. After."

"And you deduced Selene betrayed the Witches' Council and the magical community as a whole because she feared for her life?"

A tightness settled in Preston's chest at Ryker's words. Yes, he loved Selene, but he wasn't blind to her faults. What his brother-in-law truly wanted to know was if Preston believed she'd betray their family if the opportunity arose to save her own hide. He didn't have an answer.

"Yes. I believe Selene feared for her safety. But remember, she also sacrificed her own life for Holly's sake. She'll do what's right, Ryker." If he told himself that often enough, Preston might believe it. He needed to examine if that was the real reason he didn't want her to go to the Nether, should the situation arise. He didn't want her put in the position to choose between his family and hers again. She might not care to lose her life a second time for a bunch of strangers.

Ryker smacked him on the back and handed off the unlit cigar. "I trust your judgment, my friend. Now, do me a favor and get rid of this, will you? GiGi will make mincemeat of me if she believes I even *thought* about smoking it."

As quietly as he arrived, he blended into the darkness. Presumably to skulk in the shadows and keep watch. Ryker wasn't one to trust Alastair's hired security team.

With a snap of his fingers, the cigar was no more, and Preston headed into the house to join the meeting taking place. Selene gave him an undecipherable look when he arrived, then turned her attention back to whatever Damian was saying.

Preston crossed to stand beside her and laid a hand on her tense shoulder. With his thumb, he caressed the stiffness from her neck, and eventually, her hand came up to clasp his. He was forgiven. *For now.* He'd have to wait until they returned from the other dimension to see if she would once again, since he had every intention of preventing her from going.

He caught his brother's inscrutable gaze. Al's dropped to their hands, and the smallest hint of a smile tugged at his lips. Preston had to have faith that Alastair would pick up any ill intentions on Selene's part. Hell, if it came to it, Damian could and would read her mind to protect them all. Hopefully, it *wouldn't* come to that.

"They'll need to be revived and given powers to cross the threshold to the Nether," Damian was saying. "And there lies the dilemma. Infusing Zhu Lin or Victor Salinger with magic is like signing your death warrants. They won't care if it costs them their own lives if they can take their revenge on all of you for putting them in the grave."

"I agree," Selene said. Once again, tension tightened her shoulders. "Victor is heartless, and his hatred of Alastair runs deep. If you hand him a magical loaded weapon, he'll pull the trigger."

"Then the trick is not to give him a weapon at all," Alastair promptly replied with an unconcerned shrug.

"How do you expect to get around it, Al?" Preston was worried, but his curiosity woke. His brother was as devious as the day was long, constantly ready with some Machiavellian plan his incredible mind had conjured in a split second.

"The illusion of magic should work. We don't infuse them with magic; we create a magical cloak they can't utilize. Just long enough to get them through any portal we open." Alastair cast a sharp look at Damian. "It should work, right?"

"In theory. However, we will need a trio of gods or goddesses to open the portal. We can't do it ourselves, and they are the only ones with the magic to do so."

Alastair lost his satisfied air. He crossed his arms and used one hand to rub the spot between his brows. Seeing him stumped was new for Preston.

"Set will help us," Spring said. "He could probably influence his sister Nephthys. But if Isis remains stuck in the Otherworld, I don't know where we'd find a third."

"What about Athena?" Summer asked. "She helped Quentin once. She might be willing to do it again."

Damian grimaced even as he shook his head. "I can't be one-hundred percent sure, but I fear we'll need a counterbalance there, too. One good, one neutral, and one to oppose the good."

"As in an evil goddess?" Knox's expression turned grim. "We all know of one. Nothing ever goes well when she's involved."

"Serqet." Spring looked like she'd eaten the soil from one of her beloved plants. Preston was surprised she didn't spit in her distaste. "Lovely. Just freaking lovely."

"Are there any other evil entities you can think of with the same power?" Selene asked. "Someone not likely to thwart your plans and save her horrid minions, Zhu Lin and Victor?"

"One with evil intent? No." Knox scrubbed a hand over his face and sent an anguished look at Spring. "I can't do it, sweetheart. This plan won't end well for any of us, and especially not for you and me."

She reached over and clasped his large hand between both of hers, bringing it to rest over her heart. "I buried Zhu Lin once. I can do it again, babe."

"Serqet isn't likely to let us get away with only providing power to get those fuckers to the other dimension. She's going to insist they be amped up." Winnie's hand went to her throat as if she were recalling her almost death at Zhu Lin's hands. The man had been obsessed with her and had attempted to draw on her immense abilities to make himself stronger. When it hadn't worked, he'd tried to kill her. "If the rest of the Désorcelers know their leaders have returned, will they rally around them? How much harder will it be to put those rabid asshats down afterward?"

No one had answers, and they all seemed to share the same fear.

Finally, Castor rose. "Do I bring them here or not?"

"Not here. We should find neutral territory." Preston blew out a breath and ran a hand through his already mussed hair. "I want our families' homes to be as protected as possible."

"Aren't you all forgetting something?" Summer's expression was pure faked innocence. When she had their attention, she pointed to Damian and asked, "Who's *his* opposite?"

No one. The answer was no single magical being had as much power as the Aether. *He* was the balance in their world. Damian wanted to swear up a storm, but clamped his jaw shut. He didn't want to tell them they were fighting a losing battle, or that the odds they faced if they brought gods, goddesses, and old enemies into the mix would quadruple.

As he looked from person to person, he could see the hope they held for this futile plan. The heavy weight of responsibility rested on his shoulders alone. Sabrina had been right. Damian needed to save them, as his mother had done before him.

At the thought of his mother, a wild, impossible idea struck. "What if we use Isolde? She was tainted with the Evil once. It might work. It's possible there are enough black deeds in her past to make her my counterpart."

"Bring Isolde *here?*" Evie had remained quiet the entire meeting, sitting off in the corner and sipping on a glass of wine. "It's risky, dear boy. If she's been reinfected, she could start the whole cycle over again."

"I'm curious about one thing," Spring said, interrupting what would've been Damian's response. "If it piggybacked on you to the

Otherworld, Grandma Evie, then why didn't it take over your body or hitch a ride back here?"

"I can answer that," Preston said. "When Evie was recalled to the Otherworld, her Guardian abilities were stripped from her. It's my assumption, based on what we know of this monster, that it would've had nothing to feed on once she had no magic left. It would've sought another source."

Summer leaned forward. "But was all her magic taken away or only the Guardian part?"

"All of it initially." Evie took another sip as a thoughtful expression crossed her face. "Isis restored my natural-born abilities after. It must've been removed at that time."

How odd Damian had never thought to question what two virtual baby witches had! Why hadn't he? Because he didn't want to consider the woman who'd raised him might be infected? Might, even now, be carrying the Evil within her.

Evie's eyes took on a shuttered look as she purposely blanked her thoughts, and Damian had his answer. His heart started to hammer, but he kept his face neutral with the exception of a small, indulgent smile.

He needed to separate her from the others without suspicion on her part.

A golden burst of light filled the yard outside the windows beyond Evie's shoulder, and Damian was floored to see Isis step through the rift. His heart picked up its pace as a look of supreme distaste flashed across Evie's face. Or the woman who should've been Evie.

"Serqet," he said softly.

She flinched before she faced him again.

He couldn't wait. He had to find out how she'd possessed Evie's body. "Where is she? Where's Evie?"

Serqet's lips curled in a sneering smile, and her viciousness made it gruesome. His stomach lurched, and he knew real fear. With a simple wave of her hand, she transformed to her true form. He was relieved to see her presence was not possession, but just a glamour to fool them. His distraction over the Evil had blinded him to the enemy in their midst.

"Consider her like Sleeping Beauty. It will take Prince Charming to wake her with his kiss."

Which meant none of them could help her. Her recovery was beyond their ability and required Nathanial's touch.

"She'd better be back to one hundred percent when she wakes, or I will hunt you to the end of time," he snarled. Enraging a goddess wasn't the smartest thing to do, but this one held little power now and was certainly no match for him without it.

"Temper, temper, Aether," she purred with a smirk and a glance around. "They're all feeling the effects of your fury."

Sure enough, those present looked ill. Damian's emotions had caused a hard magical punch of sorts. With supreme effort, he dialed it back, envisioning an impenetrable bubble around him to protect the others. That done, he turned furious eyes back to Serqet. "Where's Evie's body?"

"Enjoying a long sleep, like your poor mother did."

"She must mean the rose garden," Alastair inserted. "I'll go check."

"Take a few of your guards and Ryker, Al." Damian never removed his watchful gaze from Serqet. Had he detected satisfaction? Reading her emotions wasn't exactly easy for him due to what she was. "And be extremely cautious of traps."

"Always."

Alastair strode out of the room, cellphone in hand. He stopped only long enough to speak to Isis at the base of the terrace stairs. Based on his grim expression when he looked back toward the house, Damian assumed whatever she'd told Alastair wasn't pretty.

"The blasted games you deities play!" Damian snapped at Serqet. "You haven't a care for human life."

"Not true. I care a great deal." She shrugged and sipped her wine. "More than I should, in fact."

"As long as it suits your needs, you do. Otherwise, everyone is expendable."

From the corner of his eye, he noticed Knox shuffle Spring to the back of the room and position her behind him. He caught the Goddess's attention in the process. Sadness and longing flashed before she hid it behind a wall of disdain.

Damian understood in an instant that all her machinations were a result of her hurt at Knox's defection all those centuries before. *A woman scorned.* It didn't matter she was a breathtakingly beautiful goddess who could have almost anyone she desired. She was female first, and her ego hadn't been able to deal with not being worshipped forever by the one man she'd truly loved.

Damian approached her, putting himself between her and those she would intentionally hurt. "Isn't it time to let go of your grudge, Exalted One?" he asked softly, infusing understanding and compassion in his tone. He pitched his voice too low for anyone else to hear. "You could have any one of a million men as your consort. Why continue to obsess over Knox? If you truly love him, you should want him to be happy."

There was a vulnerability in the dark-brown eyes she turned on him, and the resemblance to his mother jerked him to a halt. He'd known he was a descendant of Isis but failed to remember a quarter of his DNA came from the goddess in front of him. The first Aether was created from the four siblings: Isis, Serqet, Set, and Nephthys. He'd gained his powers from each of them, and it made him the ultimate being. Perfect in every way. In all the years since, each descendant of the first Aether had the same traits. The only difference being gender and the strength of their magic. Damian was, of course, the strongest of his line. Perhaps due to the Thorne blood mixed with the Dethridges'.

"You don't understand!" Serqet's eyes took on the wild look of a trapped animal. "You never could!"

"I believe I can and do, Exalted One," he said kindly. "My wife left me, taking my child. She tore my heart in two." Sure, it wasn't a brilliant idea to lay bare his soul to someone like Serqet, but he needed to force a connection. "I know the desire to strike out and cause pain."

She seemed to come back to herself, and the panicked look left her. "But she didn't leave you for another, did she? She simply feared your power. Feared for your child. She didn't leave you because she no longer loved you."

"True," he allowed. "But is it very different? I could've forced her return. Kept her prisoner and caused her untold emotional pain until she hated me. But why?" Damian stepped to within a foot of Serqet and stared down into her confused eyes. "What good would it have done but cause us both more angst? Revenge isn't all it's cut out to be, Dearest One. And I think you know this."

Her mouth firmed, but she said nothing.

"Tell me true, Serqet. How many years have you denied yourself the chance to be happy? Don't you want someone to care about again? Someone who cares about you?"

She looked beyond him, and whatever she saw there made her close her eyes. "Too many." When she lifted her lids and met Damian's direct gaze, she seemed drained of her lifelong fury. "Would you consider being my consort, Beloved One?"

"I'd be honored, but it would mean leaving my daughter, and that I cannot do. Even for you, Exalted One." He cupped her cheek. "I mean no insult, but Sabrina is my life."

"I, too, had children." Her love for her offspring was obvious by the soft light in her eyes and the gentling of her tone. "They were cursed by my hatred."

"Perhaps we can work to undo the curse. Together."

Lifting her hand to place on top of his, Serqet smiled. Her first genuine smile without hatred or wicked intent. "I'm proud to call you one of mine, Damian Dethridge."

"And I'm proud your blood courses through these old veins, my queen."

"You're a charmer, child. Very similar to how I once was."

He grinned. "I've no doubt. Your beauty hasn't diminished, has it? I imagine you'd still bring legions to their knees with a simple flirty glance."

"Perhaps." Her smile turned coquettish as she became thoughtful. "Your wisdom has helped me. I'll grant you one boon."

"Must I name it now, or may I keep it in my back pocket for a future date?"

She laughed, a wholesome, amused sound. "I'll allow you to use it at your leisure, child. Now, I must speak with my sister." She became serious. "Give me a quarter of an hour and send out Knox Carlyle. I should like to speak to him."

"I'll see it's done, Exalted One. And I apologize for my show of disrespect. Put it down to my concern for Evie."

"Thank you, Beloved."

"It's you who is owed the thanks," Damian said. "It isn't easy to set aside your feelings for the greater good." He bowed and backed away to allow her access to the French doors.

As Serqet sashayed away, Damian prayed he'd done the right thing and that she truly meant what she'd said. He detected a residual resentment, but those emotions were normal. After all, he still had pent-up frustration and anger toward his wife for leaving him. It didn't mean he loved her less or that he hadn't forgiven her. It only meant he was still working through his hurt. One didn't get over it in an instant.

From his vantage point, he saw the two goddesses converse. An understanding smile graced Isis's face, and she stepped forward to hug her sister. They turned their faces upward as if they sensed his regard. Isis gave a short nod. Maybe this was their turning point. Two sisters who had once been close, again finding common ground and renewing their love for one another. With a small wave, he turned away to speak with Knox.

CHAPTER 13

The tradition continues… No chances will be taken or fates taunted here!

CHAPTER 14

"$\mathcal{E}$vie is indeed in the rose garden. Laid out on an altar," Alastair said grimly. "I can't wake her."

"I imagine only Serqet or Nate will be able to do so," Preston said grimly. He watched as the two goddesses strolled the grounds with Knox beside them, the moon lighting their path. Periodically, the young man would nod, but otherwise, he didn't react. "What do you suppose they are talking about?"

"I'm not sure." Damian checked his watch. "But it's getting late, and I should check on my family."

"We'll meet again first thing in the morning." Preston shook his hand. "I don't know if what you did will help Spring and Knox in the long run, but I'm grateful you tried."

"No one likes to feel as if they've been betrayed. When he fell for Spring, that's exactly what Knox did to Serqet. Her bitterness shouldn't have come as a surprise. Gods and goddesses feel a slight the most. Enough to wage wars." Damian looked toward his estate although it couldn't be seen from where they stood. "I can't say I wouldn't have felt the same."

"But would you have taken it to the extreme of wiping out

anyone with your sibling's blood?" Alastair countered. "I'll never trust Serqet. She's the master of games."

"It would be difficult for anyone to hide their emotions and thoughts from me, Al." Damian shook his head when Alastair would've spoken. "I'm not saying she couldn't do it, but usually I can sense something lurking in the background."

"And this time?" Alastair asked.

Preston had to acknowledge his brother's concern was valid. He'd never trust Serqet either. The risk was too great.

Damian grimaced. "Resentment is still present. But I asked myself how I would react if I felt betrayed. We can't expect everything to be hunky-dory immediately, gentlemen. However, genuine regret was in her emotional makeup, as well. We'll have to move forward with caution, but also with the hope she's changed."

"She could've killed Evie," Selene said softly. "She had the opportunity. She also didn't strike out at anyone while she was within our inner circle."

Spring snorted, and the cynicism was odd coming from her. "She wouldn't have wanted to give herself away. She was on a fact-finding mission."

Preston wrapped an arm around her shoulders and gave a light squeeze. "We won't let our guards down, baby girl. If she intends you harm, she'll go through the rest of us first."

"I know you mean well, Dad, but don't get on her bad side. Let Knox carry the weight of her grudge. He's an old pro at her games." The compelling candid eyes she turned on him proved she was wise beyond her years. He was happy to see her intelligence coupled with innate kindness, and that her strong will hadn't been trampled by the torturous events of her past.

"We'll all stick together. It's the Thorne way," he said firmly. He'd be damned if anyone hurt this beautiful young woman again.

She sighed her resignation and gave a small shake of her head as if to say he was impossible.

"I've not always been there for you, Spring, but please, let me have this," he said gruffly.

"You've been the best of fathers," she declared loyally as she embraced him fully. "Never doubt it, Dad."

Preston found himself getting choked up, and he held her tighter to express all the emotion bottled up in his throat. She didn't complain about the fierceness of his hug, and he was glad. He needed this moment.

Opening his eyes, he saw Selene watching them. The longing on her face tugged at his heartstrings. She'd missed out on parental love. Oh, maybe not when she was young, when her mother was alive, but after. And her father had definitely been a coldhearted bastard. Preston had never met the senior Salinger, but he'd heard the stories circling about the witch community when talk of his son, Victor, arose. The general consensus was that the apple hadn't fallen far from the tree.

"She's lovely, Dad." Spring's sweet voice caught his attention. "She looks like she could use a hug, too."

Mischief lurked in her smile, and Preston bussed a kiss on her smooth forehead. "I'll get right on that."

Spring walked away, but not without holding up her hand for a high five from Alastair.

His brother caught Preston's I'm-on-to-you-two glare and grinned.

Making his way to where Selene sat, Preston smiled down on her upturned face. "Spring believes you need a hug, too."

"Does she?" Selene's tone was cool, but her eyes twinkled in direct contrast.

He offered a hand to help her stand. "I've been ordered to show you love."

"I don't want it if it isn't freely given, Preston."

"Who said it wasn't freely given? I'm all for hugging you any chance I can get." With that said, he opened his arms. A ghost of a smile touched her lips as Selene stepped into his embrace. But she wasn't fooling anyone with her reserved routine. Especially not him. "Much better," he murmured.

"Mmhmm." She tightened her arms. "You give the best hugs. I

can see why Spring insisted on sharing."

"She's a giver. Like her father."

Selene laughed and snuggled deeper. After a moment, she pulled away and touched his cheek. "Thank you. It was the extra boost I needed today."

"Let's go get some rest. Tomorrow promises to be challenging."

"I assume there are enough beds to accommodate us all?"

Preston hadn't expected her to drop her guard and have sex with him so soon, but he had hoped she might decide to stay the night with him and allow him to hold her as they drifted to sleep. It had been too many years since he held a woman he cared about in that way. His disappointment was keen, but he refused to let it show. "I'm sure there are. My children will head to their homes for the evening. It isn't safe for all of us to be in one location without our amped-up wards."

Selene cast him a sharp look. "I hadn't thought about it, but I suppose it isn't the smartest thing. Can I help you put wards in place tonight?"

"I'm sure the Drakes' standard charm will work. I'll be the only Thorne, with the exception of Mack, in residence. The likelihood of anyone knowing I'm back on the earthly plane is nil."

Sebastian, ever the dutiful host since they'd arrived unannounced, chose that moment to approach and offer to take them to their assigned rooms for the evening. As Selene waited, Preston excused himself long enough to speak to his brother on the pretext of ensuring Evie's welfare.

Selene made small talk with Sebastian as her mind turned over the question of whether she should ask Preston to stay the night with her. When he returned to her side, he seemed distracted and remained quiet on their trek through the house.

"What do you intend to do about Evie?" Selene asked.

Startled from his thoughts, Preston looked down at her as if he'd forgotten she existed. "Alastair has created a temperature-controlled dome around her body to protect her from the elements. He'll have guards watch her throughout the night."

Sebastian stopped in front of a door on the third floor. "Aunt Gwennie and I will reinforce the spell protecting the entire estate before we turn in. Evie will be well cared for."

"Thank you, Baz," Preston said, his voice gruff with emotion.

Selene could only imagine how difficult it must be for someone like him to be unable to revive Evie with a simple spell or snap of his fingers. It also had to weigh on him to know he'd missed Serqet in their ranks. She'd gotten the better of them all, and none would've been the wiser without Damian.

"We love her, too." One side of Sebastian's mouth quirked up. "She posed as my Aunt Teddie for as long as I was alive."

"I know she'll be in good hands," Preston assured him with a pat on Sebastian's back. "Now, which bedroom is mine?"

Sebastian pointed. "The one next door, just there. And Selene, this suite is yours. Should you need anything you're unable to conjure, please don't hesitate to call downstairs."

"I'm sure I'll be fine." She smiled her thanks.

"I'll bid you both good evening." With the barest indication of a bow, Sebastian's long strides were eating up the distance to the stairs.

Selene turned her face up to Preston and smiled. "I see no point in sleeping in separate beds, *agápi mou*. Would you care to join me?" Where she'd gotten her courage to ask, she'd never know. But she wanted him with her tonight, if only to hold her and share his warmth. She desperately wanted to feel the solid strength of a man's arms around her again. And she wanted that man to be the one standing before her.

"Not thirty minutes ago, I was dreaming of the moment when you'd offer. However, I'm afraid I'll be poor company." The heavy regret in his tone felt like rejection all the same.

"It's not a problem." She spun to flee. "Sleep well."

His large hands gripped her shoulders and prevented her from sailing through the door to her room. "Don't even think about rushing off without a parting kiss, my love."

Relieved he wasn't rejecting her in general but was preoccupied with the thoughts in his mind, she didn't let him see the smile forming on her face. Instead, she leaned back against his hard chest. "Based on our previous kisses, I'm not sure you'll be able to settle for one, Preston."

His laughter rumbled, and she felt it chase along her spine. "Most likely, I won't, but let's give it the old college try."

He turned her to face him, and his heat enveloped her without him ever fully embracing her. All around her, the air sizzled, and the glimmer of a flame lit his cognac eyes and gave them a red glow. This fire elemental could burn her without trying. She lifted the few inches to close the distance between their mouths. He didn't take it beyond a mere tasting, but Selene was consumed with desire all the same.

When he drew back, he traced the line of her lower lip with the pad of his thumb. A sadness hung over him, and he possessed a general sense of tiredness—as if he'd journeyed a long way and hadn't quite found what he was looking for. "Good night, darling."

"Stay with me," she blurted, horrified by her need to keep him close. "I don't care if you're moody or preoccupied. I simply want you to sleep beside me. Nothing more."

He watched her, and she was sure his eyes missed nothing.

Achy and desperate for him, Selene wasn't entirely ashamed of her feelings.

"I'd like nothing better."

Clasping his hand, she led him to her room and shut the door. She feared the awkwardness of climbing into bed with him, a virtual stranger, but his confidence overrode her nervousness. Why she was acting like a stammering virgin, she had no idea. She'd seduced many men in her lifetime when the urge took her, but perhaps her anxiety stemmed from loving this particular one. Preston mattered.

"Normally, I sleep naked," he said with a mischievous side glance. "But I can conjure pajamas if it bothers you."

"Your boxers should serve well enough." Some of the old Selene returned enough for her to say, "I enjoy the sight of a muscular chest."

Preston barked out a laugh. "Good to know. Come to bed, my love. I want to hold you, and you can help me chase away my demons."

"I can definitely do that," she said softly as she settled on the mattress, beside him. "I'll be whatever you need tonight, Preston."

"I only require you to be yourself, Selene. The fierce, beautiful woman I've come to admire."

Her heart melted, and she willingly went into his arms. She lightly stroked the planes of his chest until his breathing deepened and evened out. Closing her eyes, she joined him in his slumber.

CHAPTER 15

The dawning light filtered through the slit in the heavy curtains surrounding the bed. Selene immediately became aware of the fact she was alone. Disappointment hit her hard. Although she hadn't thought about Preston's early morning exit before going to sleep, she was irritated he hadn't waited around long enough for her to wake.

She'd just sat up and threw back the duvet when he stepped from the *en suite* bathroom. A plush towel was wrapped around his waist and hung low on his hips, taunting her with its precarious position. His deep auburn hair was slicked back and still damp from a shower. He only needed a trident and he'd easily pass for a sea god.

Selene's mouth went dry.

The searing heat of his gaze warmed her in all the right places as his eyes slid down her body. They paused overly long on the exposed length of her legs.

"Good morning." The huskiness of his voice only added to the ache forming between her thighs.

"Good morning," she replied softly. "What time is it?"

"Still early."

"When do we need to meet the others?"

A small smile tugged at his lips as if he guessed where her line of questioning would lead—or where she wanted it to lead. Right back to bed!

"We have time yet."

Time.

That one word sobered her. Time was running out for all of them. Should she grab what she could with both hands before the world as they knew it was gone? Before the Evil had its way and took over, destroying all the beauty and love to be had?

"What is it, Selene?"

A shiver ran the length of her spine. Preston had immediately picked up on her mood shift, and the only person who'd been able to do that in the past was Victor. Many times, he'd noted and used the slightest change to manipulate her. Was that what Preston was doing without her realizing it? Was he playing her?

With as much grace and confidence as she could muster, Selene rose to her feet. Wrapping in the robe left by their host, she avoided Preston's all-seeing eyes.

She attempted to pass him, but his arm shot out and effectively halted her.

"Selene. Talk to me, love. Where did you go just now? It's like your mind went on a side trip."

Lifting her chin, she met his concerned eyes. "It's nothing. Old ghosts creeping in to haunt me."

"Nothing I've done?" He seemed troubled that he might've.

The chilling tension left her, and she placed her hand atop his. "No. Nothing you've done, Preston. It was the idea of time and how little we have left if we don't find a way to stop the Evil."

"That's not all, though," he said with a frown.

"I thought your brother was the empath." She tried to sound teasing, but her tone fell flat.

"He is, but I'm observant. Especially with people I care about."

Placing her palm along his chiseled jaw, she attempted a smile. "Thank you for caring. I'll be fine after a shower." She looked down the length of his tall frame, pausing where the towel rested below his ridged abdomen. Once again, the moisture fled her mouth as she silently counted the visible muscles. "Too bad you didn't wake me so I could help you with all the hard-to-reach places."

Her words had the desired effect, and his body's reaction was immediate.

Glancing up beneath her lashes, she shot him a wicked look. "But you can help me reach mine."

He moved so fast, she squeaked.

Without giving her a second to think, he swept her up into his arms and charged for the bathroom.

The large space was filled with his scent along with the refreshingly clean smell of soap. The combination was heady, and Selene soaked it up.

Preston set her on her feet and cupped her face between his large palms. "I just have one question—shower or bath?" A slow, seductive smile curled his generous mouth and made her weak.

"Shower."

Without ever removing his gaze from her, Preston waved a hand in the general area of the Roman shower stall. The handles turned, and the overhead rainfall showerhead released a deluge of water. The hand-held wands sputtered, then settled on a steady stream.

"Hot?"

"Is there ever any question with you around?" she asked in disbelief.

His roar of laughter sent color rushing to her cheeks the second she realized he meant the water temperature and not her internal thermostat. "Hot is fine," she mumbled.

Preston wove his fingers into her mussed hair and cradled the back of her head as he lowered his lips to hers. All the previous embarrassment fled along with any coherent thoughts she might consider forming. The boldness of his kiss shot a thrill along her skin, from crown to pinky toes and every place in between.

Christ alive, the man had a talented tongue!

Selene thought of all the other key spots he could use it on, and her knees gave way.

Quick on the draw, he wrapped his sinewy arm around her back and drew her against him, deepening his kiss. She moaned into his mouth and held on for dear life.

Walking her backward until they were under the spray, he hoisted her up. She experienced a second of panic when she remembered her clothing, but it faded as she felt the skin-on-skin contact.

Thank the Goddess for witchcraft.

Her breasts were squished against the hard wall of his chest, and she shifted to increase the friction. Her nipples tightened into hard buds, and she practically whimpered as he ducked his head to take one into his mouth. After he paid the proper homage to her left breast, he dedicated an equal amount of time to her right. She deeply appreciated his thoroughness.

Selene didn't realized she'd said it aloud until he chuckled. This time, she didn't give two flying flips about her silliness. She smiled down into his face as he lifted her and pressed her back to the tiled wall.

"Stay," he murmured an instant before he dropped to his knees in front of her.

She gasped, unsure whether it was her reaction to floating above the floor or the touch of his tongue to her core. While she'd used magic to enhance sex in the past, she'd never had it used on herself. Nor had she hung suspended in the air as her lover laved her folds and toyed with her until she screamed his name.

He surprised her when he didn't immediately enter her. Instead, he reached for the soap and turned her rag doll body to face the wall. His large hands used the slip of the suds to massage her shoulders and upper back. Working his way down her body, he cupped her buttocks and used his thumbs to massage the area between her legs.

Again, she moaned as she pressed her palms to the tile and locked her trembling knees to keep from dissolving into a puddle at his feet.

Using the hand-held wand, he directed the flow upward between her thighs. The water pressure made her catch her breath as it hit her clit, and when it turned icy cold, she cried out. Immediately it warmed, only to change to frigid again. The fluctuating pressure and temperatures were a sensation like nothing she'd ever experienced before, and she rode the wave to her second orgasm.

The smug smile on his face when she finally faced him made her roll her eyes. "I can now freely admit I was an idiot in the Otherworld for not taking you up on your offer to date the second we met."

The flash of white when he grinned set her knees to trembling again.

The man was divine.

She wondered if he was even aware of his devastatingly good looks and what they did to a woman's internal system, so she decided to ask.

His surprise was laced with a bit of embarrassment. Or so she believed when she witnessed the tinge of color highlight his cheeks. Selene loved his discomfiture. It spoke of the lack of conceit and the very real emotion he felt being with her.

Taking the shower wand, she knelt in front of him. His eyes flared wide then dropped to her mouth.

Selene magically adjusted the water pressure and ran it over the underside of his penis, teasing the tip before massaging his balls with the spray. Making eye contact long enough to shoot him a seductive look and matching smile, she took him into her mouth.

It was his turn to moan and gasp his way through her ministrations. As she felt his balls tighten, he drew back and cupped himself. He breathed in and exhaled a long moment later, stopping himself from coming by sheer willpower alone.

His lids lifted, and he stared down at her with wonder. Those soul-destroying eyes of his turned the color of molten lava, and a tight half smile curled his lips.

Selene sat back on her heels and watched him as he watched her.

"Why did you stop me?" She trailed her hands up his muscular thighs, making slow circles with her fingers as she worked her way back to his groin.

"Because I want to come inside you," he replied. The husky quality of his deep voice couldn't hide his honesty and the openly admiring look he sent her. "I want to feel your walls tighten around me as I thrust into you. I want to feel you milk every drop from me and inhale your cry of pleasure into my mouth."

"Aw, fuck," she whispered, turned on as she'd never been before.

"Precisely." He hauled her to her feet and into his arms in one smooth motion.

Wrapping her legs around his waist, Selene lowered her mouth to his.

He used his index and middle fingers to stretch her and work her to the point of exploding for a third time, but before she could, he replaced his fingers with his dick. She purred his name as she felt the fullness of him for the first time. It seemed to ignite something within him, and his hips moved faster, and the constant piston motion became harder. Deeper.

She released a gasping cry with each thrust, begging for what only he could provide.

Shifting to place her back against the wall, he cradled her head with one hand and used the thumb on his other to circle her nub. The slap of skin on skin, the delightful pressure of his superhuman thrusts, the rasping moans he released as he lightly bit down on her nipple, all worked to send her spiraling over the edge.

He followed right after, and the shout of her name echoed off the walls around them.

With his face buried against the hollow of her throat and his ragged breath hot against her sensitive flesh, she felt herself grow aroused again. She'd done this. She'd had the power to bring this man to completion and have him cry out for her and her alone. It was a heady feeling.

Wearing a satisfied smirk, she tightened the walls of her vagina.

His groan was her reward. "Fuck, but you're going to kill me."

"And you me. But we'll die extremely satisfied and happy," she teased.

"You know it."

Scooping her up, he tossed her over his shoulder and gave her a light tap on her ass.

"Let's have round two in bed. I don't think my legs will hold up to that again this soon."

She laughed and caressed the beautifully rounded ass in front of her.

His second go rocked her world even more than the first, and Selene was ready to alter her initial impression of him as a sea god and declare him a bed god. She puffed out a breath, which was ragged since she was in short supply after what they'd just done.

He chuckled. "Did I hit all those 'hard to reach places,' my love?"

"Most assuredly. And then some."

His laughter was deeper, more full-bodied this time. "Good. I'd hate to think I lost my touch after so long in the Otherworld."

"Nope. No touch lost at all." She kissed the rounded shoulder next to her. "Or if you did, I can't imagine what sex with you would've been like before. Quite possibly, it might've killed me."

He rolled on his side and propped his head on his hand. Blowing gently on her sweat-soaked skin, he cooled her body down, but with the same breath, he heated her up and sparked her desire for another round.

"I would give you all day to do that," she murmured huskily as he eased down the sheet to expose her breasts. The moment the cool air touched her skin, her nipples contracted. "I'm not sure I've met anyone who uses their magic to such an amazing degree."

"Unfortunately, we don't have all day, but I'm willing to steal a few more minutes to delight you with my talents," he said.

She moaned his name when he sucked one of her tightly budded nipples into his mouth. "Delight away."

CHAPTER 16

"We have to get dressed and go down, my love."

"I know, but I don't want to ruin my postcoital bliss."

He laughed and stood up.

As he slid into his boxer-briefs, Selene used the last glimpse to admire his tight, toned ass. She wasn't sure of his exact age—probably close to seventy—but damned if she could see where he'd been touched by time. Like most warlocks of his caliber, his body had stopped growing older at the forty-year mark. Genetics played a large part in a witch's aging process. The Thornes were exceptionally blessed, and Selene was thrilled about it.

"Are you planning to lie there and ogle me all day, or are you joining the rest of us to save the world?"

"Tough choice. I'll pick option one since I like ogling you."

He grinned over his shoulder. "If you go that route, it won't only be ogling you're doing."

"Preston Thorne, are you saying you'd dismiss your responsibilities as a hero and stay in bed with me?"

"In a second. I'm hoping you're the honorable one here. I need you to force me out that door to deal with this mess."

Selene expelled a long breath and climbed to her feet. "You really did kill my high. As soon as everything is back to rights, I'm chaining you to my bed for a good month." She held up a hand when he would've spoken. "No, don't argue. You owe me that, at least."

"Who's arguing? I was going to suggest two months minimum."

A girlish giggle escaped Selene, and it surprised her. Rarely before had she experienced this level of teasing, and she loved it. With each layer of her reserve Preston peeled back, another fun part of her emerged. She adored him for waking her up to all she was.

"Sold. Two months to the ridiculously handsome man in the gray button-down shirt." She pressed herself against him. "I'm afraid we have to seal our deal with a kiss."

He gave her a quick hard peck. "That's all you get. Anything more, and we'll never leave this room."

She grinned and reveled in his matching smile. "You're onto me."

"And stop trying to tempt me with sexy talk."

"'You're onto me' is sexy?"

"Absolutely. Especially when I want to be *on* you."

Laughing, she escaped to the bathroom. She peeked around the opening to say, "I'll meet you downstairs. I'm sure you want to check on Evie."

"I do. Thank you for understanding."

"I'd be a selfish person if I didn't, *agápi mou*. Go now."

After he left, Selene sat on the edge of the tub and pressed her hand to her heart. This morning had been a revelation. He wasn't the first skilled lover she'd been with, but he was, by far, the most considerate. Perhaps their feelings for one another heightened the experience, but events had left her shaken and frightened of the future. If things should go wrong, if the Evil should come out the winner in this skirmish and if Preston's soul was obliterated in the process, she'd never recover.

If she dug deep enough, she'd probably have to acknowledge she'd avoided relationships for this exact reason. Previously, she'd been terrified of her half brother's reach. Now, he needed to be brought back to balance the scales of good and evil to make the

Thornes' plan work. If he could strike down Preston to make Selene miserable, Victor would do that very thing.

Closing her eyes, she prayed to the Goddess they would succeed. Any other outcome was unimaginable.

PRESTON FOUND HIS BROTHER ON THE TERRACE, A CUP OF COFFEE IN hand and a grim expression on his handsome face. "Al? What's happened?"

"Isis and Serqet consulted with Set. They will be the three who go to the Netherworld."

"Did Isis say why she chose now to leave the Otherworld? I thought the risk was too great?"

"She's been watching our progress from her side and wanted to speed up the process. Apparently, things are taking a turn for the worse there."

"I'm glad she's here. I would think having Isis on our side is a good thing."

"It is. But they've picked the witches and their counterparts who will accompany them."

A sliver of unease pierced Preston. "Who?" But he feared he already knew.

Alastair straightened from where he rested his elbows on the railing and turned toward him. "Damian and Isolde, of course. Spring and Zhu Lin. GiGi and Harold Beecham. You and Delphine. Selene and—"

"Victor," Preston finished for him. "*Fucking hell!* The sickest individuals with the greatest grudges against us all, a goddess we can't trust, and our cousin who would likely shoot me through the heart herself in place of her henchman this go around."

Preston understood the pairings. One of the two had ultimately been responsible for the other person's death to a degree. Although his sister, GiGi, hadn't killed Beecham, she'd set up the plan and provided her husband with the knife. The pairings drove the stakes higher and made their task fraught with danger.

"I tried to take Spring's place against Zhu Lin, but Serqet wasn't having it, and her siblings agreed there had to be a male-female balance among the pairings as well."

"Spring killed Lin, GiGi set up Beecham, Delphine ordered my death, and Victor killed Selene," Preston said, easily figuring out the connections. "Doesn't it throw off the balance having the Aether there? After all, he killed Isolde."

"Technically, that was a joint effort by him and Nathanial."

"Right." He ran a hand through his hair and met his brother's probing gaze. "What else aren't you telling me?"

"Nothing. I'm waiting on the others to arrive to inform them of the decree from our godly trio."

"Then what's your thoughtful look for?"

Alastair's lips twisted. "I'm curious how well you slept, little brother."

Preston glanced down at his person. Nothing seemed to be out of order. "Why?"

His brother laughed. "You look more relaxed than normal. I imagine your lovely companion from the Otherworld is responsible."

"Shut it, Al. I don't kiss and tell."

"It could be argued you just did with that statement." Alastair chuckled when Preston shot him the bird. He quickly sobered, staring down into his mug. "I've missed these moments with you, Pres. Having you beside me whenever the world turned upside down or we needed to fight scum like Lin, Salinger, and Beecham. It's not the same without you here."

Preston's chest grew heavy, and he was forced to blink back the tears forming behind his lids. He swallowed hard against the rising tide of emotion. "I know, Al. I know."

Alastair smoothed his tie with one hand and pointed his cup toward the house. "Go. Have a hearty breakfast to keep up your strength. I fear you're going to need it."

Alastair watched Preston stride away, and with each step separating them, he wanted to call his brother back. What he hadn't said—and what he desperately needed to—was how much he loved him. How proud he was of the man Preston had become, and how grateful Alastair was to call him kin. He wanted to tie him up and shove him in a closet to protect him from what was to come.

Of the two of them, Preston was the better man.

Regret for the lost years settled heavily on Alastair's heart: the ones spent at odds over Aurora, the ones lost when he was kept prisoner by Zhu Lin, and the most recent ones since Preston's death. If Alastair could trade places with any of those journeying to the Nether, he would in an instant. Sitting this fight out went against his nature. As did failing to protect those he loved. He'd failed all of them at one point or another.

With a grimace of distaste, he tossed his coffee in the bush below the balcony railing. The lone figure under the tree caught his attention, and he set the mug down before descending the steps to join her.

"I'm surprised you'd risk speaking to me, Alastair Thorne."

"I've risked a great many things in my life, Exalted One. The least of which is speaking with a goddess who looks upon me without favor." He offered up a self-deprecating smile. "But you wouldn't have made your presence known if you didn't wish to talk to me, Serqet."

Her eyes narrowed marginally, but she gave a quick nod to acknowledge he was correct. "My sister has impressed upon me the severity of this upcoming trial. You understand it is in my nature to take advantage once the danger has passed?"

"I do." Dread curled in his belly and shook its tail like a rattlesnake. "Are you warning me to be on guard?"

"Not from me, child. Not this time. But I would urge caution regardless. Your enemies bear you great ill will, and they won't be keen on returning to the Underworld. They've lived there twice as long as those in the Otherworld and a hundred times that of those on this plane." Her gaze was void of standard spitefulness, and Alastair could physically feel the truth of her warning. "Their souls have been tortured. Should they get the opportunity, they will try to remain here, Alastair. Be prepared."

"Is this your way of offering my family an olive branch?"

"Yes. The Aether helped me to see what I've always known. He took from me a good portion of my hatred and bitterness with his touch." She must've recognized the surprise on his face for what it was. "He didn't tell you that part, did he?" She smiled and shook her head. "He's worthy to hold the honor of Aether, and he uses his powers wisely. As I should've done from the beginning."

"I'm glad he was able to ease your suffering, Exalted One. It seems none of us choose who we love, not even your kind, huh?" He softened his comment with an understanding smile. "For what it's worth, I'm glad you hold Damian in esteem. Maybe it will give our side the boost we need."

"If I can repay his kindness, I will." She looked beyond his shoulder to the house. "I believe your family is returning. But first, I wish to give you something to give Knox." Serqet held out a chain mail bag.

Alastair's heart began to hammer, the sound drowning out all other noise. He couldn't seem to look away from the item in her hand, nor could he lift his to accept her offering.

"Don't be afraid, child," she said gently. "I'm returning it to your family to use or to dispose of."

"Don't take this the wrong way, Exalted One, but if I never see that wretched necklace again, it will be too soon."

She laughed, and the sound was as light as the air around them. "With the help of my sister, I've tweaked the curse. The Red Scorpion will bring with it great power without the death sentence."

He lifted his gaze to meet hers. Honesty shone back, and he could detect no falsehoods. Still, he was filled with trepidation. "How do I protect the others from it, should the need arise?"

"You hold no trust for me."

"No offense is meant when I say I don't. But I do find it difficult to reconcile the woman in front of me with the goddess who spent centuries trying to wipe out my family. Trust doesn't come easily to me, of all people."

Understanding was in the smile she gave him. "Here. Take my gift, Alastair Thorne, and be grateful for it."

"I've never known a gift from the gods not to contain a catch. Hence my inability to swear without summoning locusts," he said dryly.

Her eyes twinkled as she said, "You are wise to be wary of our offerings, and because you are, I'll promise you this; no death shall come to you or your bloodline as a result of my pet here. Fair enough?"

"What about those things worse than death? You could cause my pecker to fall off."

He was only half kidding, and yet she laughed as if he were the greatest jester.

Then he recalled her words. "My bloodline? What about the extended family?" His tone grew hard, but he was damned if he could help it. His in-laws would be protected if he had to lay down his life to do it.

"I cannot promise that, child. My deal with Isis and Set was to spare your lives. Should anyone but a Thorne touch the scorpion, they risk death. Remember that."

CHAPTER 17

"Do you trust her?" Both Alastair and Damian seemed to be swayed by her change of heart, but Preston found it difficult to believe Serqet wouldn't betray them all. Of course, he had a lot more to lose. Spring was his daughter, and Selene had been paired with Victor as her counterpart. If anything happened to either woman, Preston would lose his damned mind and do something stupid—like try to end the life of a goddess. He wasn't impulsive by nature. Hell, he was more methodical and predictable than the average Thorne. But when it came to family, he'd kill first and ask questions later.

"I do." Alastair wore a thoughtful expression as he stared out the window toward where he'd met with Serqet. Finally, he shrugged and faced those gathered in the dining room. "It's rare to have someone fool me, but it isn't impossible. The best we can do is keep our eyes and ears open to be on alert to betrayal."

Damian appeared to be in agreement.

Preston's nerves got the better of him, but he pushed them aside. "Okay. If that damned necklace can't hurt us, let's give it a try." He rose and grabbed the chain-mail bag, only stopping when Spring cried out.

"Dad, don't! You haven't seen what that thing can do."

Actually, he had, through Isis's looking glass. Victor Salinger had used the twin sister of Nash's girlfriend to force him to put it on as she held Spring hostage with a knife to her throat. One nick of that poisoned blade, and Spring's life would've been forfeit. As it was, Nash had barely survived and only due to Ryanne's sacrifice on his behalf.

"The surest way to know if Serqet is lying is to put it to the test. My life has technically ended so I'd rather be the guinea pig of the group." Preston gave her a warm smile. "What's the worst that can happen? I die again, and Isis sends me back?"

Selene approached him and rested her hand on his arm to stay his motion. "I don't find this amusing in the least, *agápi mou*. Nor is it the wisest course of action."

"At some point this week, we meet with those soulless devils, Selene. We need to have a game plan and weapons at our disposal. Ones that won't backfire and kill us all."

She shot him a glare at his testy tone. "I may not be one of your inner circle, but I know my brother. He was Serqet's minion for years. On her orders and Zhu Lin's, Victor became a ruthless killing machine. But make no mistake; he enjoyed it." She released Preston's arm and backed away. "And he'll enjoy it this time around."

"I won't let him hurt you, my love."

"You won't have a choice if you're dead and waiting to be revived, will you?" She scoffed and shook her head. "I know you're fierce, Preston, but this goes beyond the boundaries of what a normal man would do or how he would react. Victor is a rabid dog."

"I tend to agree with Selene," Alastair said with a steely-eyed look at the two of them. "When Lin and Victor held me prisoner, their favorite game was torture. Victor being the more sadistic of the two. Lin hated me and wished me dead, but Victor? He was pure evil."

"Tell me. What's the alternative?" Preston snapped. "What do you, oh-holier-than-thou Alastair Thorne—"

"Sonofabitch!" Knox entered the room and immediately scooped up the bag with the necklace. "What the fuck is this doing here?" He didn't wait for an answer and stormed toward the exit.

When Preston would've charged after him, Spring latched onto his arm. "Dad, wait!"

He glared down at her. "What is it?"

"The necklace has the power to alter moods. Did you notice how angry all of you became? How quickly it happened?"

He twisted to look at his brother. The wrathful expression on Alastair's face confirmed what Spring had said. When Preston would've spoken, Alastair gave a subtle shake of his head. He held up both hands and quietly uttered the words to Granny Thorne's cloaking spell. As soon as they were free of outside prying eyes, Alastair swirled a finger as if to say "go ahead."

"So I was right. Serqet hasn't removed the curse," Preston said grimly.

"It would appear so. The other option is she failed to remember that fun side effect of the blasted thing." Alastair's tone was equally grim. "Dethridge, what do you think our next move should be? How do we go about cutting her legs out from underneath her?"

Damian uncrossed his arms and ran a hand through his hair. "I don't know. Fighting a goddess is new territory for me. I try not to piss them all off as you are all wont to do."

The air around them crackled, and Alexander Castor stepped through a rift in the corner of the room along with Quentin. Castor glanced around in his confusion. "Where are they? The timing—"

"Unless I miss my guess, they've cloaked themselves."

Cupping his hands around his mouth, Castor called out, "Come out, come out, wherever you are!"

Quentin cast him a scathing look. "You think this is a game, old man?"

"Son, you'll learn all the world's a game, and we are mere chess pieces to be sacrificed at the whims of the gods. Some of us are kings and some, the lowly pawns."

"I'll be sure to note that in my diary of useless things my sperm donor told me." Quentin didn't bother to hide his disdain.

"How many times must I apologize to you, boy?"

"Don't bother. You're wasting your breath."

From his place in front of the two, Preston could practically feel the tension. Quentin's hatred was real, and he wondered why a son would despise his father to such a degree. With a quick amendment to Alastair's initial cloaking spell, Preston added their names and altered the charm to encompass them. Castor laughed when they all appeared. It seemed Quentin was correct in assuming everything was a joke to his father. It bore consideration.

Preston purposefully reached out a hand to shake Quentin's first, letting Castor know where his loyalties lay. The truth was, Preston wasn't as trusting of Alexander Castor as his brother and cousin were. "Hello, son. Let's update you on what's happening."

Castor narrowed his eyes as he registered the slight but returned to his jovial self within seconds.

"I should go find Knox," Quentin said after hearing what Preston had to say.

"I'll go. He hasn't heard the worst of it, and I fear he'll want to choke Serqet with that necklace when he finds out I'm one of those going to the Nether." Spring gave her father a quick kiss on the cheek. "We'll find the proper weapons and plan accordingly, Dad. It's what we're good at."

After Spring left, Preston turned to Alastair and Damian, effectively ignoring Castor. "We need to speak to the trio. I want Spring removed from those going." By trio, he referred to Isis, Serqet, and Set. His tone was hard when he said, "None of my children are to be put at risk. Not. A. One."

"They can't be budged, Pres. I tried."

"Then we try again," he snapped. "I mean it, Al. I'm not allowing my daughter to go there. Not Spring. Autumn, I'd consider. She can handle her own. But Spring is innocent."

"You aren't giving her enough credit, brother, and you're allowing the past to influence your thinking." Alastair rubbed the back of his neck, a sure sign Preston's high emotions were chipping away at him. His expression turned contemplative, and he shot a sharp look at Damian. "Tell me what you know of the Nether, Dethridge. Would enchanted items and spells work, other than the one we intend to use to trap the Evil there? Say, if I created tanzanite rings for us all to communicate telepathically, can it be done?"

"There isn't much information about the Netherworld, Al. I can see what my ancestors may have written in our records, but no one can go there without the Yin and Yang balance, both male-female *and* the good-evil. It's likely why there isn't much information on it." His look was sardonic as he rhetorically asked, "Who in their right minds would go anywhere with the person who most wished them dead?"

"Enter the Thorne family," Preston muttered. "If this bullshit works, I'll be a monkey's uncle."

"Well, technically, you're a monkey's grandfather, does that count?" Quentin teased.

"No. Summer's ape is a menace."

Alastair chuckled. "He's quite sweet, if a bit mischievous."

"Okay, back to the subject at hand. Time is short." Selene pinned all the men with a hard look. Here was a woman used to issuing orders and expecting to be obeyed. Preston admired her take-charge attitude. "Mr. Dethridge, please go see what you can find in your records. Preston and I will visit Georgie Sipanil. As the oldest living Council member, she may have an idea about what will and won't work." She faced Alastair. "It's well known you hold Isis's favor. Perhaps you have a female enemy sporting a grudge. You might be able to convince the Goddess that you and this person should take Spring's and Lin's places." Next, Selene turned to Caster and Quentin. "Speak to Athena, if you can summon her. She seems to know the most about your family's history. Before we go into the Nether, I want to know what you two are truly capable of."

Preston grinned in the face of her directives. Selene was simply amazing. She caught his eye, and a light blush tinted her cheeks.

"What is it, *agápi mou?*"

"You're magnificent. I feel you should be the acting commander of this op." Especially if she prevented Spring's endangerment with her militant planning.

Selene rolled her eyes, but a small smirk danced on her lips. "Someone had to. The testosterone in this room was suffocating. Nothing was getting done but posturing."

"Apparently, we need more Yin and Yang energy," Damian quipped.

She chuckled. "Agreed."

"Perhaps we should bring in the lovely Vivian for more female balance." Castor's grin was pure wickedness. His quip earned him a glare and a magical shove from the Aether.

"Leave my wife out of this," Damian growled. He signaled Alastair, who murmured a spell to counter their cloaked enchantment.

"I forgot how territorial you were in regard to your mate, Dethridge." Castor conjured a mason jar of what looked to be moonshine. "Anyone up for a swig to get this party going?"

"Are you never serious, Castor?" Preston shoved the hand offering the rotgut.

A sneer twisted Alexander's lip. "Why do I need to be when the lot of you are serious enough for a hundred people?"

Hands curled into fists, Preston stepped into his space and stood toe-to-toe with him. "Maybe because my family's lives are at stake? How about that, you fucking asshole?"

"It's not like the Thornes don't continually come out on top, right?" There was a steely edge to Castor's words, and Preston hoped like hell either Alastair or Damian could tell what was behind them. If Alexander Castor was a liability, he needed to go, seventh elemental or no.

But Quentin's reaction was swift and immediate. He grabbed his father by the throat and slammed him into a wall. Castor brought his hands up, and electricity danced along his fingertips. Quentin didn't appear concerned that he was about to be shish kabobbed.

Their pose was like a sculpture of two larger-than-life Titans ready to go to war.

"I fucking dare you, old man," Quentin growled.

"Do you think I don't have control over this power after so many years, boy? I could kill you and shock you back to life in the blink of an eye." Castor's eyes turned icy, and Preston shivered at the contempt.

When he would've stepped forward to intervene, Damian halted him with a hand on his shoulder.

Don't intervene. Castor's anger is an act.

Preston frowned as Damian's voice echoed in his mind.

This was all an act? Why?

A jolt shot through him, and he almost cried out from the strength of the current. Along with the energy came a vision of Damian's conversation with Castor early that morning. The two men felt it was best to make Castor appear recalcitrant and have him throw verbal barbs whenever possible. All in an effort to fool Serqet into believing he was being forced to help the Thornes and not through any desire of his own.

Preston gave an infinitesimal nod of his chin, but he had no doubt Damian could clearly see what was in his head: acknowledgment of their plan.

The Aether gave his shoulder a light squeeze before releasing him and stepping forward as if his intent was to take Preston's place in reprimanding Castor.

"Very amusing, fellas, but your anger is enough to turn me off my breakfast," Alastair said drolly. "Do you intend to rein it in, or is it to be a shoot-out at the O.K. Corral at high noon?"

The blue sparks jumping along Castor's fingers disappeared, and Quentin gave a grunt as he released him.

"Try not to be such a fucktwat all the time," Quentin snapped.

"Try to remove the stick from your ass," Castor countered. "I thought you'd be a chip off the old block. Apparently, you're as humorless as your mother."

Rage flared on Quentin's countenance, and his lips pulled back in a snarl.

Alexander had thrown the wrong comment into the mix.

Preston punched Castor in the face. Not hard enough to take him down, but definitely hard enough to hurt. "Mamas are off-limits, you prick. Without exception."

Quentin laughed for the first time in the two days since he'd learned his father was alive. "I love the fuck out of you, Mr. Thorne."

"Call me Preston, my boy. We're family." He patted Quentin on the back and strolled away, whistling an off-key tune.

CHAPTER 18

"Preston Thorne." Georgie Sipanil held out her gnarled hands in welcome. As Selene watched them, they embraced, and Preston took great care when enfolding the pint-sized woman in his hug. Although her joints were twisted with age, they were the only thing giving away the elderly witch's age. To look at her, one would believe she was in her late fifties. She was attractive and had an ageless quality about her.

"As I live and breathe, Georgie girl, you've become even more beautiful since my passing."

"Oh, go on with you, you scamp!"

Selene didn't fail to notice the pleasure lighting Georgie's eyes or the pink splash of color darkening the woman's skin. Preston's charm was as fabled as Quentin Buchanan's. Seeing it in action, Selene could now understand why. This Thorne had magic in his honeyed words as well as those fabulously skilled hands of his. She felt her cheeks heat as she recalled their early morning acrobatics. Preston had stolen her heart and captured her soul. Oddly, she wasn't bothered by it.

Georgie had a diminutive stature, and it screamed fragile. However, the woman in front of her was made of pure fire-forged steel. Many a time, they'd met at a Council function. Every single one of those occasions had reinforced Selene's belief that Georgie was the stuff of legends and wouldn't tolerate bad behavior from anyone. This geriatric spitfire held those around her to a higher standard, and oddly, people met that standard to avoid disappointing her.

Turning her attention on Selene, Georgie's expression became reserved. "Ms. Barringer. I'm surprised to see you here."

"Because I'm supposed to be dead, or because I'm working with the Thornes?" she asked coolly.

The elderly woman's lips twitched as if she wanted to smile. "Come. I'll order tea."

"I can conjure whatever you'd like, ma'am," Selene offered.

"I still have the power to do the same, young lady. I simply like to keep my staff hopping. They grow bored otherwise."

Preston laughed and tucked Georgie's arm through his. "Who in their right mind could ever be bored in your presence, my darling Georgie?"

"You're as charming as your rogue father, my dear. And his father before him." Georgie allowed Preston to assist her into a large wingback chair. Her diminutive size made her appear like a child sitting in an oversized grown-up's seat. He tucked a blanket across her lap and squatted in front of her, turning his face into her palm as she cupped his cheek.

These two had a deep affection for one another, and Selene wondered if perhaps Georgie viewed Preston as the grandson she never had. *Or perhaps it went deeper?* Georgie would've still been in her prime when Preston was young and carousing around.

A small kernel of jealousy popped inside Selene as she watched him kiss Georgie's palm before standing. The other woman was still attractive at her advanced age.

Georgie tilted her head slightly but met Selene's gaze with a steady one of her own, as if sensing where her thoughts had gone. With a slight shake of her head, a reminiscent smile formed on the councilwoman's wide mouth as she said, "I was courted by Preston the First. *Until* he found his one true love and promptly forgot I existed."

"It's not possible to forget you exist, Georgie-girl," Preston protested, not defending his grandfather, but refuting the fact anyone could fail to remember her.

She waved a hand as if to shoo him off. "Nonsense. We all know Thornes only love once. I'm not complaining—*much*. I'm giving Ms. Barringer insight into our history and why I hold you in high regard."

"Why *do* you hold me in high regard?" he asked with a teasing gleam in his bright eyes.

"You're a rascal and a charmer like he was. You might've been my grandson had things taken a different turn."

"I'd have been honored."

"Of course you would've. You'd be a fool not to be. Now sit. It hurts my neck, craning to look up at you both."

Selene sat on the smartly designed leather sectional across from her. "Thank you for the insight. I know next to nothing about Preston, other than the rumors one hears in our community."

His head jerked in her direction, and his face showed his surprise. "You can ask me anything, my love."

"There hasn't been time since we arrived here."

He acknowledged her words with a snort. "True. We've been going hell-bent for leather since we stepped through the portal."

"Which brings us to the reason you're here," Georgie concluded.

"Yes."

They filled her in on what was happening and what they knew to date, only leaving out information harmful to their cause should the wrong person be scrying or listening at keyholes.

"Is there anything you can tell us about the Nether, Ms. Sipanil?" Selene asked.

"Call me Georgie, my dear. The friend of my friend and all that."

"I'm glad you're willing to set aside formalities in this situation."

"Make no mistake; I'm doing it for Preston. I trust his judgment.

Please don't disappoint me and turn out like that horrid brother of yours."

"That will never happen," Preston assured her, clasping Selene's hand in his larger one. "Ms. Barringer has a sterling character."

"Does she?" Councilwoman Sipanil's voice contained a hard edge, and Selene knew she'd hate what was coming. "Tell me, Preston. Has she told you about her part in spying for Victor Salinger while under the guise of our liaison for the Greek Witches' Council?"

Selene's heart picked up its pace. The hammering was so loud, it drowned out all but the high-pitched ringing in her ears. She'd wanted to be the one to break the news to Preston, not have someone else throw it in her face in front of him. Now, he'd believe she was hiding things, when all she'd wanted was to find the proper time to tell him. Selene feared she'd faint dead away.

The pressure applied by Preston's fingers brought her back. His grip wasn't exactly painful, but it did speak to the tension in his frame.

"She has," he lied smoothly. "She regrets her part in all of that and has assured me she's no longer in league with Salinger."

Selene wasn't sure how she kept her jaw from dropping to the floor, but she managed.

"Hmm."

Slowly, Selene raised her gaze to meet the shrewd eyes of the woman across from her.

Georgie knew Preston had lied.

Selene gratefully accepted a cup of tea from Georgie's employee and smiled her thanks. After taking a sip, she set her cup into its matching saucer and placed it on the coffee table. "Councilwoman Sipanil—"

"Georgie."

"Uh, *Georgie*. I'd like to formally apologize for my past actions. It would've taken a stronger person than me to thwart Victor. I'm deeply ashamed, and I know nothing excuses what I've done." She clasped her hands together and set them in her lap. "If it is any consolation, I skewed any details I gave him. I made sure to provide only the barest of information to keep myself alive."

"I know." The sternness left Georgie's features, and she gave Selene a thoughtful look. "I also know you helped Holly Thorne-Buchanan and her husband, Quentin. You saved lives that night, Ms. Barringer."

"Holly is a lovely woman, and my conscience wouldn't allow me to let Victor hurt a pregnant woman."

"And had she not been heavily pregnant?"

The woman before her was sharp and missed nothing, but Selene was tired of the games. "I'd have tried to help her regardless. But any life-saving wasn't done by me, Ms. Georgie. The Thornes have Quentin and Athena to thank. I died that night, in case you were unaware."

"I've been fully informed of the circumstances. Alastair Thorne was forthcoming about his part in stealing the Cheirotonia Scroll from our vault in his attempt to revive Aurora Thorne."

"Then you also know I betrayed the Council when I gave Holly information as to the vault's whereabouts and on how to open it," Selene stated flatly. She stood and brushed her hands down the length of her fitted navy dress. "I believe we are both aware I'm not to be trusted, Councilwoman Sipanil. But I care about Preston, and Isis has entrusted her faith in me to help fight the Evil. So what you think about me doesn't concern me in the least." She looked down at Preston. His expression was inscrutable, and Selene's stomach tightened. "I'll wait outside while you make your request."

Preston remained quiet as Selene swept from the room. The confirmation of her involvement in Victor's activities was a punch to the chest. He couldn't say he hadn't had his suspicions, but he'd hoped she'd open up to him and tell him about the past at some point.

Despite what she might believe, he wasn't angry—or at least not with her. Preston's hatred of Victor, however, rose to the highest degree.

"I'm thrilled she's grown a spine," Georgie said.

Preston whipped his head around to stare at her. "Selene's tough," he snapped. "She was in an impossible situation, Georgie. None of us could say we wouldn't do the same. Victor had the full force of the Désorcelers at his back."

She inclined her head in a regal nod. "I understand you love her, and I understand you will defend her to your last breath, my boy. But be cautious. Please. I'd be heartbroken if anything happened to you a second time."

"The welfare of the entire magical community is at stake here. I intend to be very careful." He rubbed the spot between his brows and released a heavy sigh. "What can you tell me about the Netherworld? Anything?"

"No one goes there. It's universally known it would cost your life if you did." She grew thoughtful as she sipped her tea, and Preston stayed silent to allow her to piece together her thoughts. Finally, she said, "Very few know the secret to a safe crossing. There has been one or two brave souls who've tried it, I believe."

"Who?"

"Alexander Castor comes to mind. I'm sure that's how he died. It must've been close to thirty years or more now."

Preston wanted to swear a blue streak. First, over the fact Castor hadn't been forthcoming about the Nether. Second, that his fact-finding mission was a virtual bust. "Nothing else? No files or books hidden in the ever-moving vaults of the Council?"

It wasn't common knowledge that the Witches' Council had charmed the chambers containing their rarest or deadliest spellbooks and artifacts. Each room was on a timer and moved from one spot to another on an hourly basis. They were also cloaked to keep their location unknown to any but those in the loop. Georgie, as head of the Council, would have the information on how to access them.

"Possibly. I'll convene an emergency meeting of the Council's members to discuss this at length. Be prepared to present your case in one hour's time. Together, we'll convince the others to provide access for your family to search the vaults."

"Thank you, Georgie." Preston rose and crossed to her. He lifted her hand to his lips and kissed her knuckles. "We'll be there."

"I'm counting on it." She patted the hand covering hers. "Now, go find your young woman and tell her she needs to treat you right or she'll incur my wrath."

"I'll do that. Oh, and for the record, Castor is still alive."

As Preston strode from the room on the heels of her gasp, he sent a silent prayer to the Goddess that the WC would work with them on this matter. If they decided to be reticent and hold back helpful information, they would all suffer for it.

CHAPTER 19

"Did she tell you what you needed to know?"

Preston didn't answer Selene immediately. Instead, he studied her set features and wary eyes.

"I understand if you don't wish to tell me the details after what you've learned." Her voice held only the slightest tremble, and she forged on. "However, we are required to work together to conquer this threat. As such, I'd appreciate it if you tell me about any relevant information you discover." This time, there was pure irritation in her tone. As if by remaining quiet, he was thoroughly pissing her off.

Biting the inside of his cheek to stem his amusement, Preston dropped his gaze to the ground. If he lost it and laughed while she was in a state of high dudgeon, he would never live to tell the tale.

"Fine. Keep your secrets, you tosser!" she snapped.

His brows went up, and the hilarity he'd been holding back erupted. "Tosser? How very British of you!"

"I am British. I was born in England." She crossed her arms, and a muscle ticked in her jaw. "My time was split between England and Greece. I know how to properly insult a person who deserves it."

"But I don't deserve it, my love." Preston shifted closer and ran his thumb along her jawline. "I don't deserve it at all." Dipping his head, he kissed her, leaving them both breathless when he drew back. "Am I irritated you didn't tell me about your part in Victor's schemes yourself? Yes. Do I believe you can't be trusted? No."

She opened her mouth to speak, but he silenced her with his index finger against her lips.

"Please. Let me finish. You wouldn't have been in the Other-world if you were a bad person, Selene. The sorting of a soul may take minutes, hours, or days, depending on past transgressions. You were there for just a few moments before you were allowed to enter." She didn't look as if she really grasped what he was telling her, so he said, "You're a good person. Isis recognized it right away."

"But I *did* do those things."

"It's not who you are now. Hell, I doubt it was who you were then." He played with a strand of her inky hair. "Did any deaths result from your actions?"

"No! Or if they did, I didn't know about them. I tried my best to make sure that never happened."

"Exactly. Now, in answer to your first question, there were no details to learn or share with you. Georgie doesn't know about the Nether personally. She's going to convene the Council for an emergency meeting and go from there."

"I'm sorry, Preston."

"She put you on the spot to test your merit. I think she admired you for standing up to her."

"I should go back in and speak with her."

Selene looked as if she'd rather eat nails, so Preston slung an arm around her shoulders. "Nah. I think the Council meeting is soon enough. Let's go. There's something I'd like to show you."

"What is it?"

"You'll see when we get there. Hold on tight." She wrapped an arm around his. "Nope, not tight enough." He shifted to embrace her. "That's better."

Her laugh was his reward. Without another word, he teleported them to Thorne Manor—or rather, the pond where he and Alastair used to fish as children. Her appreciation was heard with her breathy sigh and a cry of "Oh, Preston!"

"This is my estate. Or rather, my children's estate now."

She shot him a wry side look. Selene understood all too well the challenges their deaths presented now that they were both alive and kicking again. "You really *do* trust me."

As she'd guessed, he never would've brought her here, to the place his family was most vulnerable, if he believed she might betray him to their enemies. He held out his hand and conjured food for the ducks. "I thought you could use some downtime. Things have been intense for the last few days."

Love or something like it softened her features, and she placed her palm flat over the area of his heart. "Thank you, *agápi mou.*"

"Take time to do what you love." He dumped the duck food into her hands. "I'll wait for you. Then I'd like to show you my home."

"Will you walk with me and tell me about growing up here?"

Over the next few minutes, he spoke of his childhood. Of the love his parents bore their three children. Of racing around, playing cops and robbers with Phillip Carlyle. He told her of the clearing with the standing stones and, eventually, of his antique shop. The one place he escaped to when the world weighed him down. He'd found solace there after Aurora left him for Alastair, and again when his girls were teenagers and he needed a break from all the drama associated with young women.

Selene laughed as he detailed this escapade or that. The amused twinkle in her eyes nearly did him in. They'd just reached the porch when the phone in his pocket vibrated.

"Dammit," he muttered after he read the text. "We have to head back. It's time for the Council gathering."

"Will you bring me back here someday?"

Her words were tentative, as if she wasn't sure he'd still be committed to her tomorrow, never mind next week.

"Without a doubt." He lightly kissed her temple and teleported them to the reception hall at the Witches' Council. They'd need to sign in before they would be allowed into the main chamber.

Preston and Selene weren't there five minutes before they encountered their first problem.

"I DON'T UNDERSTAND. WHY DOES IT FALL TO THE THORNES TO TAKE on this Herculean task? How do we know this isn't another of Alastair's games?" Councilman Smythe asked. With his wild gray hair and bushy brows, he reminded Selene of a wizened old owl.

"My family is the strongest, Smythe," Preston responded with a hard edge. "And my brother has never played 'games' when it was a matter of great importance. Never would he risk the entire witch community."

The room was packed with people from all the magical families. At least two representatives from each. Selene had never witnessed such a large gathering as this, and the sheer numbers were overwhelming her.

Spring touched her arm and smiled. "It's okay. Dad knows what he's doing."

"I have every confidence in him. I simply don't understand why any of this is up for debate," Selene returned quietly.

As if he'd heard her, Preston said, "This isn't up for debate. We are going to the Netherworld, with or without your approval. What remains to be seen is if you'll have our backs and be prepared with a backup plan should anything go wrong."

"What about the Aether?" Councilwoman Hall asked. "The job of Damian Dethridge is to provide balance between good and evil. Shouldn't he be the one to see to this?"

"I fully intend to."

All heads spun toward the back of the room. Damian emerged from the shadows and swept the room with a chilling glance. Gasps echoed around the chamber as he strode down the aisle toward where Preston and Alastair presented their case. Dressed all in black, he was an imposing yet romantic figure. Radiating mystery and strength at the same time.

"Isn't he dreamy?" a woman whispered from directly behind her.

Spring smirked as Selene rolled her eyes.

"I've spoken at length with the Thornes, Sebastian Drake, and the goddesses involved in the plan." Damian tilted his head toward Preston. "Isis has put him in charge of eliminating the Evil. Not me. However, I plan to provide the support needed to conquer it, whatever that entails," he finished grimly.

Selene suspected he was thinking about his daughter's prediction. When he turned his head to meet her gaze, she shivered. How was it possible he had access to everyone's thoughts and still managed to single out one particular person?

"Because yours had to do with my daughter."

Damian's voice in her head sounded exceptionally loud, and she jerked in her seat, drawing Preston's concerned gaze.

She waved him off and decided to keep her thoughts on the topic at hand.

A hint of a smile tugged at Damian's mouth, and all eyes turned to see what had him amused.

Heat climbed Selene's neck and rapidly warmed her cheeks.

Preston frowned but turned his attention back to the Council members gathered at the high table. "Look, we don't need your permission to tackle this threat. We need your knowledge of the Netherworld. None of us want to be blindsided by something on another plane we weren't prepared for." He released a breath and asked, "Will you give us access to the vaults to look for the information we need?"

"Mr. Dethridge, it's my understanding you intend to cross over with a handful of the others?" Georgie Sipanil was seeking clarification for the benefit of the other members. She herself already knew this, based on her conversation with Preston and Selene.

"Your understanding is correct."

"And to balance the Thornes' and Ms. Barringer's crossing, you will all need to resurrect some unsavory characters?"

"Also correct."

"The Enchantress among them?"

"Yes."

Gasps, louder than when the Aether appeared, ricocheted off the chamber's walls. Those who hadn't been in contact with Isolde still would've heard rumors of her reign of terror. Damian would've needed to report to the Council that she was truly dead and that her body had been destroyed. From there, the story would've leaked out and made the rounds.

"What is the risk to the magical community as a whole should she be resurrected and escape?"

"The Evil—the one that caused my mother to murder others for their magic—left her upon her death. Should she return to the earthly plane, the community will be safe."

"Why should we trust you?" someone from the gallery shouted.

Alastair graced the person with a quelling look. "He's all that stands between you and death, you fool."

Councilman Smythe frowned and leaned forward. "Let me make sure I have this straight. You and your family wish to comb the vaults on the off chance there's information to be found regarding the Netherworld. This will give you unlimited access to spells and ancient artifacts no one should have the right to." He held up a hand when Preston would've spoken. "You also intend to resurrect five unsavory characters—four of which are this community's most lethal enemies—and grant them magical abilities. In addition, if your trip to the Netherworld doesn't work, you want to take down magic on earth and the Otherworld, leaving us vulnerable to the Underworld and these resurrected enemies who would possess magic. Do I have this correct?"

"No one could call you slow, Smythe," Alastair drawled.

Preston closed his eyes and shook his head, and Selene suspected he wanted to gag his brother.

"I'm the balance," Damian reminded them. "The moment the Evil is transported to the Nether, I'll remove the power from Beecham, Lin, and Salinger."

"What about your mother?" the first heckler shouted, seemingly unable to contain himself.

The Aether's visage was a frigid mask, and his eyes were deadly as he faced the man in the third row. "What's your problem, Harris?"

Harris paled. His already pasty skin turning startlingly white. His fleshy jowls wobbled, expressing his fear. Maybe he'd assumed Damian didn't know him or had no way of identifying who he was, but right then, he looked as if he was soiling his pants.

Selene pursed her lips to hold back a giggle.

Alastair didn't bother. His mocking laughter echoed around the room. "Yes, Harris. Please, tell us. What *is* your problem?"

The other man looked as if he'd swallowed his tongue as his skin turned an alarming shade of purple. He didn't speak. Instead, he jumped up and ran for the exit.

"Was it something I said?" Alastair called after him. With a shrug, he turned and faced Damian. "I don't know why people can't take a bit of ribbing."

A flash of brilliant white teeth was Damian's response, and all the women present heaved a collective girly sigh.

Selene pressed her fingertips to her mouth when she witnessed the Aether's irritated expression. Preston caught her eye and winked.

With a loud clap of his hands, Preston turned to the high table. "So. What's it going to be? We save the world, or it goes to hell in a handbasket?"

CHAPTER 20

"That went better than expected."

Preston glanced up sharply, pausing in cutting his steak. "Really, Al?" He snorted before consuming a forkful of the meat he'd dipped into aioli.

"We've gained permission to search the Council archives. Score one for our team."

Preston swallowed the food, downed a mouthful of wine, and sat back. "Yes, but we have a limited time to do it, and each of us is saddled with a member of the high table. I don't trust them not to take what we learn and screw us over."

"Well, now you sound like me, little brother. I'm the untrusting one of the two of us." The humor lurking in Alastair's eyes triggered an answering reaction inside of Preston, and they laughed.

They both knew Alastair was busting his balls. Neither of them were particularly trusting, but Preston could usually get around people easier than his brother. He tended to be less grating on the nerves, and he was a whole lot more diplomatic in nature.

Raising his voice to be heard over the din of conversations around them, Preston said, "There are seven known vaults. Given the whole of our families, minus those left behind to protect the children and the estates, we can divide into teams of four." He looked at the people surrounding the Drakes' dining room table, then to those standing just beyond their chairs. "I believe the eldest, most experienced members of our group should lead a team. Alastair, me, Ryker, Rafe, and Gwennie. The exceptions will be Spring and Nash. They specialize in research and artifacts, so they'll head up two of the groups. Any questions?"

His cousin Leonie raised a hand. "What if we don't find what we're looking for before the vaults shift?"

"Each of you will have a timer set to the exact number of minutes needed for teleportation, performing the spell to unlock the door, and conducting a search of the contents. It will leave you with roughly forty-eight minutes inside." He gave her a stern look. "Once the timer goes off, you get the hell out and close the circle. No exceptions." He leaned in to stress, "If you feel the floor of the vault move, get the fuck out. There's no need to take chances. You'll have a list of places where your vault will bounce next, and you'll need to follow closely on its heels so you can repeat the process. You'll lose a few minutes with each round, so be sure to take that into account when you set the timer."

"The WC has given us exactly five hours total. After that, all the vaults will shuffle to undisclosed locations," Alastair added.

"What if we don't get out in time?" Winnie's husband, Zane, rested his hands on her shoulders. He looked uneasy about the entire mission.

"Your insides will be scrambled," Damian said flatly.

Several people gasped and looked alarmed.

Preston pasted on a warm smile although he wasn't close to feeling it. Inside, he was cold and eaten up with worry he refused to show. "I suggest you don't forget to set your timer when you happen upon the first location and make it a point to get out when it alerts you, without delay." He shoved aside the rest of his meal and stood. "We understand this is dangerous. Any of you hesitant to take the risk, please know we won't hold it against you should you choose to remain behind. Most of you have children to consider."

Liz Thorne stepped forward. "You're taking the greater risk by going to the Netherworld, cousin. To help the rest of us, I might add. The least we can do is research what might make it safer for you in the long run."

Alastair gave her an approving nod. "Well said, child."

"Thank you, Liz." Most of them had been at the emergency Council meeting, but Preston needed to make sure they were all clear on what might happen should he and the others fail. He explained in great detail what they intended. "Questions?"

Other than a few wary glances being exchanged, everyone remained quiet.

Preston checked the pocket watch Alastair had given him earlier in the day. "The Council members should be here soon. Take the time to indulge in this nice buffet our hosts have set out for us, then meet on the lower lawn in twenty minutes."

He left the room to find Selene. The sheer volume of people had overwhelmed her, and she'd decided to spend the time visiting Damian's wife. Selene had informed him earlier that the two women had gone to finishing school together.

Damian joined him and held out a hand. "Come on, I'll teleport us to my home."

They arrived within seconds to find Sabrina waiting on the bottom step of the sweeping staircase. "Papa!"

"Beastie." Damian knelt on one knee and braced for the impact of her small body as she flung herself into his arms.

As Preston watched them embrace, he recalled similar greetings from his own children. Spring was the most like Sabrina Dethridge in her enthusiasm and unfailing love. How he'd never seen it back then or cherished those moments for the rare treasures they were, was beyond him. He'd been foolish to believe those days would never end.

"Don't be sad, Preston." Sabrina separated from her father and clasped his hand. "You'll have more babies to love."

"I'm old for children, sweetheart," he said dryly.

"Papa is over two hundred," she pointed out.

Preston chuckled at Damian's put-out expression. Leave it to a kid to keep you humble. "I stand corrected."

"Miss Selene wants babies."

"Aannndddd that's enough of that." Damian tossed Sabrina over his shoulder and stalked off down the hallway. "Where's your mother, beastie? I need to talk to her about obtaining magical duct tape for your trap."

Sabrina must've heard all of this before because she giggled at the threat.

Preston followed, shaking his head in amusement. These lively interactions between Damian and his daughter made him smile. He was happy to see their family unit back together and thriving.

For the first years of Sabrina's life, Damian had been a doting father. Then, Vivian had allowed her sister to play on her fears, and she'd stolen their child away in the middle of the night. Damian had been like a wounded animal in those days, living a solitary existence. No one other than Alastair and Preston had dared approach him. They'd encouraged a conversation between the couple, but Damian had refused for reasons he didn't care to divulge. Eventually, he'd retrieved his family. Although, as Preston understood it, Damian and Vivian were putting on a show for Sabrina's benefit. Their relationship was still fractured.

"Viv, our gremlin is spilling secrets again," Damian said when they found her and Selene. "I think we need to send her to a boarding school for wayward witches. Don't they have a good one at the North Pole?"

Sabrina giggled. "You're so silly, Papa!"

He shifted her from his shoulder to cradle her in his arms. "Silly is intended for those who are kidding. I assure you, I'm completely serious." A twinkle belied his words. "Now, what punishment should I impose?" He squinted his eyes in thought, then flared them wide. "I know—"

"Not broccoli, Papa! You can't use that again."

"No? Hmm. All right. I suppose I'll have to think of another." He rubbed his nose against hers and set her on her feet. "Run along, you troublemaker. The adults need to converse about serious issues."

Sabrina opened her mouth to argue but quickly caved to her father's stern, warning look. With a shrug, she teleported away.

"Where do you suppose she went?" Vivian asked, placing her teacup and saucer on the side table next to her.

"Most likely right outside the door to spy. She's missed her calling. We should give her to the Witches' Council to run their Intelligence Department." A faint giggle sounded behind them, and Damian made a face. "Begone with you, beastie, or it's gruel for your dinner tonight," he boomed out.

Preston grinned. The threat was empty, and they all knew it. The child had the ability to conjure whatever she wanted to eat whenever she wished.

"How did your meeting go?" Selene asked with a small smile. "Is everything ready for us?"

"Pretty much. Everyone's been briefed, and we've stressed the need to stay within the timetable for each jump. I don't know how much plainer we can make it."

She studied him for a moment. "But you're worried they won't heed your warning," she finally concluded.

"Yes and no." He accepted the tumbler of brandy Damian had poured for him. "None of this feels right, and I'm not sure what's bothering me."

"Possibly the consequences should we fail?" Damian grimaced and downed his drink in one shot. "The fact I'm forced to consume the Evil and will potentially go mad like my mother isn't exactly making me excited for what comes next, either."

"We need to put safety measures in place, Damian," Vivian said softly. The wariness in her eyes cut Preston. He could only imagine how the Aether must feel to receive such a look from his own wife. "If you... if..."

Oddly, Damian seemed more resigned than irritated. "I know, Viv. We have time yet."

"Not a lot."

Preston met Selene's worried gaze with a solemn one of his own. She probably felt as he did—that they were intruding on what should be a private conversation.

"It's all right, Pres," Damian assured him with a slight twist of his lips. "My wife and I don't require tender moments alone. Right, love?"

Vivian's pale blue-gray eyes cooled, and her mouth tightened. For a long moment, the husband and wife stared at one another, seemingly fighting a silent battle of sorts. Damian was the first to look away. He ran a shaky hand through his hair and walked to the cabinet to pour himself another drink.

"I'm a right prick. I apologize." After he downed his second tumbler of brandy, he set the glass on the sideboard and faced them. "Vivian's correct. We don't have a lot of time to create an unbreakable spell that will prevent me from finding her and Sabrina should I turn as evil as my mother before me."

Selene pressed her palm to her chest and shifted to look at Vivian.

Preston sat beside her. "That's been weighing on you all this time, Viv?"

"Yes," she said tearfully. Turning tear-bright eyes on her husband, Vivian said, "If it were only me, I wouldn't insist on this, Damian. You know that. But I can't *not* protect Sabrina."

"I *do* know." The Aether closed his eyes with an expression of profound grief on his face. "Let's get this over with. It's better if you both disappear before I become a monster."

"No, Papa!" Sabrina cried as she flung open the door.

They all faced the tearful child.

"Beastie. There's no other way to protect you." The anguish in Damian's voice tore at Preston's heart.

"No. You don't have to send me away, Papa. I swear it." She ran to her father and flung her arms around his waist. "I swear I'm not lying. You don't have to send me away."

Vivian crossed to them and squatted down to wipe the tears pouring from Sabrina's eyes. "Darling, it's just a precaution. We can come back when this is over."

"But we won't. If we leave, we won't. We have to stay, Mama. We have to," she sobbed out.

"Bloody hell!" Damian lifted Sabrina into his arms and hugged her tightly to him. "You're killing me, my darling girl. Please don't cry. We'll work this out."

"No, Papa. You're just saying that. You're going to try to put me to sleep so you can cast your spell. But if you do, we won't come back."

Pure torment resided in Damian's obsidian eyes as he stared at Vivian over their daughter's head. "I don't know what to do, Viv. I honestly don't."

"Trust your daughter, Mr. Dethridge," Selene said. Her voice was strong and sure. "Didn't you tell us she was an Oracle? I believe she's trying to tell you what she's seeing."

CHAPTER 21

"How did you get so wise, my love?" Preston asked Selene as they strolled across the bridge dividing the Dethridge and the Drake estates.

"I don't know that I'm wise per se, but they were both ignoring what Sabrina was trying to tell them. They were caught up in safeguarding her, and they failed to understand the Oracle would protect herself first, should the need arise. Mainly because she knows she's the only one with her abilities."

"She's still a child, Selene."

"Yes, but she also has the capability to weigh all possible outcomes. It comes with her gift." She tugged him to a halt. "Sabrina doesn't want to lose Damian. If she truly believed he'd kill her to steal her power, she'd flee and only return if she could figure out how to help him at some later date. She'll determine the best course of action and see it through, Preston. I'm sure of it."

"Goddess preserve us, I hope you're right." He tugged her into his arms and touched his nose to hers. "This whole thing is terrifying me."

"You have much to lose."

"And you don't? Damian doesn't? The entire magical world doesn't?"

"It's not what I meant, *agápi mou*, and you know it."

He inhaled deeply and released her. "I do know. I'm just on edge."

"Is it the sense of doom you're experiencing?"

"Exactly that."

"I feel it too. Is it just nerves, or is it something much more dire?"

He shook his head and focused on the water beyond her shoulder. "Perhaps a mixture of both, but other than Sabrina, who can say?"

"I can't believe we only have a few minutes before everything is put in motion." Selene clasped her hands in front of her, and Preston had to assume it was to halt her trembling. He'd felt it moments ago when he held her. Deep down, he was experiencing a similar fearful reaction.

"We haven't had any real time together, you and me," he said softly. "One night of sleeping in each others' arms. One morning of making love. Some hand-holding. It isn't enough."

"No. It really isn't." The stark longing in her eyes called to him. Preston wanted nothing more than to lead her to the grassy bank by the stream, strip her bare, and make love to her for countless days and nights. But in less than ten minutes, the Council would be on their doorstep, ready to carry through with this dangerous plan of theirs.

"I wish I hadn't wasted our time together in the Otherworld. I love you, Preston. More than I've ever loved anyone in either of my lifetimes."

"Can I tell you a secret?"

"Of course." She'd said it stiffly, as if maybe she was upset he hadn't immediately declared his undying affection. He almost smiled.

"We've had more than this single lifetime together, Selene. We've been soul mates throughout many lives before."

She frowned as his arms encircled her waist. "I don't understand."

"You've no doubt heard the saying a Thorne only loves once." She nodded, and her brows met. Preston was forced to kiss the tip of her delicate nose at the adorableness of her confused expression. "There's a reason for it. When we meet our soul mates, we recognize them instantly. Their aura burns brighter than any other. For me, yours is near blinding."

"I assumed yours is as bright as it is because you're a powerful warlock."

"To a degree, yes. But the continual golden glow strengthens over time and becomes a beacon to us. When we see it again in any lifetime, we need to claim it for ours."

"That's the way I feel. Like I can't get enough of you. I want to consume you whole," she said, blushing as if embarrassed by her confession.

"Precisely."

"I think I understand why you're all fighting as hard as you are to end the Evil. Not just for the rest of mankind, but for your other half. If your true love were to be obliterated, where would that leave you?"

"It would leave us devastated and living a half life," he confirmed softly. "You are my true love, Selene."

"This has an awful suggestion attached, but did you know who I was as a child? Is that why you helped me?"

"Goddess, no!" He shuddered at the thought of anyone being attracted to a child. "You did display a bright aura, but we can attribute things of that nature to power or abilities. The aura you present today is thousands of times stronger than when you were a girl."

"But I thought you said Thornes recognize their soul mates right away."

Irritated at how badly he'd fumbled this conversation, he urged her toward the Drake estate and tried to form the words he needed to explain so he didn't come across as an old lecher.

"When Summer was little more than a toddler, she met Cooper Carlyle at a hometown holiday celebration. Afterwards, she told anyone who would listen that she loved him and would one day marry him." Preston smiled at the memory of her insistence. "She'd rave about his light and how she wanted to see it. We had a devil of a time keeping her from sneaking out to find him."

"It sounds like she was obsessed," Selene said with a grimace.

"To a degree, she was. But to her, his light was a thing of beauty, something young Summer wanted to hold onto for its warmth. She didn't understand adult love."

Selene's frown grew, but she remained silent.

"A child would see the pureness of light in someone that an adult might miss. It's possible, to your younger self, I would've appeared brighter than you would've appeared to me. You might've wanted to bask in the magic of the light. Like holding onto a favorite toy or stuffed bear, it would've provided you comfort." He paused to look down at her. "And had we both been children, I'd have seen right away who you were, but as an adult looking at a child? Yeah, I had no idea who you were anything other than a potentially powerful young witch. Does that make more sense?"

"I believe it does." She placed her palm along his jaw. "Also, it makes me feel better to know you didn't fall in love with a young child."

He shuddered. "Perish the thought." He allowed his hot eyes to slowly travel the length of her body and back before he boldly met her gaze. "I'm only interested in the woman you are today. For a multitude of reasons."

Selene laughed, wrapped a hand around his neck, and drew his head down for a kiss. She moaned into his mouth as he deepened it, setting her on fire with his passion. When she drew back, she touched her fingers to her mouth. "Your aura has grown brighter in the last few days."

"We are falling more in love as the seconds pass," he said. Preston cupped her face and ran his thumbs along her cheekbones. "I was blessed the day I stumbled across you in the Otherworld, Selene. It was only there I recognized who you were to me."

"I think I've loved you from the first," she confessed. "You were a hero in my eyes when you treated me so kindly in Greece. After I grew up, I wanted to seek you out and thank you for what you'd done."

He allowed her words to sink in and concluded she'd been hesitant for a number of reasons. The primary one had been her brother. "But you were worried you'd put me in Victor's crosshairs."

"Yes." She squinted one eye and wrinkled her nose. "Also, I feared you'd have feet of clay and not be the man I believed you to be. I didn't want to be disappointed."

"All the men in your life have done a number on you, haven't they?"

She nodded and exhaled heavily. "It may be one of the reasons I wouldn't date you in the Otherworld."

"Makes sense." She had no reason to trust him in one plane over another. He was no different here on earth than in the afterlife.

"Oh, I'd already decided to put us both out of our misery. But I was enjoying your games too much, so I let them continue."

Happiness bubbled up inside of him. "Good to know. I'll be sure to introduce more of the same in the future."

Selene laughed, then just as quickly sobered. "We have to return."

Overwhelmed with all the words he wanted to say but didn't have time to, Preston reached for her and held her tightly.

"This has to turn out all right. I can't lose you," she whispered. She'd manage to say what he couldn't, and Preston's arms tightened to express himself.

His phone vibrated in his pants pocket. Reluctantly, he released her and reached for the device.

It's go time, little brother.

He showed the screen to Selene. Wordlessly, she clasped his hand, and they started for the Drakes' garden.

WHEN THEY ARRIVED, IT LOOKED AS IF A SOIREE WAS IN PROGRESS. Witches' Council members milled about, and a handful of Preston's family had separated into a small group and were participating in an intense conversation.

Selene released his hand. "You should see what that's about. I need a moment to prepare myself for all these people."

"Are you okay, my love?"

He never failed to show his consideration or concern. Touched by his generosity of spirit, she patted his chest and offered up a reassuring smile. "Of course. I simply want to touch up my makeup and put on my invisible armor."

"You're already beautiful, Selene. No touch-up needed. However, I do understand the need to prepare yourself for what's ahead. Would you like me to go with you?"

"No. I think it's more important for you to see what Alastair and Nash have to say." She rose on her toes to drop a light kiss on his mouth. "I won't be but a minute or two."

"Hurry back. I don't like being away from you too long. It makes me itchy."

She experienced the same reaction when she was away from him, so she nodded her agreement. "Promise." In the blink of an eye, she'd teleported to their bedroom. Looking at the bed, she pressed her hand to her stomach. She'd been in total agreement with Preston earlier when he said they hadn't had enough private time together. She sent a prayer skyward that they would be able to save the day and have a future together when all was said and done.

"I was surprised to see you when I arrived last night."

With a small shriek, she spun around and searched for the intruder.

Alexander Castor emerged from the shadows and crossed to her. With his index finger, he tapped her gaping jaw shut.

"You are as beautiful as ever, Selene." His tone was silky and seductive, but a thread of malice underlined it. "Does Preston know how duplicitous you are?"

She shivered, and although her instinct was to flee, she stood her ground. "What about you, Alex? Should I tell the Thornes and Damian Dethridge what kind of man you truly are?"

He laughed, and the sound was pure wicked delight. "You're still as feisty as ever, my dear."

"And you're still as twisted and self-serving, aren't you?"

His eyes turned frosty, and the ice-blue stare chilled her. "I never claimed I wasn't self-serving, darling." He trailed his fingers along her jaw as that shrewd gaze dropped to her compressed lips. "What say we have a tumble for old times' sake?"

She smacked his hand away. "Not a bloody chance!" Selene crossed her arms. "Why don't you get to the point of this visit, Alex?"

"I thought we might make a pact, you and me. Should Victor and Lin come out the winner on the other side, we will need to protect ourselves by joining forces."

"I'd rather Victor put another bullet through my brain."

His mouth twisted, reminding Selene of a jaded angel. "I'm sure it could be arranged."

She was no match for him, should it come to a fight. Alexander Castor not only had the ability to travel, but he could fry all her internal circuits with a single thought.

"I won't be looking out for your best interests this time around, Alex. You left me in a lurch when you abandoned me. Victor almost killed me then." Ten years ago, Selene had wrongly believed Alex loved her, and she'd helped him escape her brother's detection after he told her Victor was out for his blood. For the six months he'd hidden out in Greece, Castor had fostered her false belief with loving touches and honeyed words. Little did either know that Victor had found out about their liaison and was waiting for the perfect moment to strike. Only through the grace of the Goddess had they discovered his plan.

"I fully intended to take you to safety, Selene."

"You're a liar, Alex. You always were."

He shifted closer, dipping his head until only an inch separated his mouth from hers. A hair's breadth remained between them when the door opened and Preston stepped in.

"What the hell is going on here?" he demanded.

The smile on Alexander's lips was triumphant, and savage victory shone in his cold, cruel eyes.

Selene's heart shriveled in her chest. *He succeeded in making Preston believe she was duping him.*

Alex kissed her—*hard*. And before Preston could cross the room, he'd teleported away.

The fury permeating the air around her was thick, and it burned her skin. With resignation and a leaden heart, she faced Preston.

CHAPTER 22

"I promise you, Preston, this isn't how it seems."

Selene looked as if she wanted to cry, and it shredded Preston's soul. He'd long been acquainted with Castor's games and wasn't surprised by this one, but *she* wouldn't know it.

"Are you planning to betray me in any way, Selene?" he asked, carefully modulating his voice to remove all emotion.

The color of her irises darkened, and disappointment clouded her face. She seemed upset he'd asked. "It wasn't my intent," she returned crisply.

"Good." His gaze snapped to her mouth. "Now, how about you gargle with antiseptic and wipe away Castor's kiss while I go kill him?" he suggested on a falsely cheerful note.

"You believe me?"

Her incredulousness bothered him. In her shaky and unsure question, Preston witnessed the pain of her insecurity. He closed the distance between them and lifted her chin the small degree needed for their eyes to meet. "Of course I do." He led her to the bathroom, and holding up a hand, he conjured a cotton wipe. Dragging it gently across her mouth, he said, "It still doesn't mean I want his lips touching yours. Nor does it mean I want to kiss you right after he has." He acted out gagging and grinned when she swatted his arm.

"I should tell you… Alex and I…"

Knowing he'd hate what she was going to say, Preston placed a finger against her lips. "Not right now. When we get through all this, you can tell me about your past, okay?"

"But it's important, Preston."

He closed his eyes and truly wanted to gag this time. "Go ahead. Tell me."

"Before I met him, Alex worked for my brother. Not by choice, according to him, and he only got away by faking his own death."

"How is this relevant to you?"

"I met him on a business trip about ten years ago. I had no idea who he was other than some handsome man who appeared interested in me."

Stomach ready to revolt, Preston nodded and drew her to the bed to sit down. "You had a brief fling."

"More than brief. It lasted six months." Her expression grew tortured, and she focused her attention on her fisted hands. "I loved him, and he led me to believe he loved me, too."

She might as well have taken one of her balled fists and struck him in the face. The impact would've been the same. Dumbfounded, he stayed silent, waiting for her to elaborate.

"But it was all a lie. Alex used me to monitor my brother's movements so he could stay off Victor's radar." She flexed her fingers and sucked in a breath. Lifting her head, she locked eyes with Preston. "He provided enough of the facts to sound sincere, and he convinced me we could both escape my brother's reach. He had an elaborate plan, but in the end, it didn't include me."

"And Victor found out about it?" Preston asked harshly, already guessing the truth.

She winced. "Yes. I paid for it every day after. He made my life even more miserable than it already was."

"What did he do to you, Selene?"

"Other than dismembering any man I cast a second glance at?"

"Jesus!"

She rubbed the spot between her brows and sniffed. "Those he didn't hurt, he turned."

"Turned? As in forced them to work for him?"

"Yes."

"Wonderful." Obviously, he meant the exact opposite, and Preston was seething on her behalf. What kind of tortured life had she lived through under Victor's rule?

"I was attracted to Quentin when I met him in Greece. Perhaps he reminded me of Alex. I don't know. But I'd have never truly started anything with him for the reason I didn't want to see him become Victor's enemy."

"Also, he's devoted to Holly," Preston said dryly.

"Yes." She smiled. "There is that."

He lifted her hand and intertwined his fingers with hers. "And you told me all this why?"

"What if Alex sides with Victor when my brother is brought back? He can't be trusted, Preston. He'll do what's in his best interests, and if it means forming an alliance with Victor, then that's what he'll do."

Her expression was earnest and void of deceit. Selene fully believed what she was saying, and her warning should be taken into consideration as they moved forward with their plans. "Damian assured me he is on the level. But I'll talk to both him and Alastair. If Castor's out to screw us, one of them will know right away."

"Thank you for your faith in me." Her voice trembled when she spoke, and it hurt Preston to think she'd never held anyone's trust before.

"No thanks necessary. I'll always accept your explanations at face value. You've done nothing to make me doubt you, Selene."

She launched herself at him, and he fell back on the mattress, laughing as she rained enthusiastic kisses down on his face.

"I love you, Preston. I love you so much."

"And I love you. But if you continue to drape yourself across me this way, we are going to screw over the entire magical community by not showing up this afternoon. I don't have any willpower where you're concerned, Selene."

She blushed, and Preston loved the hell out of her reaction. Someone as worldly as her responding like a young maiden tickled him.

"Oh, to hell with it," he murmured. Drawing her head down to his, he kissed her. If there was no tomorrow for them, he didn't want to know. He wanted to *feel*. To experience these last moments without reserve.

He rolled them over until his weight rested on hers as her fingers worked the buttons of his shirt. Preston positioned his fingers, ready to snap and dispose of their clothing, when a sharp rap sounded on their door.

"Time to join the rest of us, you lovebirds," GiGi called out. "It's time for the Thornes to save the world."

Preston swore under his breath and helped Selene stand. She looked as wobbly as he felt. Only this woman made his knees weak and his limbs tremble. "I suppose we have to wait."

"Is it terrible that I don't want to?" She ran her hand down the bared skin of his chest and sighed. "I'm being entirely selfish, but I want one more hour with you."

Fisting his hand in her hair, he gently tugged to expose her throat. He trailed light kisses along the long column of her neck, stopping to nibble on the lobe of her ear. She released a soft moan as he placed his lips against the shell of her ear and whispered, *"Me, too."*

Selene wasn't sure why Preston believed her or openly offered his trust to the degree he had, but she was damned grateful. Alex was out to start trouble, and for a brief moment, she'd believed he succeeded. But why? Why taunt Preston? Why call her deceitful when *he* was the one who'd betrayed her?

She didn't have answers and likely wouldn't get them anytime soon. Yet it made her sad to remember what she and Alex had shared all those years ago. He'd been tender and loving in the months leading up to his disappearing act. They'd spoken of hiding off the grid, using his gift to stay one step ahead of their greatest enemy.

As if her thoughts attracted his attention, Alex turned his head to stare at her. Oddly, he no longer seemed cold. He appeared almost sad when their gazes connected. But a quick blink later, his expression showed nothing of what he was thinking.

She turned away and caught Preston watching the two of them. Because she had nothing to hide, she didn't look away, and his sudden soft smile eased her misgivings. When he winked and blew her a kiss, she laughed.

She could admit to herself—and only herself—Preston and Alex were very much alike in their playfulness. Perhaps it was why she'd been standoffish in the Otherworld. Maybe she'd feared a repeat of what had happened ten years ago: a man using her for his own personal gains and leaving her without a backward glance. She should've recognized the two were cut from different cloths. Preston was open and honest, family-oriented. Alex was secretive and selfish, leaving his motherless son to fend for himself. Two very different individuals, indeed.

"Do you love him as much as you once loved me, darling? Does he know what we were to each other?"

Had she been paying attention, Selene would've never let Alex approach her again, but she'd been distracted by Preston's playfulness. Hell, the subtle shift in Preston's expression should've alerted her.

Pasting on a cold smile, she faced Alex. "We were nothing to each other, Castor. You made sure of that by leaving me to face Victor alone."

He studied her for a long moment. "I never left you, Selene. You were the one who told Victor I was alive. I barely escaped and was on the run until recently."

"I never said a word to him until *after* you left me, and he already suspected the truth. And at that point, he didn't give me much of a choice," she said coldly. "Had you taken me with you as you promised, you would've saved me years of his viciousness."

A flash of pain crossed his face but disappeared just as quickly behind an impassive mask. "You're a liar. You were then, and you are now." He looked to the person behind her. "Don't trust her, Preston." His eyes locked on hers. "She's liable to cut your heart out while you're sleeping."

Preston wrapped an arm across the front of her chest and drew her backwards to rest against him. "Keep your digs and innuendos to yourself, Castor, and stay away from her. She's under the Thornes' protection now."

Tears burned behind the lids she closed. She brought her hand up to grip Preston's forearm, tightening it to silently convey how much his words meant to her. He gave her a brief squeeze in answer.

A sneer curled Alex's lips. "She has you buffaloed, man. Don't say I didn't warn you."

"Wanker!" Of its own volition, her leg shot out, and her foot connected with his balls. As Alex bent double and squeaked out a breath, Selene gasped and looked around. The shock on everyone's faces equaled her own surprise.

Quentin was the first to start laughing, followed quickly by Preston.

"Selene Barringer, you are my hero," Quentin said as he applauded. "I've been wanting to do that my entire life."

"Fuck off, you shit," Alex snapped. "I went back and tried to make up for my past sins."

"Too little, too late, asshole."

Alex gingerly straightened and glared his fury. "I should leave the lot of you to your fate!"

"Didn't you tell Quentin to remove the stick from his butt?" Alastair said as he joined their small group. "I could suggest the same to you, Castor."

"She only gave you a light tap, you pansy," Preston said, shifting

Selene behind him and out of strangling distance of Alex's hands.

"How about I do the same to you and then you can show me how easy it is to shake off the pain?" Alex offered with a growl.

Selene shoved her way through the sea of testosterone and faced him, chin raised high. "I'm not sorry. You absolutely deserved that and more."

He stared at her for the longest time before something softened in his eyes. "I suppose I did." When he graced her with a wry, somewhat apologetic smile, her heart picked up its pace. A smiling Alexander Castor was a dangerous man. Especially to the average woman's heart.

He grew deadly serious, and it didn't seem to fit the man she'd known. "I don't know exactly what happened back then, but maybe we were both played. A woman only has that kind of pent-up rage when she's been wronged." Regret shone brightly in his brilliant eyes. "I'm sorry I didn't come back for you, Selene." He reached to touch her, but Preston knocked his hand away.

"Pretty words, Castor. It remains to be seen if you're being truthful. You aren't known for your honesty."

"Touch me again, Preston, and we're going to throw down. Threatening evil entity or not."

Preston's eyes darkened with his anger, and he held up his hand to display a rotating fireball. "I'm game."

A wave of water doused the flames and soaked Preston's sleeve as Alastair positioned himself between the two men. "Sorry, fellas, but subduing the Evil comes before the measuring-your-dicks contest."

Selene pressed her fingers to her mouth to curb an inappropriate laugh. Quentin didn't bother to hide his amusement, though. He guffawed like Alastair was the funniest comedian alive. Most likely, he enjoyed someone else zinging his father with their sarcasm.

"It's time," Damian said with a tone as hard as granite and features to match. "Everyone pair up and be prepared to teleport to the vault location you've been assigned."

CHAPTER 23

Preston clasped Selene's hand and led her toward where Georgie Sipanil waited under the oak they'd used to first return to the earthly plane. About ten feet away, he halted and faced Selene.

"Castor seemed legitimately sorry back there. And while I wouldn't dream of telling you how to live your life, I will urge you to be wary of Greeks bearing gifts."

"Who's the Trojan horse in this case? Alex or me?"

He grimaced. "Obviously, I'd place my bet on Castor, and that's why I'm warning you. His about-face was pretty fast."

Selene shifted closer until they were chest to chest, and wrapped her arms around his neck. She urged his head down and kissed him in full view of everyone. "Thank you, Preston. You have no idea how much your unconditional love means to me. I've never experienced anything like it."

"So you don't think I'm telling you to be careful because I'm jealous as hell?"

"You are?"

"Abso-fucking-lutely!"

She laughed and patted the area over his heart. "Alexander Castor holds no appeal for me anymore, *agápi mou*. Only *you* do."

Staring at her, seeing honesty and love reflected back at him, Preston released a ragged breath. "I'm glad. Let's not keep Georgie waiting. We don't want her to get cranky."

He'd lowered his voice to whisper the last bit, but the council-woman heard him anyway. "I'll show you cranky, you rascal," she threatened with an indulgent chuckle. Turning her attention to Selene, she said, "Preston is right. Be careful who you trust, dear."

Georgie drew out a timepiece to consult "I'm taking you to the Athens vault. I'm afraid Alexander Castor will need to join the three of us. Whatever we find there will be weapons crafted from the Greek gods. Due to his bloodline, he's got the best chance of wielding them."

Preston wanted to swear up a firestorm when Georgie called Castor over to their group and explained her reasoning. "Quentin could do the same thing, couldn't he?"

Alex's grin held a triumphant edge. "Sorry, buddy. I'm closer to the source, being his father and all."

When Selene entwined her fingers with Preston's, he relaxed—and maybe he appeared overly smug with righteousness when Castor's attention dropped to their joined hands.

They waited the next four minutes in silence. Finally, Georgie spoke. "Now. Join hands. Or rather, Alex, take Selene's hand."

It went against every fiber of Preston's being to allow Castor to touch her, but he stuffed down his possessiveness for the sake of their mission. He didn't miss Selene's shudder or that her hand tightened in his. Their gazes locked, and she gave him an encouraging smile. All he could do was give a barely discernible nod. The muscles bunched in his shoulders and neck were too tight for him to do anything more.

Within seconds, Preston's cells began to warm from the impending teleport, and he closed his eyes. When his body began to cool, he opened them and surveyed his surroundings. The door to the vault was five feet to his left, directly behind Georgie.

"Preston, conjure the candles for the ceremony," she ordered as she moved to a blank wall. A wave of her hand caused the illusion to fall away. The real vault door appeared as the mirage faded.

"Neat party trick," Castor said approvingly as he stepped forward.

Georgie gave him a narrow-eyed stare. "You'll do well to forget what you see after this is over, Alexander."

"Ms. Georgie, I'm hurt. You used to call me 'young Alex' and hold me in high esteem."

"That was long before you allowed your loved ones to believe you were dead, you rotten boy." She softened her words with a stroke of her hand down his arm. "Go create the circle. We don't have a second to lose."

"Yes, ma'am."

Castor lifted his arms and magically drew a chalk circle an inch outside the pillar candles Preston conjured. Once that was done, he created a pentagram in the center, making sure the points all touched those same candles. He shot Preston a look, giving him the go-ahead to light them as they all stepped within the circle's boundary.

The wicks smoked a second before fire turned them black. The flames soared high, then settled at a steady height, flickering and snapping when their group of four joined hands and their combined magic met.

"These vaults were designed to only allow one person in at a time, or they will seal shut with all of us inside. After the meeting today, we tweaked the spell to allow three people into the chamber. However, it only gives us forty-eight minutes, and then we must be out." Georgie gave them all a stern look. "No exceptions. We *all* must be out. To delay could cost your life. Understood?"

Preston grinned. "Yes, Ms. Georgie." He handed a timer to Selene. "You get to be timekeeper, my love. But it won't hurt my feelings any if you leave Alex a few extra minutes inside the vault."

"Hardy-har-har," Castor said, without an ounce of laughter in his voice.

"Here I believed you to be the jovial sort, Alex. The last few decades have turned you into a complete bastard."

"Preston, when this is all over, remind me to smash my fist in your face about, oh say, twenty times or so, won't you?"

Had it been anyone else, Preston might've laughed at the response. As it was, he was beginning to hate Castor with a passion. He suspected the feeling was mutual.

"Enough! You're acting like recalcitrant children," Georgie scolded. "We need to concentrate."

Preston bit his tongue to keep from saying "he started it." He was sure he would indeed sound like a bratty kid. "Apologies, Ms. Georgie," he said instead. "Please continue."

She lifted a silver brow as if to warn him to behave.

He grinned.

She had his number.

Once again, they all joined hands for the length of time it took Georgie to say the reverse cloaking spell and for the vault to grant them access.

"Start your timer, Ms. Barringer," the councilwoman ordered as she stepped toward the opening. "Gentlemen, follow me."

Preston had been inside a Witches Council's storage room before. Each one was vastly different although the general layout was primarily the same. The organization was a key feature and top-notch. Small typed labels identified an item and the date it was created. Below the label, in a smaller font, was a paragraph detailing what the artifact was rumored to do. No dust coated any of the collection, and he assumed the reason was magical.

The geeky antiquities collector in him could've stayed lost in this chamber for days. The man whose mission it was to help defeat the Evil knew his time was limited. With a regretful sigh, he began reading the item descriptions on the top shelves while Georgie scanned the items on the lower shelves. Alex began on the wall farthest from them.

"Ms. Georgie, how do you want us to handle an item if we believe it might be useful to the cause?" Preston asked.

"Tell me what you find, and we can determine together if we should hand it off to Selene."

They worked in relative silence for thirty minutes when they heard Selene call out a ten-minute countdown. It was smart for her to allow an extra few minutes for them to abandon the vault.

"I feel like we'll never finish in time," Castor grumbled. There are too many damned magical artifacts here."

Georgie looked up sharply. "Less complaining, more searching, young man."

"Seriously, how do we get through all this? Will it scramble the contents when it relocates?" Alex asked.

"We'll follow this vault to the next location. The interior will remain the same, so remember where you left off," she said.

They were one minute away from their cutoff time when Preston spotted what might be a useful tool. He was about to reach for it when the floor rumbled. *"What the fuck?"*

"Get out now!" Georgie hollered over the noise. "The vault is preparing to leap."

She was behind him, and he knew she'd never make it to the opening if he left her to fend for herself. Without thinking of his own possible demise, he sprinted to her and scooped her up.

As if the sound came down the length of a long tunnel, he heard Selene scream his name. He caught Selene's horrified expression on the other side of the opening and knew they weren't going to make it out in time.

Even as the knowledge settled in Preston's chest, his mind rebelled against death. Not his. He'd been there before. But Georgie's. She didn't deserve to go out this way. She should die peacefully in her sleep with her family and friends surrounding her to mourn the magical community's greatest loss.

The floor shook again, and a ringing began in Preston's ears. The noise was deafening, and he wanted to throw up his hands as Georgie was doing to protect his eardrums. He staggered for the exit, but the door was two-thirds of the way closed and they were still four yards away.

Who knew this fucking vault was so long?

With a suddenness that halted him in his tracks, all sound ceased and the door slammed into an invisible barrier, leaving a small opening for a person to squeeze through.

"Hurry, goddammit!" Alex shouted. "I can't hold this for long."

Weak with relief, Preston bolted for the exit and set Georgie on her feet for her to precede him out the door.

Alex was on the other side, sweating and swearing, with his raised arms trembling from the effort to freeze time. As soon as Preston cleared the entry, Alex's arms dropped and he fell to his knees, panting. "What the fuck took you so long? Did you decide to take a Sunday afternoon stroll?"

Preston chuckled as he hugged Selene tightly to his chest. "It seemed like a nice day for one."

With a snort, Castor climbed to his feet and accepted a hug first from Georgie, then Selene.

"Thank you, Alex," Selene said in a low, shaky voice. "I don't know how the timing went sideways regarding the vault, but we're all indebted to you."

He ran a trembling hand down her silky black hair and gave her a cocky smile. "All in a day's work, darling."

Seeing them together, Castor so god-like with a panty-melting smile and Selene so exotic and mouthwateringly beautiful, Preston felt sick to his stomach. They were a stunning pair, and had Victor's machinations not separated them, Preston suspected the two would still be together.

He felt Georgie's hand on his back a second before she spoke. "We have no time to waste. We must get to the next location. We'll have less time to search."

"How about we start in the back and work our way forward this time? That was a helluva mad dash to make," Preston said with feeling.

They agreed to cut each search by five minutes to eliminate any repeat of what had happened. In the end, they came away with three potential items to use, along with a mysteriously ancient grimoire with no family name attached.

"Let's get back to the Drake estate and plan for tomorrow morning's adventure," Alex said, looking as worn out as Preston felt.

"It seems like it's been a day from hell." Selene rested her head on his shoulder and sighed. "I want a long bath and a full bottle of wine."

Castor looked as if he intended to offer to share, and Preston glared in warning, his arm tightening around Selene. "Don't."

"I was only going to say it sounds like a brilliant idea. We should all do the same," Alex said, but the devil danced in his ice-blue eyes, and Preston wasn't fooled for a second.

CHAPTER 24

Selene rested her head back against the rim of the tub and sighed. The day had taken an emotional toll on her. First, the confrontation with Alex and the fear Preston wouldn't believe their kiss was all a game on Alex's part. Second, the scene in the garden when Alex had accused her of betraying him to Victor. And finally, the mishap with the timing of the vault and the real fear Preston was going to die.

In that two minutes, everything became clear. She loved Preston a thousand times more than she'd ever loved Alex. Yes, her feelings for him had been true at the time, but nothing like the deep-seated knowledge that she'd never have recovered had he not saved Preston today.

Selene had just lifted a handful of bubbles and blown them into the air when a knock sounded on the bathroom door. Believing it was Preston, she called out, "Come in."

Alex strolled in with a wine bottle in one hand and two glasses in the other. "I believe you mentioned a bath and wine, darling."

"Get out!"

He placed the wine glasses on the vanity top and tapped a finger on the cork. Within a second, it worked its way free of the neck with a tiny popping sound. "You're fully covered by the bubbles, and Preston is in a powwow with his cronies. This gives us the perfect time to talk."

"Alex, I'm serious. You need to leave. Should Preston find you here, he'll never believe this is innocent." Her heart hammered in her chest, and although Alex was correct about the bubbles hiding her nakedness, she was uncomfortable as hell. Not about her body—she was confident and content with who she was—but with his nearness and how this would look should he be discovered here with her.

"Relax." He handed her a full glass of wine. "You are much too uptight these days, Selene."

"Yes, well, death will do that for a girl," she retorted.

His grin sent her heart into overdrive. She might love Preston, but she still had eyes in her head. And Alexander Castor was fucking gorgeous. If she had enough to drink, a woman might forget anyone else existed.

He perched on the tub's edge and sipped his wine. "Tell me what happened."

She frowned, not quite sure what he wanted to know.

"The day before I left you, my future self arrived and told me you'd betrayed me to Victor," Castor explained. "I now have an idea why, but I need you to clarify the events for me."

Wanting to sit up, but knowing she risked exposing her breasts, Selene placed the wineglass on the wide marble shelf next to her and hugged her knees to her chest. "I don't know what you're talking about, Alex, or why you'd tell yourself something that wasn't true, but I swear I never betrayed you to my brother." She closed her eyes against the loathsome memories of the past and sighed. "I couldn't do that to you. To us."

When she opened her eyes, he was staring at her. The fierce love in his expression stole her breath away.

He dropped his attention to the water, and he trailed his fingers through the bubbles. "I believe you," he said softly.

"You do?" She hated how tentative and hopeful her words

sounded, and she swallowed hard when he lifted his gaze to meet hers.

"I do." With a weary sigh, he downed his drink and rose to his feet. "Bear this in mind for the future, darling. If Preston mistreats you in any way, I'll murder him without a second thought."

"Alex!" she cried out, shocked he could even *think* Preston might misuse or mistreat her. "He's the best of men. He'd never do anything to harm me."

"No, I doubt he ever would, either. It's the only reason I'm not going to make another play for you."

"I love him." Tears filled her eyes. "More than you could possibly know."

Alex's face reflected a profound sadness. "I believe my future self lied to my younger self so you could have this relationship with him."

"You're not that selfless, Alex," she said gently. "Isn't that what you habitually told me?"

"It's nice to know I can still surprise those around me," he quipped.

"Thank you." Her gratitude came out as a breathy whisper. "For loving me enough to let me have this, and for saving him today."

"You can repay me by being happy, okay?"

"What about you? Do you get your happily ever after?" She pressed a hand to her heart. "It would wound me to think you don't."

"Future me hasn't given away the plot yet. He's a dick that way."

She laughed, as he'd meant her to. "I did love you, Alex. Maybe I still do now that I know you sacrificed your wants for mine."

"This is exactly why I didn't tell younger me the truth. He wasn't noble in the least and would've tried to use it to his advantage." He nodded toward her wine. "Enjoy your private time. I need to get back, or your new beau will get suspicious."

"You make it sound clandestine," she said dryly.

"I live for clandestine, remember?"

She couldn't prevent her happy smile. "Thank you."

He blew her a kiss and strolled out the way he came in. Selene shook her head. Alexander Castor was one in a million.

PRESTON WAS ABOUT TO LEAVE THE BATHROOM AS UNDETECTED AS he'd arrived when Selene spoke.

"You can show yourself now, *agápi mou.*"

He nearly swallowed his tongue in his surprise. With a few mumbled words, the cloaking spell dissolved away, and he met Selene's twinkling eyes. "How did you know I was here?"

"I didn't until Alex turned to leave. You stepped backward to avoid a collision, I assume?" At his nod, she pointed to the towel rack. "I caught a glimpse of movement in the mirror."

"Clever deduction."

"Isn't it, though?" she teased.

They smiled at one another.

Her expression shifted to serious. "I'm assuming you heard what he said?"

"Yes. Everything."

She raised her brows in question.

He grinned at her arch look. "Castor had a gleam in his eye when you mentioned a bath earlier. You didn't really think I wasn't going to watch him like a hawk after that, did you?"

Her laughter made his sneakiness seem less stalker-like. "What is it they say about people who listen at keyholes?"

"In this case, I heard only great things, for which I am eternally grateful." He took the spot Castor had vacated and reached for her wine. After pressing it to her lips for her to take a sip, he took a drink. "It's hard to believe he tricked himself into leaving."

"I know. But I still don't understand how Victor learned he was alive?"

"Me either. Perhaps someone your brother hired to watch you?"

"That's the only explanation." She sipped from the glass he held to her mouth. "Is your day of planning finished?"

"Why? Do you have fun activities in mind?" He heard the hopeful note in his voice, and he mentally laughed at how boyish it sounded.

"This tub is big enough for two."

Her seductive suggestion went right to his dick. The thing had been knocking on the door to his zipper since the second he stepped into the bathroom and saw her. It had only relented during her heartfelt conversation with Castor.

With a snap of his fingers, Preston divested himself of his clothing and stepped into the tub, behind her. He drew her against him, wrapped his arms around her waist, and released a contented sigh as she rested her head against his shoulder.

"This is every man's fantasy," he said huskily as he cupped her breasts.

"A bath?"

"A bath with a hellaciously sexy woman such as yourself."

"Hmm." Her response sounded prim, but he glimpsed the wicked smile forming on her face.

He groaned when she wiggled her ass and pressed back into his erection. "I honestly thought I was exhausted until one second ago."

"Oh?"

"Yep, I'm raring to go."

She snorted and shifted to straddle him. "You're raring all right."

"Now you're just talking dirty to make me horny. Keep it up."

When she threw her head back and released a throaty laugh, Preston fell more in love. Before that moment, he wouldn't have thought it possible, but the free-spirited woman in his lap was a siren.

"Here or in the bed?"

"Here works for me," she replied huskily.

He wasted no more words.

CHAPTER 25

*S*elene woke in the middle of the night to find the room empty. Frowning, she shifted to her elbows and squinted into the shadowed room.

No Preston.

Shoving back the covers, she climbed from the bed and padded to the bathroom. When she came out, he still hadn't returned. She threw on a robe and descended the stairs to find him. It took roughly ten minutes, due to the sheer size of the house, and she had the errant thought that she should've scried to find him faster.

As she stepped outside and the bottoms of her feet connected with the cool stone of the terrace, she curled her toes. Witches could easily warm their cells with a simple thought, but she appreciated the chilly temperatures after the time spent in the Otherworld, where the weather was consistently perfect.

Preston was nursing a tumbler of alcohol by the railing. His gaze was thoughtful as he looked out over the expanse of manicured lawn. "I thought you were sleeping." His voice, although soft, was deep and rumbly. The sound filled Selene and drew her forward.

"I'm not sure what woke me, but I think my subconscious

must've realized you were gone. It's only been two nights, and you've spoiled me. I don't want to sleep alone ever again."

He smiled but didn't turn her way.

"What's troubling you, *agápi mou?*" She placed her palm on his bent back and rubbed circles, hoping to soothe the tension.

"Everything." He heaved a sigh and drained his drink. After setting the glass on the wide stone rail, he straightened and faced her. "Three of the women I love most in the world are going to the Nether with our greatest enemies tomorrow. I don't know how to wrap my mind around it."

She nodded sagely. "I don't suppose anything will ease your mind until we're all back here and your enemies are tucked back in hell."

"I hate this." He compressed his lips and shook his head.

"I know."

"The bitch of it is that not one of us is sure it's going to work."

"I know that, too."

"Goddammit, Selene. I want to smash shit and set things on fire. But all I can do is shove my anger down and hope the Evil can be vanquished without Victor and Lin getting the upper hand."

"You're not worried about your cousin Delphine or Harold Beecham?"

"Delphine, no. I believe she felt regret for my death. Beecham's wily, but not like Lin and Victor. It would take planning for him to make a move against us."

"Are any of the tools we found today going to help?" She was grasping for straws, but his grimness was flaying her nerves alive. One of them needed to be confident they could make it through the upcoming trial.

"Possibly. We'll also have the tanzanite rings Alastair is designing for our group. They will allow us to communicate without words. If one of us notices something off, all the others will receive the message."

"Don't take this the wrong way, but I love your crafty brother."

Preston cracked a smile. "He's handy in a crisis."

"I'm handy regardless." Alastair stepped from the darkened corner of the patio, startling them both.

"What is about powerful warlocks hiding in shadows?" Selene muttered.

"It gives us an advantage over cunning witches," Alastair quipped.

She rolled her eyes but found it difficult to hide her amused smile.

"You were listing potential tools to help your cause," he said, giving Preston an encouraging look. "What else do you think can be utilized?"

Preston scratched at the stubble on his neck and half sat on the flat stone behind him. "I'm not sure, Al. We discovered an ancient grimoire today. It's not attached to any family names I recognize. Georgie took it away to study."

"I take it she stayed here?"

"Yes," Preston and Selene chorused.

"Spring and Knox found binding bracelets and a teleportation disc." Selene rubbed her upper arms, suddenly chilled by the thought of needing to use the items to escape. She sent a small surge of magic to her cells to warm herself. "I suppose if things go tragically wrong, we can imprison the others and teleport out of there."

"Quentin discovered a transmutation wand and a mending stone," Preston added. "That's about the extent of it."

"All worthwhile items, but hardly anything that might give you an advantage." Alastair tugged at the cuffs of his dress shirt as a thoughtful expression settled on his classically handsome face. "We can only hope Damian or Georgie discover something in their research tonight."

"If I know my daughter, and I do, Spring will be up all night finding spells to use and bottling potions."

"Nash will be right beside her," Alastair assured Preston.

"Al, should this go drastically wrong—"

"Don't, Pres. I'm not losing you a second time."

"You might not have a choice."

Alastair's anger crackled along the current of air and shoved into Selene. She stumbled and was saved from falling by Alastair himself when he reached out a hand to steady her. "I'm sorry, Selene. I sometimes forget myself."

"No harm done," she assured him. "Since it doesn't seem like any of us will get any sleep tonight, let's take a turn reading our heavenly grimoire so Ms. Georgie can get some sleep."

Preston's head whipped around, and he practically shouted when he demanded, "What did you say?"

Unsure what had caused his reaction, she glanced at Alastair, only to find him frowning, too. "Um, that we should relieve Ms. Georgie?"

"No, *before* that. You called it a 'heavenly' grimoire." Preston locked eyes with his brother. "Do you think it's possible, Al? After all this time?"

Selene had never felt as confused as she did at that moment. "I don't understand."

Alastair, still sporting a deep frown, was the one to explain. "It's rumored to be the first grimoire in existence. There was the Book of Thoth, of course. It's basically a spellbook for godly entities. But when the first mortals were granted magical powers, they were gifted with a grimoire from those gods."

"The Heavenly Grimoire," Preston stated. Excitement had crept into his voice, and oddly, it gave Selene hope. "If the book truly is the first, it will have spells modern witches have never seen."

Selene looked back and forth between the brothers, trying to process what they were telling her. She was sleep-deprived, and her brain took a second to catch up. "Wouldn't *someone* have practiced them at some point? Most spells today are rooted in the old ways."

"It remains to be seen. Or, in this case, read." Preston grinned. "Let's go annoy Georgie."

"I suspect she'll love it if it's you." Selene crossed her arms and raised her brows. "Maybe I should leave you alone to charm her into letting you have the grimoire?"

"I can flirt with or without you there."

She sputtered a laugh. "You're a cheeky devil, Preston Thorne. That's for sure."

"And he continues to become more cocksure the older he gets," Alastair said with a chuckle. "Go, brother. Work your charm on Georgie. I'll entertain Selene with tales of your wasted youth."

"I believe you're confused again, Al. I was the least troublesome of the three of us. Mother always said so."

With a hearty laugh, Alastair slapped him on the back. "She told each of us kids the same thing, depending on whether or not the other two were outside digging up trouble."

Selene loved their teasing. She was certain she could listen to them go at it all night. Yet, it made her sad to think she'd never developed a closeness with her brother. Quite possibly because he was completely mad and became a sociopath when he grew to adulthood. That tended to put a damper on relationships.

PRESTON FOUND GEORGIE SIPANIL FIRMLY ENSCONCED IN SEBASTIAN'S study with a teapot hovering in the air in front of her and pouring steaming liquid into a cup all on its own. He grinned. Ah, the fun of magic. One could simply enchant an object to do their bidding. Sure, most of the younger crowd liked to hide what they could do, but those like Georgie and her ilk performed simple tasks without a second thought.

She hadn't noted his presence yet, and he didn't alert her. He enjoyed watching others. It allowed him to glimpse beyond the general surface of a person. Looking at Georgie, someone would see a woman who appeared to be in her late fifties. Her hair had turned white long ago, and she didn't bother with a glamour spell to alter the color. She didn't need to. She was still a striking woman. Her nose was on the long side, and her mouth was too wide for most conventional tastes, but her eyes were large and lavender, like Elizabeth Taylor. Although petite and wiry, Georgie was a powerhouse of magic and energy. The only indication she was in her late nineties was her misshapen hands. Witches didn't escape the rigors of things like rheumatoid arthritis if it was in their genetic makeup.

Preston's gaze dropped to the gnarled hands turning the stiff page of the grimoire. It was most probably made of some type of human skin or leathered animal hide which lent to the stiffness. Georgie didn't appear bothered by what she held. She seemed intrigued.

"Are you going to stand there all day, boy?" she asked.

"I thought I was being stealthy."

"You're being creepy." She shot him a censuring look. "Come. Sit beside me and have a cup of tea. I want to show you what I've found."

When he settled next to her, she plopped the heavy spellbook in his lap. "Flip back to the page with the silk marker."

Overcoming his aversion to the idea of human-skin pages, he did as she ordered. The entire two-page spell was in a language he had never learned to read. "I can't make it out. What am I looking at?"

"The spell to get to the Netherworld."

He gaped at her, and she tapped his chin as she chuckled.

Preston focused on the weathered pages again, wishing like hell he'd had the affinity for languages Spring had. "How difficult is it to carry out, and what do we need to accomplish it?"

"A teleportation disc, for one."

"Isn't it great Knox already snagged one from a vault." He smiled. "What else?"

"That's it, other than seven elementals."

"Wait, we don't need Lin, Victor, and the others?" Hope began to build in his chest.

"Oh, no. We do. Each elemental needs a match, and those opposites need to have enough magic to get them through the portal. But no more than that." Her smile was triumphant.

"And to get back? Do we need those same matches?" He prayed like hell they didn't.

Georgie's smile faded, and she looked troubled. "There's no return spell."

Preston simply stared at her, convinced he'd heard wrong. "Pardon?"

"There's no spell to return to this dimension."

He jumped up and flung the spellbook on the sofa, swearing a blue streak as he went. Once again, the desire to break things nearly overwhelmed him. Not one prone to violence, he was bothered by his need to get physical.

"Preston, my boy, please take a seat. Your pacing is distracting."

He shifted to glance back at her, seeing she'd already picked up the grimoire and was thumbing through it. "How the hell do we safely return home, Georgie? I can't let my family go if there is no way back." He didn't try to hide his worry. If anyone would understand, it would be her.

"I know, my dear. It's why no one is going until we have a solid plan."

After striding to where she sat, he squatted in front of her and clasped her hands. "I love you, Ms. Georgie. You'll never understand how much you mean to this family. To me, in particular."

Placing her misshapen hand against his cheek, she smiled. Her lavender eyes were lit with affection. "I believe I do. I love you, too, and I intend to see you live to see your great-grandchildren running about."

He swallowed past the lump of emotion in his throat and blinked back the stinging moisture from his eyes. "I've no doubt if it can be done, you'll be the one to do it," he said huskily. "When you have it worked out, just tell me what you need, and I'll move heaven and earth to get it for you."

"That's what I like. A can-do attitude." She patted his cheek and gestured to her teacup. "Hand me that, won't you?" After she took a sip, she sighed. "Perhaps it's why I adore your family so much. There isn't one Negative Nelly in the bunch. Rascals and rebels, yes. But once any of you set your mind to something, you do it."

"We aim to please."

"Go on. Go *please* that young woman of yours, and leave me to my research."

"I've already done that. Multiple times." He used his forearm to swipe at the imaginary sweat on his brow. "She's insatiable, Ms. Georgie. Take pity on me and marry me already."

Her eyes crinkled at the corners, and she trembled with her laughter. "You rogue!" she finally managed. "Be gone with you."

"Fine, but it's heartless of you to lead me on this way." He heaved a dramatic sigh. "How many men's hearts have you crushed with your dismissal?"

"Countless."

"Just as I thought!" Preston stole a quick kiss, causing her to blush prettily. With a wink, he strolled away, whistling a bawdy tune she was sure to recognize.

Her burst of laughter made him grin.

Goddess, he adored that woman!

CHAPTER 26

"Preston, it's time to wake up." Selene brushed his thick auburn hair back from his forehead. "Wake up, *agápi mou*. We have work to do."

His lashes fluttered, and when he turned his sleep-heavy gaze her way, Selene's heart stuttered in her chest. This morning, his expressive eyes were golden and filled with love. They smoldered and told her exactly where his mind went first thing.

"You wore me out last night and again this morning, my love. Surely I deserve a bit of rest?" he teased.

He shifted more fully on his side, and his erection brushed the flat plane of her stomach.

"Your words say one thing, but your actions say another." Although heat curled low in her belly and her breasts grew heavy with want, she gave him a brisk kiss and a no-nonsense glare. "We don't have time for this right now."

"I say we do." He rolled on top of her, bracing himself on his elbows and pressing his penis against her already wet core. "They can't start the party without us."

"True." She reached down and stroked him. His moan brought a satisfied smile to her lips. "In that case, I'm up for anything."

His eyes flared wide. "Anything?"

"Anything you can do within a fifteen-minute window of time."

"Challenge accepted!"

She meeped when he forcefully plunged into her, and he paused to ask, "Too hard?"

Wrapping her legs around his hips and crossing her ankles, she locked him in place. "Not at all. I was merely surprised you went straight for the prize." She thrust up so he was fully embedded inside, and she contracted the walls of her vagina, tightening around him. "I don't mind it hard. I prefer a hard man."

He barked out a laugh that morphed into a groan as she shifted her hips and thrust again. "Fuck! You're going to kill me, but I'm going to die a happy man this time around."

She stilled. "Don't joke about dying."

His gaze seared into hers. "I'm sorry, Selene. I'll not leave you if I can help it."

"Same," she whispered past her suddenly aching throat. She suspected the tightness was due to the thick emotion she was experiencing at the possible loss of Preston, but she wouldn't explore that line of thought.

Their next kiss was tender but packed with the love they shared. Once they broke apart for air, they began to make love in earnest. Neither could get enough of the other, but it wasn't for lack of trying on Selene's part. Nor Preston's, based on the fierce thrusts and mind-drugging kisses.

When she came, light burst behind her eyes and she screamed his name. With a few murmured words of endearment and a hoarse "fuck, yes!" he finished shortly after her.

Too spent to do more than flop her arms and legs on the mattress, she smiled her happiness. "That wasn't even close to fifteen minutes. I feel cheated."

He nipped her shoulder and rolled onto his back in an imitation of her pose. "You're such a demanding wench. I don't know why I bother."

She giggled and stretched. "Maybe because I give great head."

"Mmm, true enough." He rolled on his side and propped his cheek in his hand, using the other to toy with the tight bud of her nipple. "I'd say it's one of my favorite things about you."

With a light punch to his shoulder followed by a feather-light kiss to his lips, she sat up. "Well, it's a good thing you're a silver-tongued devil the rest of the time. You're a bit of an idiot in the mornings."

He laughed and tackled her back against the pillows. "I said *one* of my favorite things. I have about a million of them."

"Nice save."

"I thought so." His grin faded, and he grew serious as he gazed down at her. "I don't know when I'll have another chance to say it, but these moments spent with you have been the happiest of my life, Selene."

The icy fingers of premonition danced along her skin. "Don't talk like this is goodbye, Preston. Please, don't."

"It's not my intent, but we certainly need to say what we feel, so there are no regrets on either side."

She sandwiched his beloved face between her palms. "Then I'll tell you the same. These moments spent with you have been the happiest of my life, both the one before and again this time around." She kissed him with a fervor that stole the breath from them both. Panting, she locked eyes with him. "I love you so much, and I intend to hang onto this forever. *Fuck* the Nether, and fuck the Evil, too."

His wide, radiant smile was brighter than the sun and warmed her chilled heart. "Well, with that kind of fierceness, I've no doubt you will."

She laughed and hugged him close.

"Is now a bad time to tell you I'm turned on again?"

"Really? This soon?"

"It's those incredible breasts. Anytime they press against my chest like that…" He sighed as if he was put out. "I really have no choice."

"I think we still have four minutes of our allotted fifteen. What can you do with it?"

"Oh, my love. Did you just throw down the gauntlet? If so, I'm about to rock your world."

"You've already done it, but I'm not opposed to a repeat performance."

Selene was radiant when she and Preston joined their group for breakfast, and Alex swallowed a bitter pill of regret. Not that she didn't deserve to be happy, but he was distraught that he wasn't the one to cause her glowing smile.

He dropped his gaze and concentrated on the hot inky liquid in his mug. Everyone believed he was lighthearted and carefree, but he wasn't. He was weighed down with a life full of disappointments and a whole host of sadness.

Closing his eyes, he rested his head back against the high edge of the parson chair he was sitting in.

"Castor?"

Alex lifted his lids to find Preston standing over him, understanding and compassion on his face.

"I wanted to thank you," Preston said in a low voice.

"For what? Brewing the coffee?" Sure, Alex was being a flippant ass, but he wasn't a damned saint.

"I think you know. But in case you don't, thank you for freeing Selene to be with me. Thank you for sacrificing your relationship so we could be happy."

Those damned shrewd eyes saw everything Alex was trying to hide, and to cover his feelings, he ever-so-casually focused on the task of drinking his coffee. Preston wasn't going away without a response, so Alex finally said, "Think nothing of it."

"I owe you a debt."

He slammed the mug down, not caring if he cracked the ceramic cup, dinged the wood of the table, or captured the attention of everyone present. "No, you don't. I didn't do it for you. I did it for *her*. Now shut the fuck up about it already, all right?"

A slight smile twisted Preston's mouth. "Sure."

"Good." Shoving back his chair, Alex teleported from the room to the gateway of the secret garden. He needed to see Evie, even if she couldn't talk to him. She'd been the one woman who treated him like one of her own. The one woman who'd loved him unconditionally when his own mother took off for parts unknown. Goddess, he missed her.

When he rounded the corner, he stopped short.

A lone figure dressed all in black sat on a bench at the center of the enclosed grounds.

"Where does a guy gotta go to find alone time around here?" he called out.

"I wouldn't know. Everyone's been up my ass, lately," Damian called back. "You might as well join me. We can be miserable together."

Alex had only taken one step before his friend said, "But don't come without fortification. I need a scotch."

"It's not even nine in the morning."

"I don't care about the time."

"You wouldn't. Hell, I wouldn't either if I was as ancient as you." Alex desperately wanted a drink, and he was seriously considering going back for the booze when he had a thought. "You're the fucking Aether. You can't conjure that shit?"

Damian snorted a laugh then held his hand about eighteen inches above the stone-slab bench where he was sitting. As Alex approached, he saw a crystal decanter materialize and fill with scotch.

"That's what I'm talkin' about," he said approvingly. "Are we drinking straight from the bottle, or are you going to whip up a couple of tumblers to go with it."

"You're not demanding in the least, are you?"

If he were in the mood to be open and honest, he'd tell Damian how much he'd missed his dry-as-dirt humor, but Alex was trying to run from his feelings, not explore them. "Nope. I'm a fucking delight to be around."

"Pfft. Keep telling yourself that."

"So, about this kid of yours, I heard Mackenzie singing her praises." He took the proffered glass of alcohol from his friend. "She must take after your wife."

Damian grinned. "One hundred percent. Except in looks."

"Damn shame, that."

"We are agreed." They clinked their tumblers and, like the synchronized drinking buddies they used to be, downed their scotch in one swallow.

Ignoring the burning of his esophagus, Alex gestured to their surroundings with his glass. "This place is depressing. Why are you haunting these digs?" He cleared the hoarseness from his throat and nodded his thanks when Damian refilled his drink.

"This was where my mother was entombed."

"Huh. Well that's a bummer. I mean, unless you like the cloying scent of roses."

Damian laughed as Alex had intended. "At the time, there was only one magical plant with black roses and blood-sucking thorns."

"Let's not discuss blood-sucking Thornes. I've had my fill already."

His friend paused in taking a sip and shot him a side glance. "The relationship between Preston and Selene is killing you, isn't it?"

"Yeah. Next subject."

"I believe you're the one who brought it up," Damian pointed out lightly.

"Then I'm ending it. *Next subject,*" Alex growled.

"You should slow down, my friend. Glenfiddich sneaks up on you if you aren't careful."

"I'm immune to its charms. Too many years spent guzzling the stuff."

"I see."

And Alex figured perhaps he did. The Aether could read his thoughts and emotions if he so chose, but it wasn't as if Alex was trying to hide the fact he was salty as fuck over the dissolution of his relationship with Selene.

"When do we head to Stonehenge? I'm sick of standing around and doing nothing but talking."

"I'm waiting for Isis and my mother to arrive. We need to discuss the details of our trip to the Netherworld."

Alex nodded and rose to his feet, too keyed up to sit for long. "Georgie Sipanil found a few interesting things in the Heavenly Grimoire." He glanced over his shoulder at Damian and made a face. "Alastair's name for it."

"Not his. That's actually the name of the first grimoire in existence, so it must be the one she has."

"Yeah, well, apparently there's a way into the Nether, but no way out."

Damian scrubbed his hands up and down his face. "Right. Lovely."

"I'll be honest, man. I've no interest in dying for a lost cause."

"Me either, but it's better than the alternative."

"Which is?"

Rising to his feet, Damian crossed to his mother's grave marker. "Allowing me to roam free after consuming the Evil," he said grimly.

It took a second for the words to sink in, but when they did, Alex lost his shit. "No! Fuck. No! Why wasn't I informed of that little nugget of information?" All he got for an answer was a tight-lipped look. "You are *not* doing that, Dethridge." He pointed his finger in Damian's face. "Not in a million years. Get that thought right out of your head. Leave that fucking plague in the Otherworld and let the souls be obliterated, but you are not consuming the Evil."

"I don't have a goddamned choice, Alex!"

The suppressed fury in Damian's voice was coated with helplessness and pain. The two of them stared at each other, both knowing full well the Aether wouldn't walk away from his responsibility.

"Damian, man, *come on*. You have to understand there's no stopping an eviled-up you like the last set of wannabe heroes did your mom. If you turn nutso and decide to go on a murdering rampage, there's nothing and no one able to prevent it or take you down." He pointed to the marker with Isolde's name. "No tomb will hold you."

"My daughter's an Oracle."

Alex felt his knees weaken. "Shit. She saw it, didn't she?"

Damian gave him a clipped nod.

"What else?"

"Other than crying her heart out and ripping mine to shreds in the process? Not much."

"No indication it would all be okay?"

A thoughtful look crossed the Aether's perfect features, and he frowned as he stared off toward his estate. "She assured me if I sent her away, she'd never come back. But I can't make heads or tails of it, if I'm being honest. My ability to see the future is gone. Yet I can't see her putting herself in the path of danger, knowing what she must become."

"I agree. Any kid of yours would be much more clever than that."

"Exactly." Rubbing the spot between his furrowed brows, Damian sighed heavily. "I'm damned if I know what to do."

Alex had to laugh. The Aether *always* knew what to do, and made sure he did it. "You're like a mere mortal now, my friend. It's refreshing to see."

"Fuck all the way off, Castor."

"Been there, done that, got the t-shirt."

The air around them contracted, and a golden light created a vertical seam in the garden. It split, and two women walked out. Alex had met the one in his travels, and he bowed his head to acknowledge the Goddess. His eyes were drawn to the other woman, and he nearly swallowed his tongue. She was incredible and perfect in every way. The female version of Damian.

Isolde de Thorne. The Enchantress.

Alex had heard rumors, but she'd been long buried by the time he arrived on the scene. A damned good thing, too, because he'd be the first in line to offer up his power had she summoned him. What was it about dark-haired, dark-eyed women that brought him low? He was an absolute sucker.

Other than to give him a curious look, she paid him no mind. Her focus turned to her son.

"Damian." There was a wealth of love and pride in the one word.

"Mother."

Damian crossed the divide between them and embraced her tightly. The shock on her face made Alex's heart hammer. No one should ever feel unloved or uncertain, but he knew all about that.

Tears streamed down Isolde's face as she hugged Damian back. She appeared pathetically grateful for his affection.

Alex wasn't sure what had gone down in the past, but it warmed him to see them set aside their differences. Also, he didn't do emotions well, and as a result, his mouth opened and sarcasm poured out. "Touching reunion. Did you know your son has decided he wants to follow in your footsteps and consume the Evil? No?"

Damian glared in his direction and gave him a mental slap in the form of a blinding headache. Bending double and pressing his hands against his head to keep his brains inside, Alex shouted in pain.

"What the fuck, man?"

"I could say the same, Castor." Damian pulled back his magic. "Let me make my own confessions in the future."

"Done. Now repair the damage before I die from an aneurysm or something equally tragic."

As the Aether, Damian could've very well killed Alex if he wanted. "You're fine, you big baby."

Isolde watched them as if she was confused they were friends.

Alex grinned. "It's my charming personality," he told her.

With a roll of his eyes, Damian snorted. "You'd have to have a personality to be charming."

"Ouch, buddy. That stung." Alex placed one hand over his heart and the back of his wrist against his forehead in a dramatic pose. "I'm not sure my heart can take the hurt."

Isis glided forward, one seductive hip sway after another. "Alexander Castor. I'm surprised you came out of hiding."

"Only for you, Exalted One." He bent into a low bow, and when he straightened, she was grinning.

"False, but you get credit for the lie."

He grinned in return. The Goddess had never let him get away with bullshit. Perhaps it was why he liked her the best of all the deities.

"I'd like to request a favor, my beloved queen."

She raised her black brows, and her kohl-lined eyes narrowed. "Ask."

"I request you don't let Damian consume the Evil, no matter what happens."

"Castor!" The Aether was clearly appalled by Alex's lack of manners. "Were you dropped on your head as an infant? This is not your concern." Damian's diamond-hard tone could cut glass.

"Sorry, man, but it totally is. I'm going to have to hero up and try to take you down, which we both know I'd never be able to do. Of course, it would result in my death, and half the women in the world would expire from the grief. I'm simply trying to save us all the trouble."

Damian shook his head. "You arrogant shit." This was actually said with deep amusement and a whole lot of affection.

Another light split the clearing, and out walked Nathanial Thorne. With a suddenness that stunned him, Alex felt tears fill his eyes. There stood the only father figure he'd ever known. The man who'd helped shape him and who'd taught him right from wrong. A true hero—unlike Alex.

Rooted to the spot, all Alex could do was stare through his blurry vision.

"Hello, my boys," Nate said gruffly. "It's been way too long."

CHAPTER 27

"I wondered where you'd gone to, Castor. Now I see you had a date with these two lovely ladies and Nate. You could've told us there was a party."

Alex smiled and shook his head when he heard Alastair's humor-filled voice. With a single glance over his shoulder, he noted the Thorne brothers. Preston held the hand of a young, dark-haired child who could only belong to his best friend.

"I thought I told you to stay away, beastie," Damian said sternly, striding to where the little girl stood, unrepentant and smiling. "Are you ever going to do as you're told?"

She held up her arms for him to lift her, apparently confident she wasn't in too much trouble. "I wanted to see Grandpa Nate. But I didn't come alone. You told me I have to have an adult with me if I gallivamp around."

"Gallivant," Alex corrected helpfully as Damian returned to the center of the garden with his daughter. "Nice way to dodge an order, kid."

"I'm Sabrina."

"I'm Alexander Castor."

"I know. Papa broke the cupid when I told him you were hiding."

"For the love of all that is holy! I'm going to lock her up until she's a hundred," Damian vowed.

She giggled and patted her father's cheek. "No you're not, Papa."

Other than to narrow his eyes in parental warning, he remained silent.

"She's a chip off the old block, Dethridge," Alex said with a laugh. "I think I adore her."

Sabrina tilted her head and studied him for a few seconds. The urge to hide from her all-seeing eyes was strong. When she opened her mouth to speak, her father clamped a hand over it.

"No predictions," Damian warned.

With an exasperated glare, she peeled his hand away. "I wasn't, Papa."

Nathanial laughed and held out his arms. "We all know you were, darling girl. Now come. Give me a hug, and tell me what I need to do to wake my wife."

She dove into his embrace and kissed his cheek. "I missed you, Grandpa Nate."

"I missed you too, princess."

"I have to pay respects to the Goddess first. Papa will scold me if I don't," she said in a loud stage whisper.

Alex bit the inside of his cheek to hold back his laughter as Damian did a face-palm.

Isis and Isolde had watched the entire scene unfold with indulgent smiles, and they stepped forward when Nathanial set Sabrina on her feet.

"Hello, Beloved."

"Hello, Exalted One." The girl executed a perfect curtsey and smiled prettily. "It's a pleasure to see you, ma'am."

This time, Alex couldn't hold back the laugh. "Oh, she's too precious, Dethridge. Butter wouldn't melt in her mouth. Without a doubt, that kid is going to keep you on your toes!"

Damian groaned.

All kidding was set aside as Nathanial moved to stand beside his wife where she was deep in a stasis of Serqet's making. The ravaged look on his face stabbed Alex straight through the fucking heart. "Alastair, please take down your protective barrier. I need to touch my wife."

"Yes, sir." With little fanfare, Alastair touched the pulsing dome and murmured the words to dissolve it.

Perched on the edge of the stone altar, Nathanial smoothed a hand down his wife's lank blonde hair. "You need to wake now, my darling Evie. It's time to return home to me."

"Where did her soul go?" Alex whispered his question to Damian. "Doesn't a witch in stasis go to the Otherworld normally?"

The Aether stared at him in shocked wonder before running to where Evie was laid. "Nate! Don't touch her!"

But it was too late.

Nathanial's back arched, and a guttural cry emerged from his throat. He slumped over Evie with his face resting against the V between her shoulder and neck. Despite the tragedy of the moment, there was a beauty to the pose. As if two lovers were sleeping after a night of love.

"*What the fuck just happened?*" Alastair shouted. His vicious curse was followed by a forceful sneeze. Only the Goddess herself had the presence of mind to throw up her hands to stave off the plague of locust sure to follow.

The atmosphere around them thickened. Black storm clouds rolled in, blocking out the sunlight and turning the day to night.

Everyone burst into action at once.

Isolde pulled Sabrina to her as Damian positioned himself with his back to hers. They tucked the girl between them and raised their hands to wield their impressive Aether powers.

A fireball flared to life in each of Preston's palms, providing some semblance of light, but it was whatever the shadows were hiding they needed to worry about.

Alex drew the energy from the electrons around them, and electricity snapped from fingertip to fingertip. He was ready to fry the ass of anyone who'd try to harm their group.

"What's happening, Isis? What has your bloody sister done this time?" Alastair snapped as he checked Nathanial's neck for a pulse.

A deep frown marred her otherwise unblemished face, and she shook her head as she slowly spun in a circle.

Alex assumed she was assessing the threat and trying to make heads or tails of Serqet's newest game. It was no great secret the Goddess hated the Thornes.

"Al, I'm worried the others are unprotected at the manor with us here," Preston said hoarsely.

"Knox and Quentin won't let anything happen to anyone." Alastair used magic to shift his great-grandfather's body, laying him out flat next to Evie. A barely banked fury radiated off him, and Alex felt the continuous slap like waves crashing against the shoreline.

"It's not Serqet," Isis called out. "Or rather, not completely. The game with the Guardians, perhaps, but this…" She looked skyward. "… *this* is the Evil trying to break through to this plane."

"Fucking great," Alex snapped. "Is it only here, do you suppose, or is the mortal world witnessing this creepy-ass show? Because I'll be honest, I don't know how the scientists are going to spin this one."

"Climate change?" Alastair quipped.

Preston shot his brother a hard look. "Funny, Al. We can always count on you to infuse humor in a craptastic situation."

The ground around them shook violently, and they scrambled to remain standing. One by one, pillars rose until they encircled and towered over their group.

Alastair looked at Damian.

"Not me, Al."

They shifted their attention to Isis.

"I didn't raise the standing stones," she said, her frown deepening.

"We did." Spring stepped through the gate to the garden, Serqet directly behind her.

. . .

As he rushed past the altar where his great-grandparents laid in stasis, Preston tossed a fireball into one of the cauldrons perched on a pillar to keep the area around the others lit. Keeping the other flame burning in his right hand, he ran to his daughter. It might cost his life, but if he needed to toast Serqet to protect Spring, he would.

"Dad, it's okay," Spring said with her standard gentle smile. "We're okay. She's here to help."

Ignoring his daughter, he glared down at the Goddess. "What did you do to Nathanial and Evie?"

"That's why we're here, child. To wake them." Serqet's tone was missing her standard disdain, and she appeared genuine, which absolutely floored Preston. He'd been the one to urge caution since she had a miraculous change of heart, but if Spring was here without Knox to guard her, a peace treaty had been brokered between the three of them, and Preston needed to back off.

Alastair startled him when he placed a hand on his shoulder. "Stand down, little brother. Let's give her a chance to wake them."

Serqet and Spring moved to the altar, but Alastair held Preston back. They locked gazes and Alastair pitched his voice low to say, "If she pulls anything underhanded, I'll take action. But know, we are all on high alert." He gave a subtle nod to Alex and Damian. "They love Nathanial and Evie, too."

"It's difficult to trust a person who's made it her life's mission to destroy our line, but all right."

"Right there with you, my brother," Alastair said feelingly. He glanced up and frowned. "Does it look like there's a dome over us keeping the blackness at bay?"

Preston followed his brother's line of sight and acknowledged it did indeed seem that way. Bending down, he hefted a sizable rock. "Give this a boost when I throw it." At Alastair's nod, he said, "Here goes nothing." Whipping back his arm, Preston hurled the stone as hard as he could. It flew straight up like a rocket, halted about thirty feet above them as if it had soundlessly connected with another object, and then dropped back to earth with a soft thud.

He and Alastair shared a look. "What does it mean, Al?"

"I don't have the foggiest notion." He left to share a low-voiced conversation with Spring and Serqet. When Preston joined them, Alastair turned to him. "They didn't see the darkness until they were entering the garden. It's not visible to the outside world. Only those of us in here."

Isis had approached, and she seemed as puzzled as the others. It wasn't a good sign when goddesses had no clue what was happening.

"First things first, let's wake the Guardians. Other than Isolde, they've been around the longest and might have an idea what we are dealing with." Preston ran a hand through his hair. "Sound like a solid plan?"

Everyone gave their agreement.

"I take it you need the stones activated." Damian squatted and placed Sabrina's hand in Isolde's. "Stay with your grandmother outside the ring but where I can see you, beastie. I won't be able to concentrate if I'm worried about you."

Isolde's expression was one of wonder and love when she asked, "You trust me with your daughter?"

When he looked up at her, his smile was beatific. "Yes, Mother. I do."

"I showed him the Before," Sabrina volunteered.

"The Before?" The Enchantress shifted her questioning stare between father and daughter. "I don't understand."

"It's Sabrina-speak for prior to you consuming the Evil," Damian explained. "She's an Oracle with the power to see and share all that came before and all that will come after."

Isolde crouched until she was eye level with her granddaughter. "What a wonderful gift you've given your father, little one! The knowledge of the Before is wondrous. Thank you."

Sabrina touched her finger to the single teardrop sliding down Isolde's face. "He needed to see you love him. Love fixes us."

"Yes, darling girl, it does." Isolde wrapped her in a tight hug. Tears streamed from behind her closed lids. "I love you, too."

Preston felt his throat tighten with emotion, and he turned away.

One glance around showed all their group was affected to varying degrees.

When Isolde rose, Sabrina darted to Serqet and gave her a sunny smile. "Thank you for helping my Grandpa Nate, Exalted One."

"I haven't done anything yet, child. You shouldn't raise your hopes this will succeed. The spell I cast was conjured from my hatred."

Sabrina leaned in as if to impart a secret. "Love is stronger, isn't it?" She took the Goddess's hand in hers and brought it to her cheek. "You love like my Papa—with all of you."

A revelation struck Preston. If Serqet was as emotional as Sabrina indicated, it would make sense she'd take rejection harder than any other.

As if she read his thought, the Goddess made eye contact with him, and him alone. The vulnerability surprised Preston and made it impossible to look away. The wounded woman beneath the powerful exterior reminded him of Selene. He'd seen that very expression in her eyes many times since they met, and it cut him to the quick whenever he bore witness to such raw emotion.

Serqet's smile was gentle. She gave a slight nod, as if she could tell what he was feeling, but the invasion into his private thoughts didn't bother him all that much. Sabrina had a way of exposing them all, and it was better to own it than fall into a pattern of self-denial.

"What do you need from us, Exalted One?" Preston asked. "I'm at your service."

The Goddess's smile bloomed, and she looked remarkably young for a woman thousands of years old. "Thank you for your trust, Preston Thorne. I'll not forget this moment."

"It's doubtful I will, either," he said dryly.

"If the Aether will light the stones, we can get started."

Once Isolde and Sabrina were safely outside the circle, Damian moved from pillar to pillar, touching the symbol representing the elemental magic. When he was done, he crossed to stand on the opposite side of the altar, directly across from Serqet. "What's next?"

"This ceremony is for my sister and myself to perform. Those of you present should touch the symbol representing your magic to ground yourselves."

After they'd done as she directed, Serqet extended her arms, palms toward the sky. Isis mirrored the action. "Father," Serqet called out, her voice booming like thunder. "Hear our plea and assist us in this, our time of need."

Lightning zagged sideways above their heads.

"Father," Isis called. "We need you now to help restore the souls of these two trusted Guardians."

A second bolt of lightning danced along the top of the pillars, and Preston felt the electric vibration down to his toes. From twenty feet away, Alastair looked as if he'd experienced the same sensation. It wasn't altogether unpleasant, just different. Had the atmospheric lightning actually struck them they'd be barbecued right now, but this particular magic show was from the one god who knew how to play to the crowd.

"I shall pay the forfeit, father," Serqet said. "Their stasis was my doing. Take my life to restore theirs."

Preston and Isis registered the words first, and in doing so, recognized the problem. *They needed Serqet for the Netherworld!*

"No!" he shouted. Forgetting himself in his frenzy to stop the deal from being struck, he released the stone and ran for the altar.

He heard Castor swear and the pounding of feet as the first shimmer from the next lightning bolt formed. Hard hands shoved him to the ground, and he rolled on his back, arms lifted to instinctively fight. But Alex wasn't attacking. He was saving Preston's life —*again.*

The bolt hit Castor with the weight of a freight train and knocked him off his feet. He writhed on the ground as the convulsions racked his body. The scream of pain wasn't one Preston would forget anytime soon. His instinct was to help, but touching an electrified warlock was suicide, and he stared, helpless to correct his stupid mistake.

In the end, it was Damian who saved Alex. Abandoning the

safety of his stone, he knelt beside him. With one hand, he parted the earth, only creating enough room for the width of his forearm. The other hand he placed over Alex's heart.

The current was redirected using the Aether as a conduit.

"Miss Spring!" Sabrina shouted. "Do like Papa and touch the altar!" It was a miracle she could be heard over the increasing volume of the thunder. But Spring had, and she took off at a run. Preston swallowed the fear she would be electrocuted. If the Oracle was providing instruction, she wouldn't put Spring's life in jeopardy.

Preston felt like a damned fool for his spontaneous move. If Alexander was seriously injured or impaired because of his impulsiveness, he'd never forgive himself.

Isolde cried out when Sabrina crossed the barrier and entered the circle. Alerted to the danger his child faced, Damian started to withdraw his hand from the earth's cavity.

"No, Papa!" Sabrina warned. She didn't stop walking until she reached the altar. Climbing atop, she placed one hand against Nathanial's chest and the other against Evie's. She nodded at Spring. "Now, Miss Spring."

Using the hand not touching the altar's base, Spring parted the earth like Damian had and plunged her hand inside. The lightning's current found her immediately, and she cried out as it coursed through her body.

Preston desperately wanted to get her to safety, but he ignored his instinctive paternal response and forced himself to trust in the magic of the Aethers.

Sabrina channeled the power Spring fed to the stone base. Her tiny hands glowed red where they rested against the Guardians. *"Exsuscito!"*

Nathanial's and Evie's bodies arched upward, yet Sabrina managed to remain kneeling between them.

"I need more power," she cried.

Isolde ran to Isis and bowed her head. She spoke one word. *"Please."*

Isis nodded, seeming to understand the request. At the gesture, Isolde climbed onto the flat surface, next to her granddaughter, set her palm on Evie's chest, and took Sabrina's small hand in hers.

Isis placed her index finger in the center of Isolde's forehead, and Serqet did the same for Sabrina.

As one, they shouted, *"Exsuscito!"*

CHAPTER 28

"I have the mother of all hangovers," Nathanial complained. He huddled under a thick fur blanket with Evie tucked against his chest.

"Shhh," she whispered, ending on a moan. "You're too loud, darling."

GiGi had tended to them when they first returned to the Drakes' home, and now, she held out two glasses filled with a Pepto-Bismol pink liquid for them to consume.

"That looks frightening," Castor muttered from the comfort of his wingback chair.

"If it comes from my sister's medicine bag, it probably is," Preston replied.

Alex snorted, winced, and grabbed his head. "Don't tell GiGi, but I have the mother of all hangovers, too."

"Since I owe you for saving my life, mum's the word, pal."

"What possessed you to pull a boneheaded stunt like that in the first place, Thorne? It isn't like you're a stupid man."

"My mind took a vacation when Serqet offered herself as a sacrifice. As I understand it, we need her to stop the Evil." He grimaced and took a sip of his coffee. "What can I say? I panicked, and I can't apologize enough for what you went through."

"Look, had I been faster in processing the problem, I might have been the one running to stop her. But I didn't. The only reason I reacted fast enough to help you was the voice in my head, screaming at me to save you."

Preston paused in taking another drink and stared. "What voice?"

Alex shot a quick glance toward the Dethridges gathered on the other side of the great room. "I think it came from Damian's daughter."

"Fuck."

"Yeah. The kid is like nothing I've ever seen. I don't know if our friend realizes exactly how powerful she is."

Damian's head lifted, and he sent them a sharp look.

"I think he does," Preston murmured before taking another sip of his beverage. "Honestly, I don't think *we* know just how powerful *any* of them are. And I like it that way. If I knew, I'd probably crap my pants."

"Not you, Thorne. You and Alastair are giants in the magical world. The stuff of legends."

He snorted at Alex's drivel. "I think that lightning bolt scrambled your brain, Castor."

"Preston."

The serious note in the other man's voice caused Preston's stomach to tighten. "Shit, you're not going to say something nice to me, are you? I don't want to throw up my coffee on Baz's priceless rug."

A twitch of Alex's lips showed his amusement. "I promise not to say anything nice if you'll let me speak."

With a roll of his eyes and a wave of his hand, Preston encouraged him to continue.

"As I was about to say before you turned into a sarcastic ass, Selene deserves to be happy. If you don't think you're that man, if you're still hung up on your wife—"

"Alastair likes to remind me that Rorie's my widow," he said, effectively cutting Alex off. "And I'm fine with it. I love Selene. More than I believed it was possible to love anyone. Yes, I did love my wife, but not in this all-consuming way." He rose to his feet and zeroed in on Selene chatting with Aurora across the room. "I'll do whatever it takes to make her happy, Alex." He glanced down at the other man. "Just like you."

"Okay. Go away now. You're making my head hurt worse."

"I think perhaps this conversation makes your heart hurt, not your head, but I'll leave you to it." He took two steps and spun back around. "I meant what I said. I owe you."

"I'll keep the favor in my back pocket for another day."

Preston gave a quick nod and went to find the goddesses. They had all the power they were going to get, and now they needed a solid game plan.

FROM THE CORNER OF HER EYE, SELENE SAW PRESTON'S BRISK EXIT from the room. As she turned and met Alex's solemn gaze, she was forced to wonder if the two men had a tiff. His smile, when it came, was tired and a little melancholy. Part of her wanted to go to him and hold his head to her breast like she used to do to chase his worries away. To soothe his active mind that never seemed to find a quiet moment other than when she held him. She had a strong desire to speak to him and assure herself he was all right after the trial in the garden.

Twice, he'd risked his life for Preston, and Selene had no doubt he'd done it for her happiness. Alex had turned out to be a good man after all.

"Is it a difficult choice for you to make?" Aurora asked, pulling Selene's attention from Alex.

"What do you mean?" She pasted on a confused look and a half smile, hoping the other woman didn't see right through her.

"I think you know." Aurora's light eyes focused on something beyond Selene's shoulder. "You have two handsome men ready to lay down their lives for you. Both appear to love you beyond reason. Who do you intend to choose?"

Anger tightened Selene's chest, causing her heart to hammer and her lungs to work harder at drawing in air. "I've made my choice, Mrs. Thorne, and it isn't for *you* to question. You left Preston for another man, but don't assume I'll do the same." Until that moment, she hadn't realized she was jealous of Preston's ex-wife. Perhaps if she'd had longer than two madcap days to think about it, she'd have discovered it sooner. But standing before her was the only woman, other than herself, who he'd loved.

Aurora's eyes hardened, and she stepped a foot closer. "Don't mistake the situation, Ms. Barringer. I did love Preston. I still do. If you hurt him, I'll rip your head from your shoulders and—"

"Now, now, my love." Alastair cut her off with an arm around her waist and a kiss on her temple. "You'd be the first to say it's bad form to maim future family members."

She glared up at him, and without any concern for the roomful of people, tweaked his nipple through his dress shirt.

He dodged backward and rubbed his chest. "For fu—for the love of the Goddess, you bloodthirsty woman! I was trying to stop a bloodbath, but if you're determined to go to war with Selene, be my guest." Alastair turned his attention to Selene. "Run while you can. Aurora on a rampage won't be stopped."

With a suddenness that confused Selene, Aurora laughed and wound her arms around his neck. After meeting his challenging stare, she gave him a lusty kiss.

Embarrassed and perhaps a little hot from the display, Selene looked away, but not before Alastair met her eyes and winked. Face burning, she turned to beat a hasty retreat and ran smack dab into Alexander's massive, rock-hard chest. His arms contracted around her, and he helped her remain standing. If her nose wasn't throbbing from the contact, she might've buried it against the warm skin at the V of his shirt to sniff and savor his unique scent. A mix of fresh apples and cloves, the man smelled like a baked tart. Preston, on the other hand, smelled of cinnamon and sin.

Her head came up as she realized Alex hadn't released her yet. "I'm fine. Thank you."

"I noticed you were upset, and I thought I might help."

She tossed back her hair and met his searching eyes. "I promise I'm fine, Alex. You don't need to run to save me every time someone insults me."

"I didn't insult you," Aurora was quick to say. "I asked if choosing between Preston and Castor was a difficult decision for you."

The arrogance and smugness in her tone grated on Selene's last nerve, and she might've given her the dressing down she deserved if Alex's magnetic eyes hadn't sharpened on something over her shoulder.

She started to turn her head, but he stopped her by lightly gripping her chin.

"Yes, darling Selene. Tell us if the choice is hard for you," he purred.

"Not at all. I love Preston. Now release me."

"You heard her, Castor," Preston said, pure steel in his tone. "Release her."

Alex quickly disguised his disappointment with a dramatic sigh. "Ya know, you save a guy's life a time or two, and you'd think he would allow a reward by way of stealing a kiss from his beautiful woman. But noooo. He has to bluster and be a total dick about it."

Selene felt relief when he let her go with only a light, platonic kiss on her nose. Facing Preston, she held out a hand. "I need a break from your family." She gestured over her shoulder to Alex with her thumb and said, "And from all this false modesty."

Alastair huffed out a laugh at the same time Preston grinned.

"Come on. I know just the place," he said, and his tone indicated she'd absolutely love it.

"I thought you were meeting with the goddesses to get this wrapped up," Alex said.

Preston had an extremely frustrated air about him. "Can't find them, and they refuse to answer my summons. It's a waiting game now."

Alastair dropped his arm from Aurora's waist. "I believe Nate was the last one to speak to Isis. Let me see if he has any idea where the sisters disappeared to."

"Still want a quiet time?" Preston asked Selene in a low voice.

"Please. Just for a few minutes."

He nodded, made their excuses to Aurora and Alex, and teleported with Selene to their shared bedroom. Once they arrived, he drew her to the mattress and urged her to sit. He squatted in front of her and clasped her hands in his. As he stared at their joined hands, he rubbed his thumbs over the backs of hers. "Care to tell me what I stumbled across down there?"

"Your ex-wife making trouble," she ground out, still angry by the way Aurora had tried to manipulate the situation. "Who is she to question our relationship, Preston? What right does she have? She left you for your brother!" Selene was working herself into a fine fit, but she didn't care. The outrage she was feeling was on Preston's behalf, not her own. "It's almost like she was encouraging me to choose Alex. Who does that to someone they profess to love?"

"If I know Rorie—and I believe I do after all these years—she was testing you, my love."

"What was the point?" Selene didn't understand. She had a role to play in the upcoming drama regarding the Evil. "If I decide I want Alex back after all this time, am I going to be kicked out of your superhero club?"

He went completely still. After a long moment, he asked, "*Do* you want Alex back?"

With a few choice swear words, Selene jerked her hands away and stood up. "Not you, too! Am I so untrustworthy no one believes a word out of my mouth?"

Her tears came unbidden, and her embarrassment over her emotional state was keen. With no thought but to get the hell away from the Thornes, she teleported.

When her cells cooled, she opened her eyes. Her mother's headstone. How sad she only had one place to go, and it was to run to a dead woman. *Katherine Salinger.* Running her fingers over the engraved letters, Selene wondered why there was no true sanctuary for her anywhere other than here.

The air around her grew heavy, indicating an incoming witch, and Selene didn't bother to turn around. She'd already guessed who it would be. After all, in the entire time she was in the Otherworld, she'd never seen a trace of her mother. "Isn't it odd I never figured it out until now? All this time, I believed Victor was the instigator behind my miserable existence when it was actually you." She faced the woman who'd given birth to her. "Why not kill me outright? Why drug me and leave me to burn in the fire?"

CHAPTER 29

"It took you long enough to figure it out, my dear."

Selene looked at her mother with new eyes. Not through the love-goggles of a child, but through the eyes of a woman who'd been ill-used time and time again by those who were supposed to love her. She was surprised how much alike they were in appearance. The only difference was the hardened expression on Katherine Salinger's face and the uncaring hazel eyes staring back at her.

"I'm not your dear, Mother. I'm not anything other than a pawn. Who's my real father? Victor prefers men, so I doubt it's him."

"Oh, I never lied about your father. But he was easily manipulated. Much like yourself."

"I understand you were in league with Victor all this time. But why?"

"I'm surprised you need to ask. Power, Selene. It's the only thing worth having. It has a value all its own."

"I'd have to argue that point. Love trumps all else."

Her mother scoffed as she dropped her gaze to the tombstone with her name and the supposed date of her death. "Love trumps *nothing*. Tell me, girl. Did your love for Alexander Castor make you stronger? No." The disgust on her face tore at Selene's heart. "It made you pathetic and weak. It allowed you to be used by Victor and, by extension, me."

"You never cared about me at all, did you? All the affection was a pretense."

"Exactly. I'd hoped to mold you as I'd been molded, going so far as to create the same circumstances. Domineering parents, unscrupulous brother, and orphaned at a young age."

"But I'm not you."

"No. You're not. You're a severe disappointment in that regard. I blame Preston Thorne."

"Why?"

"He spirited you away, and we had the devil of a time locating you. He undid all my hard work."

Selene sent up a silent thank you to Preston for his foresight in hiding an unprotected child from her devious relatives. "Why do you believe it was him?" She tried to deflect her mother's growing fury from Preston. "It could've been anyone."

"He's the only do-gooder who showed an interest in your welfare at the estate sale, girl. Do you think me stupid?" Katherine waved a hand in dismissal. "Agnes confirmed it before she died."

A sickening dread and a wave of grief washed over Selene. "You were responsible for her death?"

"Of course. But she'd hidden you too well and wouldn't give you up."

Not only had her own mother faked her death, but she'd assigned spies to watch Selene when her nefarious plot failed. Agnes had been hired to care for her, and she'd paid the ultimate price. Selene's stomach churned, but she tried to appear unruffled at the news. Showing weakness wouldn't serve her with Katherine.

"She felt a mother's love for a young orphan girl," a deep male voice said from behind Selene.

She gasped and spun around. She'd been too caught up to register the arrival of anyone else.

Preston stood ten feet away with Alex beside him. The icy

disdain written on their faces chilled her to her core. "Careful. I doubt Mother is here alone," she warned. She mouthed the word "blockers."

Preston's eyes flicked to her when she spoke, and he raised his left brow an infinitesimal amount. Enough to acknowledge what she was trying to relay.

"I'll never understand how you could be so unfeeling toward your own child, Katherine," he said as he walked forward.

When he reached Selene and placed his hands on her shoulders, her mother's eyes grew calculating, and a nasty smile curled her lips. "You had Agnes groom her for your own needs, it seems."

Selene barely held off becoming violently ill at the accusation. She jerked from beneath his touch and surged forward until she stood face-to-face with Katherine. "Only your immoral, twisted brain would come up with something so disgusting. Preston and I didn't start a relationship until we met in the Otherworld."

"You don't owe her an explanation, my love. You and I know the truth." He drew her away and inserted himself between mother and daughter. "But it appears we found a counterbalance for Castor."

Selene frowned. "I don't understand."

"As if I'm surprised. You were consistently slow, girl." Katherine crossed her arms over her chest and lifted her chin. "He's referring to the Netherworld. Alexander will need an enemy to gain entrance."

Before Selene could grasp the importance of her mother going to the Netherworld, Alastair appeared from nowhere with the binding bracelets and clapped one around her mother's wrist. She momentarily struggled, but without her magic, she was useless against Alastair's strength, and he was able to secure her other wrist.

"The blockers were neutralized before we made our presence known, darling," Alex said to Selene.

"How did you know I'd come here?" she asked.

His expression softened as he gazed down at her. "You once told me you came here to be close to her."

"But why did you all come?"

Preston held up a hand. "My doing, I'm afraid. I was worried when you got so upset. The instant you teleported, I scried for your location. Seeing your mother threw me at first, but I quickly figured it out and brought reinforcements."

"But it all happened so fast!" She was having a difficult time understanding how they'd found her, reached the conclusion she might need help, and formulated a plan all in a matter of minutes.

"Your ex-beau can manipulate time, my love." Preston shared a grin with Alex. "He's helpful to have around."

Selene closed her eyes and rubbed the spot between her brows. "It appears you and Alex make a formidable team."

"It's all me," Castor said. "I'm the MVP for any team."

A laugh bubbled its way out of her. His inappropriate humor was one of the things she missed most about him. "I'm grateful." She cast her infuriated mother a glance. "If I had to guess, she showed up to finish the job she started when I was a child. What better way to throw a wrench in the plan to stop the Evil?"

"Actually, I intended to bargain. Your life for Victor's. He was more useful to me." The hatred on Katherine's face was hurtful, but not unexpected, considering what Selene had learned in the last little while.

"Then I'm thrilled we were able to thwart your ultimate goal," Selene said as she turned away.

"*You* didn't, though, did you?"

She halted.

Alex was in front of her, concern for her on his face. "Don't engage, Selene," he said in a low voice. "It's exactly what she wants so she can take another dig."

It didn't matter that Selene didn't respond, because her mother wasn't finished with her cruelty. "If it weren't for Alexander and the Thornes, my plans would be well on their way. You're useless, Selene. Plain and simple."

Burning rage replaced the concern on Alex's face, and electricity danced across the fingers of his lifted his hands.

"Alex, don't! She's not worth it." Selene gripped his wrists. "She's not worth it," she repeated on a softer but no less insistent note.

His icy eyes locked on her as he pulled back his magic. Some of his fury subsided, but not completely. "Don't ever grab me when I'm amped up again, Selene. You could've been electrocuted."

"You have incredible control. I was never in danger from you."

Preston approached the two of them and placed a hand on her lower back. "It'll save me a heart attack if you listen to Castor, my love."

"And we wouldn't want to give Preston a heart attack," Alex said dryly.

"Behave!" she scolded. Unable to face her mother again, she turned to Preston. "Thank you for following. It was foolish on my part to assume there was no danger, considering there are those who don't want peace to rule the magical community."

"You had no way of knowing. But my family, on the other hand..." He shrugged. "We're constantly faced with problems."

Preston watched the play of emotions cross Selene's countenance. She wasn't a Thorne by blood or marriage, and she didn't understand that even in times of peace, when all their supposed enemies were vanquished, there would always be a constant threat of danger. Powerful families were subject to ridicule and hatred.

He needed to give her a choice when this was over. Let her decide for herself what risks she wanted to expose herself to, simply by being his mate. "We should go back now."

She dropped her gaze, but not before he saw her reluctance.

"If you need more alone time, might I suggest the pond on my estate?" He stepped away to give her space. "No one will bother you there, and you can return when you're ready."

"Thank you," she said stiffly. In a blink, she was gone.

"You should follow to make sure she got to your place safely,

Thorne," Alex said. "Al and I can secure Katherine in the Council cells until it's time."

"She knows where she's going. And she has a decision to make."

"A decision about what?"

"You or me."

Castor snorted. "You're an idiot. She's made her choice, man."

"It didn't seem that way to me."

Alex sobered, and there was a sadness in his eyes. "You weren't listening. She loves you, Preston."

"And she loves you, too," he snapped. "I can see the way her eyes light up every time she looks at you, Castor."

Alex looked past him to Alastair. "Do you want to explain it while I deliver Katherine to the Council guards?"

"No. My brother is a bit hardheaded. He'll eventually come around when he's had time to think things through."

"What am I missing?" Preston bit out the question.

"Selene resents that Rorie questioned her feelings in the first place, little brother. It didn't help that you defended Rorie or that you followed it up with your asinine insecurity." Alastair patiently waited for his words to sink in, and when they finally did, he smiled. "There you go. I knew you'd eventually figure it out."

"Shut it, Al," Preston growled. "It seems I have groveling to do."

Castor and Alastair shared an amused look but, for once, kept their sarcasm to themselves.

Envisioning the pond on the Thorne estate, and sending a magical feeler to test for Selene's location, Preston closed his eyes and let his cells warm to teleport to her. He found her sitting on the outcrop of rocks where he and his brother used to fish.

"I wondered how long it would take you to show up," she said with a snort. "You can't seem to let me be."

"No, I can't. You are the flame to my moth, Selene."

She gave a delicate shrug of one shoulder. "Obsession isn't love, Preston."

"I'm only obsessed with your body. But I'm in love with the soul inhabiting it and the mind controlling it."

"Are you here to demand I make a choice between you and Alex?"

"No. I'm here to apologize for being a jackass."

Attention caught, she shifted to look at him. "I'm listening."

He grinned. "I, Preston Flemming Thorne III, do hereby apologize to you, Selene Anne Barringer for being a total jackass and for not accepting you at your word when you stated you loved me above all others."

"And?"

"And I will hold you to it for as long as we both shall live, never questioning your commitment to our relationship again."

"And?"

He thought for a moment, trying to figure out what else she needed. "And should my ex-wife ever say anything snarky or hurtful to you again, I'll read her the riot act and defend you until my dying breath."

"And?"

"I'm at a loss as to what else I may have done," he admitted with a sheepish grin.

"Absolutely nothing, but I wanted to see how far you'd take it."

He laughed and crossed to where she was. Placing a foot on the tree stump at the base of the boulder, he rested a forearm on his raised knee and stared up at her. "So I'm forgiven?"

"There was never anything for you to be forgiven for, *agápi mou*." She rose to her feet and brushed the seat of her black palazzo pants.

From her elevated position above him, with the sun behind her, it was difficult to read her expression. Nerves ate at Preston's belly, and he wanted to see her clearly. Wanted to see the fierce love he felt for her reflected back.

She held out a hand, and he grasped it, tugging her down and straight into his arms. He held her as a man holds his bride before crossing the threshold to a new home. Symbolic, to his way of thinking.

"I will never take your love for granted, Selene. Maybe the reason I'm insecure is that you once loved Castor with your whole heart. It's hard to believe those feelings go away. And also, I've never had someone who loves me one-hundred percent." He swallowed past the burning emotion in his throat. "Aurora loved my brother more, and I won't deny it hurt like hell when she left me. But if you were to ever pick Castor after this, it would crush my very soul."

"I'm yours." She grasped his face between her palms and stared into his eyes. The truth of her commitment shone brightly. "Now and forever."

"Thank Christ!"

She laughed and drew his head down for a kiss. When they pulled apart, she rested her forehead in the crook of his neck. "I suppose we should go back."

C H A P T E R   3 0

By the time they returned to the Drake estate, everyone had assembled in the lower garden. All the key players required for the trip to the Netherworld were present, with the exception of their enemy counterparts.

Selene's stomach was in knots. This was the worst plan she'd ever taken part in, and she feared it would end in heartache for more than one of them involved.

Damian was standing apart from the main group with his daughter and wife. A teary-eyed Sabrina clung to her father's neck, and he rubbed small circles on her back as he silently watched Vivian.

Spring and Knox shared a kiss and a cuddle. His expression was nothing short of tortured.

GiGi and Ryker were sitting on a nearby bench, and her head rested against his shoulder. He, too, looked torn, as if he were going to refuse to let her go without him.

"You and I are the only couple actually going together," Selene said to Preston. "It has to be miserable for the others."

"Yes." His tone was abrupt and hard—a clear indication he felt as helpless as the rest of them.

217

She touched his arm. "I won't let anything happen to your family if I can help it, Preston."

"You're my family, too, Selene." The intense love in his eyes thrilled her. "If anyone is going to take one for the team, it's me. Don't do anything to put yourself in danger. Promise me."

"This whole mission is fraught with danger. I won't make promises I can't keep."

"Stop being logical. It's driving me crazy," he growled.

She smiled and patted his chest. "Your children are waiting to say goodbye. I'll stay here to give you alone time."

He lowered his head and gave her a sweet, lingering kiss. Punctuating it with a quicker, harder one. "I won't be long."

As he strode off toward his daughters, Selene made a silent vow that even if she had to sacrifice herself, she'd see he got home to them.

"Your every thought is showing on your face, darling."

"Alex, if you don't stop sneaking up on me, I'm going to do you bodily harm."

"Promises, promises," he teased. In the next instant, all pretense of play dropped from him. "Please don't do anything foolish. Leave that to me."

"It would break my heart if anything happened to you," she said for his ears only. "I may want to spend whatever future I have with Preston, but it doesn't mean I don't want you to survive and find someone who'll make you happy."

"We're a sad pair. Each willing to sacrifice ourselves for the other."

She laughed softly. "I guess we are. But that's what love is all about, Alex."

"How you were ever able to love anyone after the family you had is beyond me."

"I had Agnes, thanks to Preston."

"He's a great guy, darling. A much better man than I'll ever be."

"Don't sell yourself short." She met his thoughtful eyes. "Everything you've done, however misguided, was for those you cared about."

A wry smile curled his lips. "True." They stared at one another for a long minute. She had no doubt he was remembering how free and fun their time together had been, just as she was. They had been younger and much more innocent then. Although looking back brought nostalgia for what once was, they weren't those people anymore. "I do love you, Selene."

Stinging tears blurred her vision. "I know."

"Be happy."

"That's the plan if we make it back."

"I'll see to it."

Unable to stop herself, she flung herself into his strong, welcoming arms. "I love you, too, Alexander Castor."

ALEX RESTED HIS CHEEK AGAINST SELENE'S SILKY HAIR AND CLOSED his eyes. He'd meant what he said. Whatever it took to see her safe and make her happy, that's what he'd do. Across the lawn, he saw Preston's attention swing their way. Concern and a hint of discomfort settled on his rival's countenance. Alex smiled without any form of mockery or gloating to let Preston know he understood which way the wind blew.

Preston gave him a nod but continued to watch them, his concern for Selene evident.

"Enough of this maudlin crap, darling. If you don't control yourself, Thorne will try to take it out of my hide. He's the jealous sort."

She gave him one last squeeze and withdrew.

With gentle fingers, he brushed away her tears. "Stay close to either me or Preston on the other side of the veil. Don't allow Victor or Katherine to separate you from the crowd."

"I get the impression you already know how this works."

"Damian was correct about the balance being needed to cross over. But the return trip doesn't require it. When either your mother or brother realizes they can kill or trap you there, they'll attempt it."

She lost her color, and her eyes went wide. "Do the others know?"

"Damian does. Maybe Alastair, too. But it's doubtful anyone else has been informed."

"Why not?"

"Trust issues." He cast a side glance and a slight head tilt toward Serqet. "No one's willing to take the chance she'll overhear."

"I would think she already knows."

"If she doesn't, why tell her?" He brushed a stray lock of her hair from her cheek. "Just do as I said and stay close to Preston or me. Got it?"

Selene nodded, but the light of determination was in her eyes.

Alex knew that look well, and a sinking sensation began in his stomach. He'd have to watch out for her extra carefully.

Damian approached them. "It's time. We cannot delay another moment."

"How are we going to bring the others up from hell, Dethridge?"

"We go back to the point of their deaths and remove them from harm's way."

"Without getting ourselves killed in the process," Alex muttered. "This should be fun."

"You live for adventure, Castor," Damian reminded him with a grin. The smile never reached his eyes. The Aether knew exactly how dangerous cheating death could be.

"Quentin was there for both Victor's and Beecham's deaths," Alex said. "He'll need to grab them. You go after Lin. He's less likely to give the Aether trouble."

"That leaves Delphine for you."

"She won't know who I am, so it'll make it easier to grab her." With the tips of his fingers, Alex drummed a beat against the side of his thigh, impatient to be off. He'd never been one for standing around when there was work to be done. Long waits left him irritable as fuck. "We're taking them straight to Stonehenge or the Council prison?"

"Stonehenge. I'll go there first to cloak the area and put out a general feeling of ill-will to deter anyone from venturing too close. Give me five minutes to clear the area and create an entrapment spell for when we teleport those bastards in, then follow with Quentin."

"When do you want the rest of us to join you, Damian?" Selene asked.

"Fifteen minutes should do it. We'll have secured the others, and will be ready for the ceremony to cross the veil."

With a carefree smile, Alex said, "See you there, my friend."

PRESTON COLLECTED ALL THE MAGICAL TOOLS THEY MIGHT NEED FOR the ceremony and set them on the tiled table. He crossed the terrace and signaled his brother. Within a minute, Alastair joined him. He had an air of barely suppressed excitement, and his eyes sparkled with mischief.

"I swear, Al, you live for this type of danger."

"It makes life more interesting, that's for sure. I only wish I could take Spring's place."

From his pocket, Alastair pulled a black gold ring and handed it over. The tanzanite stone looked to be just shy of a carat. The design was exceptional, with the illusion of flames licking up the sides. The tips created the prongs needed to hold the jewel in place. The piece was wide, not delicate in the slightest, and made a handsome man's ring.

"I would wear this all the time if I thought you wouldn't spy on my conversations," Preston said, half jokingly.

Alastair laughed and clapped him on the shoulder. "Perhaps we can add an on/off switch if you decide you wish to keep it."

"Brilliant idea."

"Wear it with my blessing, little brother."

"Do you think you'll be able to hear from this side of the veil, Al?"

"It's doubtful. Rest assured I'll be pacing until there's no grass left inside the Stonehenge monument. They'll probably need to tranquilize me."

"I know you want in on the action, but it's better if you're on this side for when we return. That way, if anything goes wrong, you can take care of the problem immediately."

Alastair's sapphire eyes darkened to a deeper blue. "Make no mistake, Preston. If, or when, our enemies return, they will be dealt a death blow. I'll not allow them to live to cause harm again."

"You're talking murder, Al."

"I'm talking swift justice. They were already slated to die. I'll simply be sending them back to hell."

There was a cold finality to Alastair's statement, and Preston suppressed a shiver. Something dark and angry had resided in his brother ever since he'd escaped from Zhu Lin's dungeon all those years ago. No one, not even Aurora, had been able to heal him. Rarely did Alastair show that side of him, but Preston was under no illusions. He knew very well it existed, simmering just below the civilized mask his brother wore in polite company.

Searching his own conscience, Preston couldn't say he cared all that much about the death of their enemies. They'd all done the Thornes irreparable harm at one juncture or another. "If you torture Lin or Victor more than the others in the process, I'll be appreciative," he drawled.

Alastair laughed, then gave him a tight hug. "I love you, Pres. Be careful."

"Aren't I always?"

"No." His brother snorted. "I remember a time when you ran off to confront Delphine and ended up dead for your troubles." Alastair rubbed his chest. "It felt as if I were having a heart attack that night. It was as if I could feel the bullet ripping through me. The fear for you and Nash nearly tore me in two."

He spoke of the prediction Delphine had made when the premonition struck her prior to turning into a murderous bitch.

"I never knew you experienced the pain of my death," Preston said softly. It had been swift, and he'd barely registered what hit him as he fell to the floor at Delphine's feet. Now, knowing the pain had transferred to his brother, remorse coursed through him.

Alastair gave a mild shrug as if the incident was minor, but his voice held a rough edge when he said, "Rorie was there. I never spoke of it to anyone else."

"Christ," Preston muttered. "Well, I hope you never experience anything like it again." But the likelihood that it would happen was great. As an empath with elevated powers, Alastair would be like a lightning rod for these type of physical and emotional events.

Since his brother's desire to change the subject was as obvious as the carefree arrogance he wore, Preston held up his ring. "Is everyone else's as striking as mine?"

"Damian was with me when I conjured each one, and we infused them with the wearer's elemental magic. We thought shaping the metal into the element of the wearer would be an interesting feature of the rings." Alastair lifted his hand and showed his pinky ring. "We replicated them from the one I created years back."

"Theoretically, owing to the fact we have a bit of Damian's magic, ours should be amped up on the other side of the veil?"

"Precisely."

Preston chuckled. "You wily bastard."

"Don't disparage our saintly mother," Alastair mock scolded. He grew serious. "Whatever advantage we have, I'll use if it means my family returns safely to the fold."

They were caught by the sound of a woman's throaty laugh, and they turned as one to look down at the garden.

Selene.

Preston's heart rate kicked up as he watched her conversing with Holly. His desire to rush to her, sweep her into his arms, and hide her away for a millennium or more overwhelmed him. With a concerted effort and curl of his fingers around the edge of the stone railing, he held himself in check.

"You need to marry that woman when you return, little brother."

He glanced at Alastair. A smile curled his lips as he noted the admiring look his brother shot her way. "She really is one in a million, isn't she, Al?"

"She is." A sly expression crossed his face. "I mean, she's no Rorie, but she's definitely exceptional."

"Rorie's with the right man. And if I have my way, Selene will be, too."

CHAPTER 31

Their group teleported to Stonehenge as per Damian's instructions. Zhu Lin, Delphine, Katherine, and Harold Beecham were all present and accounted for. The only two missing were Quentin with Victor Salinger.

"Where the devil are they?" Alex paced back and forth, his worry for his son getting the better of him.

"He'll be here, Castor," Holly said softly. "Quentin is as reliable as the day is long."

He smiled at her certainty. He couldn't have picked a better mate for his son if he'd spent the entirety of his life searching.

Ten more minutes crept by at a snail's pace, and his concern grew exponentially. "Fuck it. I'm going to look for him."

Alastair shook his head. "Give him another five minutes, Castor. He won't fail."

"It's not failure I'm worried about, Al!" he snapped. "He's dealing with a soulless bastard who would shoot his own sister in the head!"

Selene sucked in a breath, and Alex hung his head, regretful of his outburst. "Jesus. I'm sorry, darling. I'm…"

"It's all right." She touched his arm. "But Holly and Alastair are correct; Quentin won't fail. Like you, he doesn't know how."

GiGi sauntered forward and patted his cheek. Her sassy smile and dancing eyes reminded him of the days when she was a teenager who trailed after their reckless band of hooligans, demanding to be included. "He's a chip off the old block, Castor."

Whatever he would've said was cut off by the appearance of a haggard Quentin and an extremely bloodied, worse-for-wear Victor Salinger.

"He took some persuading, but then stupidly thought he'd give escape a try," Quentin told them with a one-shoulder shrug. "We played a game of cat and mouse for a while. You can guess who the rodent was."

Alex laughed his delight, proud as punch of the man his son had become.

Without bothering to dirty his hands, Damian swiped his arm sideways and sent Victor flying into the center of the enchanted ring. None of the occupants bothered to break his fall. Apparently, they were subscribing to the every-villain-for-themselves way of life.

Alex approached Damian. "You're up next, my dear friend."

All humor disappeared from their group. This next bit would be tricky. The Aether needed to cross the barrier to the Otherworld, call the Evil to him to consume, and meet them back here to pass through the veil to the Netherworld.

Damian looked ill at ease and too solemn for words. He met the serious gazes of those present. Through their new telepathically linked rings, he relayed his instructions.

"Be ready with the teleportation disc and the spell. There is an off chance we might get burned as we transition from one plane to the next." He addressed GiGi directly. *"Have the mending stone at hand for any who need it."*

"I'll have my wand and herbs for that. We're keeping the mending stone charged for you, Damian." She placed her hands on her hips and stared at him with challenge in every line of her body.

Alex nearly laughed. Who in their right mind would challenge the Aether the way she had?

Damian cast him a sardonic look, having easily read his mind.

"Are we not permitted to know whatever you have planned?" Zhu Lin called out from his invisible prison. His large, heavy-lidded eyes were shrewd and coldly calculating. At roughly five-ten, he had a casual sophistication enhanced by his silver-shot black hair. He didn't look like he had been affected by any of this. His arrogance would indicate he'd become the Underworld's ruler when the time came.

"No." Alastair uncrossed his arms and sneered at the other man. "You aren't entitled to know a *fucking* thing!"

Castor, Damian, Preston, and Quentin had already anticipated Alastair's uncontrolled rage and the subsequent swear word. Like synchronized dancers, they threw an arm up and fisted a hand to stop the locusts.

"You've lost your polish, Thorne. Perhaps when this is over, you'd be my guest once again." Lin's insinuation that he'd eagerly lock Alastair in his dungeon a second time set Castor's teeth on edge. The fool had a death wish.

Zhu Lin's gaze shifted to Alex, and a slyness entered his eyes. "And we'll happily include your friend Mr. Castor."

"You can't build a prison strong enough to keep me. Just ask your pal Salinger there," Alex taunted. With an airy wave at Victor, he asked, "How's it going, Vic?"

The dead-eyed stare Selene's half brother turned on him sent a shiver the length of his body. Victor was the one to watch the closest.

Salinger turned his head slightly and focused on Selene. Hatred blazed, giving life to his eyes. "Does he know what I did after he abandoned you, sister dear? The price you paid for your betrayal of our family?"

Preston stepped in front of her and cut off Victor's direct line of sight. "Shut your mouth, Salinger. We're all aware of your mind games, and they won't work here." He faced Damian. "Get on with it. I want this over before morning."

. . .

Until that moment, the Aether had been laid back and silent as he watched the animosity being slung back and forth. But Damian knew it was time to step in and put a stop to the bickering since it was becoming painful for both himself and Alastair on the empath front.

Raising his hand, Damian balled it into a fist. Those inside the enchanted ring were confused at first, but soon enough, they fell to their knees, gasping for air. He strolled forward until he was within a foot of the invisible cage. "Do you know who I am?"

Heads nodded and eyes turned wary.

"Good. If you wish to live, you'll do exactly as I say. Defiance on your part will not be tolerated." He squeezed his hand tighter. His victims began to sweat as they struggled to draw a breath and their eyes bugged out. "Nod again if you understand."

They gave a collective nod of their heads.

"Excellent." He released them from his hold. "I can crush your lungs or snap your neck with a mere thought. And your favorite Goddess won't save you this time."

As if on cue, a light split the blue sky and golden sparks spilled forth. When the rip sealed shut, Serqet stood at the center of the stone circle. She summed up the situation with a single glance, then sauntered over to Damian. "Hello, my children." She greeted them as if it were at a garden party. "I expect your full cooperation for our adventure. You might say the fate of the world depends on it."

Their confusion was understandable. Throughout the years, Serqet had lingered on the sidelines, whispering into her minions' ears and encouraging them to bring down the Thorne family. To see her about-face was disorienting. Damian could hear their thoughts, how they all wondered if this was a trick on his part or hers. They fully expected her to come to their aid.

He gestured Nathanial and Evie over. "These two are Guardians. I'm leaving them in charge of your motley crew. They not only have the ability to subdue you, but they can fry your insides with a few well-chosen words. They are unstoppable." He smiled, and it didn't hold a smidgeon of friendliness. Delphine shivered and Harold

Beecham broke out in a cold sweat. The Salingers and Zhu Lin played it cool, but wariness was behind their eyes. "Do behave. You don't want me for an enemy." He didn't say he'd considered them all enemies from the second they went after the Thornes.

Turning his back on the enchanted circle, he bowed low to Serqet. "My queen. I'm ready whenever you are."

She held out a hand, and he drew her close, lacing her arm through his.

Once again, a rift opened, and together, they stepped through it to the Otherworld.

Isis greeted them in the sorting room, and Damian absently noted the fatigue and worry in the barely discernible lines around her eyes and mouth.

"Is Set here?"

"He is," she confirmed with a tight smile. "He's to join us shortly, child."

"The three of you have enough firepower to draw this thing close?"

"Actually, a mob has already formed on the other side of the veil." A frown puckered her finely arched brows. "I'm uncertain how they knew you were coming, but there was a ripple of excitement through the crowd."

"The Evil is already anticipating taking over my body," he concluded grimly.

"That's the impression I received. Yes."

Damian had never seen the Goddess so subdued, but he understood why she now was. The task in front of them was fraught with peril, and they had no idea if this plan of theirs would work.

"What is your backup plan if I go nuclear, Exalted One?"

She knew what he was asking. If the worse happened and the Evil infected him like it had Isolde, he wanted to know if she had a plan to stop him. Her grim expression said it all, but she spoke anyway. "There is none."

"Fucking great."

CHAPTER 32

"This is a foolish idea." Set said as he joined the trio in the holding area, looking like he wanted to kick puppies and drown kittens. There was a barely controlled vibe radiating off him. It made *Damian* want to kick puppies and drown kittens.

"Got a better one?"

He glared at Damian. A mere human should never dare speak to him unless specifically addressed. Set had stated it multiple times in the past. Still, it gave Damian a thrill to dig at the god. He didn't know why seeing Set's hackles rise made him happy, but it did. Perhaps there was more Thorne blood in his veins than he believed. Damian certainly channeled Alastair whenever he was baiting Set.

"No," the God snapped.

"Do we need a magical circle, or do you want me to get right to it?" Damian's reluctance was obvious for all to hear.

"There is no need for a circle. Once we part the curtain, you'll absorb the Evil." Isis touched his arm. Her face was filled with compassion and concern. It startled him to see such a caring goddess. Deities were notoriously self-absorbed and dismissive of humans. They showed other magical beings slightly more respect, but not much. About mortals, they couldn't be bothered to care.

Nerves were beginning to get the better of him, and Damian wanted to get this thing done. He inhaled to the count of four and exhaled the same. After a few of these deep, centering breaths, he nodded his readiness.

"Remember, child, you must get every drop from the Otherworld or it will reinfect us all."

He looked at her sharply, his eyes narrowing. "You're infected?"

"I'm not certain, but I have not been myself in days."

"Open to me, my queen, and let me search your cells."

Isis placed her palms atop his, and Damian was able to send a magical feeler throughout her body. He met with resistance when he tried to access her mind. Whether by design or because she might be blocking him, he wasn't sure.

Sweat beaded at his hairline, and he pressed deeper.

Isis frowned, but this time, she granted him full access to her mind. In her thoughts he could find none of the Evil, but she did have reservations about him and what might happen should he allow the Darkness to take hold.

Drawing back, he bowed to her. "You are free of its influence, Exalted One."

Facing Serqet, he lifted a brow in question. She freely held out her hands, and he repeated the process. In her mind, he found residual hurt and resentment for the Thornes, but no madness or Evil influence.

Finally, he turned to Set. "We might as well get this over with, big guy."

The God looked as if he would rather swallow glass, but he held out his hands.

Damian pulled back after a minute. "Nothing there but an unhealthy obsession for Spring Thorne," he quipped, knowing there was no such thing happening. Set appreciated Spring's feistiness and beauty, but he wasn't smitten.

When Set laughed, he surprised Damian.

Taking the time to center himself again, Damian thought about Sabrina and Vivian. He hated to humble himself to ask a favor, but he didn't have a choice. One by one, he looked at the deities, meeting their gazes directly as he said, "Should the Darkness overtake me like it did my mother, should I become unstoppable on the earthly plane, I ask that you protect my wife and child. That you find or create a world for them to exist in without pain and suffering. Without fear of me."

Once again, Set surprised him. "We shall see to your family, Aether. I will protect them with my life."

Isis and Serqet nodded their agreement, and Damian focused on the latter. "Serqet, you once offered me a boon in return for the healing I gave you." He swallowed hard when she frowned. "I ask that you bury the last of your animosity for the Thorne family and, by extension, Knox Carlyle. They are needed to help my daughter become who she was meant to be as the Oracle. She loves and trusts them."

Gentle understanding flooded her face, and she nodded. "I know a parent's love for their child. I know the desire to provide the perfect balance of affection and learning. This is the boon I shall grant you, Aether."

He bowed low to hide the tears burning his eyes. "You have my eternal gratitude, my queen."

"We can delay no longer, child," Isis said as she stepped to the curtain. "When you have consumed the Evil from the gathered crowd, you will need to make a sweep of the Otherworld and search out the remaining Darkness."

"Of course."

"If you go mad from its influence, it will happen much sooner than it did with Isolde, Aether," Set warned. "You have months at most."

"Is there a vessel in the Netherworld where we can deposit it? One without magic?"

"I shall provide one," Serqet assured him.

It ate at his guts that they would sacrifice a mortal, but there was no choice. The Thornes didn't know about it, and if they found out before they crossed the veil, they would object. In magic, the basic rule was to do no harm. This process would harm at least one pure soul.

Feeling ten times older than his two hundred plus years, Damian said, "Part the curtain."

PRESTON WASN'T SURPRISED TO SEE SET AND THE TWO GODDESSES appear with Damian, but he was thrown when they had a fifth person with them. A teenage girl, by the looks of it. One with wide, innocent eyes, who looked one step away from losing her shit.

"What is this?" he demanded as a sick premonition began to creep in. "Who is this child, and what does she have to do with this?"

Guilt flashed on Damian's face—the only one of the four with any reservations, it seemed.

"Dethridge?" Castor's tone was hard and expectant of an answer. On this, he and Preston were in agreement. They demanded to know what was happening.

"We need a vessel to contain the Evil in the Nether," Set stated calmly.

"Fuck. No!" Preston didn't care if they struck him down for his disrespect. "No way are we harming an innocent child."

"There is no other way, Beloved," Isis told him.

Royally pissed by her serene, understanding smile, he stomped to where she stood. "You knew this from the beginning? You set me up? *Me*, who has constantly done everything you've asked?"

She reached for him, but he stepped back, too furious to let her connect or use her magic to soothe him.

"I won't be party to this," he said, crossing his arms over his chest. "Neither will my family."

"Preston." Damian's voice was tired, but there was a distinct edge.

"Do no harm, Dethridge," Alastair responded for Preston. "It's the motto all witches are supposed to uphold."

"This is the exception, Al. There's no other option, and it's too late to stop the process. I've consumed all of the Evil."

They all stared in disbelief. Preston felt the weight of the innocent girl's gaze. Those wide gray eyes reminded him of his daughters at her same age. He could no more hurt this girl than he could his own children. "I can't be party to it," he said hoarsely.

"*Sonofabitch!*" Quentin stormed to the other side of the circle to kick rocks with his hiker boots. Holly rushed after him to offer the comfort only a wife could.

Alastair placed a hand on Preston's shoulder and squeezed. "I'll go in your place, little brother."

"Who'll go in mine?" Selene asked, arms crossed over her chest and an angry gleam in her eye. "Like Preston, I find this abhorrent and want no part of ruining this child's life."

Never had a woman been more beautiful in her righteousness. Preston crossed to her and wrapped her in his arms. He let his tight hug say what the knot of angry emotion clogging his throat refused to allow. Her return embrace was just as fierce.

His family lined up, shoulder to shoulder. Spring spoke for them. "We won't harm an innocent."

Serqet approached her, and a grudging respect shone from her eyes. "You won't be. We are the ones responsible, child."

"We can find another way." Spring dared to touch the Goddess's forearm. "Please, Exalted One. Let us find another way."

Uncertainty flashed on Serqet's face as she looked back at her brother and sister. With something like sadness clouding her visage, she said, "The vessel must be free of magic and possess a pure heart."

"Why weren't we told before?" Knox demanded to know.

"We knew this would happen," Damian said as he rubbed the place between his brows. "You fucking Thornes all have this unwavering code. This bloody goodness that allows no room for gray areas. It's time you realize our world isn't black and white. Neither is magic." He locked eyes with Alastair. "You know, Al. You've always known, and you've always lived in the gray."

Alastair paled, but lifted his chin.

Preston hated that his brother's deeds were being laid out in front of him as a way to prod the others into this heartless plan. "Al has done what he's needed to protect our family."

"Exactly!" The Aether pointed at him. "Exactly, Preston. And now we are asking the rest of you to do the same. We have to protect our world."

"Use me." Spring's softly spoken words caused a guttural yell from Knox. The ground around them trembled with his fury.

"No! No fucking way in hell!" He swung her to face him and glared at the rest of them before cupping Spring's face. "You will not take her place. I forbid it."

She shook her head. "Knox." Her love, understanding, and compassion were rolled into his name.

"No, Spring. Not you. Anyone but you."

"I can't let this girl linger in that world to potentially go insane, Knox. I'll never be able to live with myself." She placed a hand on his cheek. "I—"

"I'll do it," Selene whispered. "I'll be the sacrifice you need."

Preston's heart stopped for three beats before it resumed at a breakneck speed. Through the ringing in his ears, he heard Castor swear. With dazed eyes, Preston saw him loom over her and begin to argue. But he was frozen to the spot and couldn't even tell Alex to back the fuck off.

Shoving Castor aside, she approached Preston. "I told you I would do what I could to save your family, *agápi mou*. This, I can do."

His brain kicked into gear, and he was finally able to speak. "No one is sacrificing anyone. Neither you nor my daughter are being left behind in the Nether." He turned to Isis. "Spring is right. We'll find another way."

Oddly, it was the teenager who stepped forward. "I chose to do this of my own free will."

Preston wanted to yell at her. To scream she had no idea what she was in for. But he never had the chance.

"The Oracle chose me," the girl said. "She said she'd come for me when the time was right."

"The Oracle?"

Preston wasn't sure who asked the question, but Damian was standing close to the girl with a frown dark enough to instill fear in the bravest of hearts.

"Sabrina told you this?"

"She showed me everything."

"*Sonofabitch!*" They all felt the slap of the Aether's temper. "*Beastie!*"

A ripple of energy zinged around them, and Sabrina dropped her cloaking spell. "Yes, Papa?"

"Explain yourself."

The temperatures around them dropped, and Preston could see his own breath with every exhale.

"I didn't want you to stay in the Nether." The tremble in Sabrina's voice was slight as she approached her livid father. "You're needed here. With me, Mama, and Nate."

Preston had never heard such an impressive stream of swear words as Damian released, but he didn't have time to admire the show. The ground around them pitched, and he was sure the seismographs were going crazy for the scientists in the area. Dust floated down from the shifting stones towering above them.

"Damian." The warning in Alastair's tone was sharp. "Calm down before you kill us all."

With impressive self-control, the Aether reined in his temper and pulled back his power. "Tell me everything, Sabrina. Leave nothing out."

CHAPTER 33

Their group remained quiet as they watched the Aether, Set, and the goddesses quietly discuss the Oracle's vision on the other side of the circle. Sabrina was animated, and her small hands waved toward their group as she gave her impassioned speech.

Selene wanted to bundle the girl into her arms and remove the curse of the second sight so the child could play. So she could be normal, instead of carrying the weight of the world on her diminutive shoulders.

Preston pulled Selene aside, and in a low voice, he demanded, "How in the hell could you offer yourself up for a sacrifice?"

"I couldn't bear it if you lost your daughter and Knox lost his wife. She has sisters and a family who love her, Preston. I'm nobody."

"No, Selene. You're wrong," he said with feeling. "You're somebody. To me." He cupped her face between his hands and kissed her with infinite tenderness. "And I don't want to live without you, my dearest love."

A sob was torn from her, and she threw her arms around his neck. "Oh, Preston. I love you so much, but I can't let that girl waste away in the Netherworld with no human contact, believing she's uncared for. Believing she's disposable to all of us."

"Then I'll take her place."

She drew back to stare up at him. Shock making her grow cold. "What? No!"

"I know I'm loved. By you. By my family. I'll also understand my sacrifice was for all of you, and maybe on my lucid days, I'll be able to use that knowledge to console me."

Selene listed all the reasons why it would be foolish for him to take the girl's place, but he simply watched her with a weary amusement. She opened her mouth to try again when she noticed Isolde.

The Enchantress stood off by herself. Her expression was troubled and bordered on fearful. She couldn't seem to tear her attention away from the teenager, and all the while, Isolde continuously rubbed her arms as if to ward off the cold.

"What do you suppose is wrong with her?"

Preston shook his head. "I don't know. Wait here."

<hr />

As he approached Isolde, Preston wondered what could possibly be upsetting her. She practically trembled, and sweat coated her upper lip.

"Isolde?"

Her gaze darted to him, but as quickly, returned to the girl. A deep emotion clouded her eyes, turning her irises black. "She'll go mad," she whispered. "She's only a child. A baby compared to me, and yet they think she'll be able to control it? She'll go mad in days."

"No she won't. I'm taking her place."

Her gaze snapped to him and stuck. "You're foolish if you do, Mr. Thorne. You don't know what it's like. The voices. The constant pressure inside your skull. You'll do anything to relieve it." She looked away and swallowed hard. "Anything. Even murder innocents and steal their magic to feed it. To make it happy for a short time so you can have peace."

"How long did it take for you to give in to its demands?" Fear began to build inside him, but he tamped it down.

"I'm not sure. A few years at most. I wasn't as strong as I believed myself to be." She frowned and looked across the circle toward her son. "He's emotionally stronger than I was. But he also possesses more magic. The Evil will be feasting on it even now, growing more powerful by the minute." Isolde closed her eyes. "It is supremely foolish to delay, Mr. Thorne. Every moment wasted is a moment the Evil grows stronger and taints Damian's thoughts."

Preston's internal alarms were sounding, and his anxiety tried to get the better of him. "What do you think we should do?"

"Let them use the girl. Sabrina selected her for a reason."

"I can't—"

"You can!" she snapped. "Trust her. Trust her visions and stop trying to be a bloody martyr."

"I'm not!"

"You *are*." She waved a hand to encompass his family. "You *all* are. But if you take her place and there is one cell with magic left in your body, the Evil will use it to escape and return here. No one will be safe."

"But—"

Again, she cut him off. "That girl is mortal. With no magic, the Evil will eventually die. Sabrina will know when the time is right to return for her. She's young enough, and she can be healed."

Preston finally understood why it was important for the teenager to be their sacrifice. Isolde had known all along, and while it didn't sit well with her—her body language and agitation were clear indications—she wouldn't fight what had to be done.

"Your family... she'll hate you all with a burning passion once she understands no one is coming for her right away." Isolde turned her sad obsidian eyes on him. "Be prepared for another enemy, Mr. Thorne."

"The cycle never ends, does it?"

She glanced over his shoulder. "They've come to a decision. And if I'm not mistaken, so have you."

"Yes. I suppose I have."

"Who plans to fuel up the miscreants?" Alastair asked when their party all gathered together again.

"We do." Set eyeballed Preston with attitude. "Are you prepared to do what you must?"

"Yes." And he was. Isolde's explanation had made him see they truly had no choice.

"Good. Anything other than the current plan is a fool's errand and waste of our resources."

"But—" Spring and Selene began to argue.

The God huffed out a breath, his irritation with the interruption causing him to snap. "Enough!"

Lightning flashed overhead, and thunder boomed on the heels of the fading bolt.

"Set—uh, Exalted One—" Spring tried once more to object.

"Child, you must listen to me now. You are pure of heart, but not of body. And should we remove your magic, the faint echo of it will linger. It is enough for the Evil to cling to, and it will escape." Set had softened his tone for her, his favorite human, but his face hardened and his voice became cold when he said, "I will hear no more. This is Ra's will."

Ra. The father of the deities present, and an all-powerful god with a short fuse. Way shorter than his son's, and that was hard to imagine.

Preston curled his pinky around Spring's. "It'll be okay, child. I promise."

Her dismay grew stronger when she realized this was actually happening, and she couldn't save the girl. "Dad... *please.*"

He hugged her tightly. "It'll all be okay," he promised gruffly.

After releasing her, he hurriedly drew the girl aside. The humane side of him wanted to save her, but the hardened warlock who'd seen and learned too much in his life knew he couldn't. Not yet. "What's your name, child?"

"Annabelle."

"Annabelle is lovely. Do you have a surname?"

"Walker."

"Well, Annabelle Walker. It's a pleasure to meet you. I'm Preston Thorne."

Solemn-faced, she extended her hand. "It's a pleasure to meet you, too, sir."

He shook it with a smile. "Where are you from? Do you have family?"

"Pennsylvania. It's where my mom, dad, and brother are." She bit the cuticle of her thumb. "The Oracle, was she telling the truth?"

"Of course," Preston assured her with as much warmth as he could muster, having no idea what Sabrina had shared.

Tears seeped from her large gray eyes. "Brandon will live? The cancer will go away?"

"We'll make sure of it."

"She said you'll set him up with a scholarship. You do things like that."

Preston turned his head enough to see Sabrina smiling in his direction. "Yes. I do things like that. He'll have the best education money can buy, Annabelle. I promise."

"Good." She scuffed the dirt with her sneaker, not meeting his eyes. "Sabrina also said you'd help Dad find a job. Brandon... well, Dad had to be there for him. My mom couldn't."

Because she was small for her age, Preston drew up the pant legs of his slacks and squatted so he was looking up into her angelic face. "Annabelle."

The tears streamed faster down her pale cheeks, but she bravely met his steady gaze.

"I will see your family wants for nothing, child. Your brother will live a long, healthy life. Your mother and father will be taken care of as well. The mortgage paid and financial security for life." He brushed back a lock of her light-brown hair. "And when you return, you'll have all the finest things, too."

Sabrina had approached as he was speaking, and when he finished, she grabbed Annabelle's hand with hers. "See, Annie? I told you Preston is the best." She hugged the older girl around the waist. "You'll be scared and sad for a little while, but you don't have to be. When you come back, I'll teach you magic, and we'll be great friends."

"What kind of magic?"

With a quick peek over her shoulder, Sabrina shifted her tiny body to hide her hands. With a snap of her fingers, she conjured a candy bar and handed it to Annabelle. "All the best kinds," she promised.

Wide-eyed, Annabelle turned to Preston. "Can you do that too?"

"I can. I can also make fire dance along my fingertips. Do you want to see?"

With a wondrous smile, she nodded, laughing when he showed her his party trick.

He rose to his feet and placed a hand atop the crown of her head. With a simple word, he infused her with a sense of well-being. "That should see you to the other side, my dear. From there, the goddesses will help you."

"Mr. Thorne?"

"Yes?"

"Thank you, sir. For what you're going to do for Brandon and my dad."

His smile was a struggle, but he managed. "My pleasure, child."

As he walked back to where his family was gathered, his heart was battered and his legs leaden.

Damian removed the enchantment from the prison ring, allowing Set entry. In less than five minutes, the Thornes' greatest enemies had enough juice to teleport and most likely would've, had they not each been shackled with a pair of binding bracelets.

Hatred and promised retribution shone from Zhu Lin's eerie chartreuse-colored eyes, but Preston paid him no mind. Set wouldn't let him hurt Spring; she was his favorite human. Not that Preston wouldn't protect his daughter at all costs, but for the moment, she was safe.

Delphine Foucher cautiously approached Preston, Alastair, and GiGi as they conversed. "Cousins…" At Alastair's lifted brows, her dark-amber eyes turned to a muddy brown as her creamy-mocha complexion paled a shade. "We're still blood kin, Alastair," she said.

"Something you failed to remember when you had my brother shot through the heart by your henchman, Delphine."

"Beecham held my daughter. I had no choice."

Preston couldn't feel kindly toward Delphine. She'd done atrocious things on Harold Beecham's behalf. "You tried to poison

Rorie. You drugged Summer and attacked Thorne Manor, holding everyone inside hostage to draw Alastair out."

GiGi tossed her glossy blonde hair over her shoulder. "Don't forget she gave Beecham the ability to wield black magic against Ryker."

"Trust me, nothing is forgotten," Preston assured his sister. He balled his hands, trying to get his temper under control. "And don't you *dare* try to say you had no choice, Delphine. At any time, you could've come to us. We'd have helped you get Leonie back."

"You've brought us forward in time, haven't you?" Delphine asked softly. When he confirmed they had, sadness flooded her face. "That means everyone in your family survived my attack, and I died."

"Everyone, but me. And yes. You were a casualty of your war against the family."

"I have no memory of those final moments," she said sadly. "How is Leonie? Did you save her?"

She faced a wall of cold stares.

GiGi was the first to relent. "Your family is happy, cousin. Leonie's planning her wedding, and Armand is well. He talks about you all the time."

Tears welled in Delphine's eyes. "Thank you for caring for them, cousin."

"I didn't do it for you, and I don't give a damn about your gratitude." GiGi crossed her arms and lifted her chin. "Don't dream of double-crossing us in the Netherworld, Delphine. I'll rip you apart, limb by limb."

"Understood."

"Good."

Delphine seemed as if she wanted to say more, but she shuffled away with her head bent.

"How the mighty have fallen," Preston murmured.

"It's an act."

GiGi and Preston turned to Alastair.

"I feel her resentment and her desire to break free," he told them. "Stay on guard. The both of you."

"Should we separate them all? Curtail their ability to plot against us?" GiGi asked.

"I wish you would've thought of that earlier, sister." Preston ran a hand through his hair. "They've had plenty of time to come up with a plan while we were all arguing about Annabelle."

Alastair's dark-blond brows rose. "Annabelle?"

"Our sacrifice." He told them what he'd learned about the girl's family. "Al, will you see to Brandon's cure and her family's care should I not return?"

"Of course."

"And Selene, be sure she's safe and happy, too."

"You're coming back to us, little brother. Isis won't let her favorite consort die."

But they all knew she wouldn't have a choice. She couldn't control death in the Netherworld. If he died, there would be no resurrecting him.

"Here."

Preston looked down and saw the knife Alastair was offering him. "What's this?"

"You each have a ring. Now you'll each have a magical weapon."

"What does it do?"

"You visualize what you want it to do, and it does it: stab, cut, slice. It wouldn't hurt my feelings if it found its way to Lin's black heart."

Alastair tugged at his cuffs and straightened his tie. Only he would turn up to a shindig like this one dressed to the nines.

Preston tilted his chin at his brother's outfit. "What's with the business suit, Al?"

"I believe in dressing for success," Alastair replied dryly.

A laugh escaped Preston, and he clapped his brother on the shoulder, pointing toward Damian. "He's preparing. We should go."

The three sibling deities met and placed themselves back to back in the center of the Stonehenge monument. Raising their arms, they repositioned the thirteen-foot pillars and the smaller bluestones until they created one large circle roughly three hundred and fifty feet in diameter.

Isis ushered everyone into a smaller circle, stationing one counterpart directly across from the other. Inside the ring was Annabelle, who looked frightened but still bravely held up her head. She stared at Sabrina in the far distance, seeming to take courage from the pint-sized Oracle's smile. The three deities and Isolde moved, placing themselves to represent the North, South, East, and West points.

Damian took a moment to speak to Alastair and hug Sabrina goodbye. He lifted her up and clutched her to him as if he never wanted to let her go.

Preston understood the sentiment, and his attention shifted to Spring. His beautiful daughter. The youngest and possibly the brightest of them all. Goddess, how he loved her.

As if she sensed him, Spring turned slightly to look at him.

"I love you, Dad," she mentally projected.

"I love you, too, baby girl," he silently returned. *"It goes without saying; be on alert and don't let your guard down."*

She smiled, and although the day was overcast and the situation was gloom, Preston felt as if she'd somehow blessed their mission. He placed a hand over his heart.

Damian returned and strode to the center of the circle. "Are you ready, Annabelle?" he asked the girl in a kind voice.

"Yes, sir."

"You'll feel your body warm to the point of burning as we teleport to the Netherworld. Keep holding my hand no matter what. It's imperative you don't let go."

"I understand," she replied in a small voice.

"Excellent." He gave her an encouraging smile.

The hardened visage he turned on their enemies was meant to intimidate. "I'm going to release you from your shackles. Don't attempt to flee. The deities can track and return you in an instant. Should you defy me, you'll pay a price."

Katherine Salinger cried out as she and the others gripped their heads as if in severe pain.

Preston shared a solemn look with his sister. They'd never seen this side of Damian, and it was worrisome. He prayed this small torturous act was all to show he meant business and nothing else.

"That's a sample to show I'm serious," Damian continued. "Should you break my rules, the next time will result in brain damage. Nod if you understand."

Five heads bobbed in unison.

"You should know I can read your thoughts." His eyes sharpened, and he pinned Victor with a lethal stare. "I wouldn't try it, Salinger," he snarled. "I'll drop you where you stand."

Victor paled but gave a slight incline of his head to show he wouldn't enact whatever devious plan had formed in his mind.

Preston suspected it had to do with Sabrina since Damian only turned feral to protect her.

With a simple snap of his fingers, the Aether dropped the binding bracelets from their enemies' wrists. Holding his hands parallel with the earth, palms facing downward, he closed his eyes and murmured a few words. The teleportation disc resting at his feet, originally the size of a dinner plate, expanded to approximately fifty feet in diameter.

"Step onto the disc and walk forward until you are shoulder to shoulder," he instructed.

When they complied, he nodded to the deities and his mother. "Complete the circle."

"Are you ready, child?" Damian's expression softened marginally as he looked down at Annabelle.

"Yes, sir," she answered with wide-eyed wonder.

"Take my hand." His gaze drifted to his daughter. "I intend to be back soon, beastie, but should the unthinkable happen, Alastair will see to your care. You do everything he says."

"Yes, Papa." She grinned. "But you'll be back."

He lifted a brow, and a sardonic smile curled his mouth. "If you've predicted it, my darling girl, I have no doubt."

The realness and love in their exchange gave Preston hope that Damian was keeping the Evil locked up tight.

"Guardians!" he called out.

Nathanial and Evie shuffled forward, aligning their bodies with the sun. They raised their hands and chanted. The deities and Isolde dropped their heads back, lifting their faces skyward and their arms out to their sides, palms down.

Preston felt the first blast of magic hit his feet as the teleportation disc turned from silver to black. Trepidation unfurled in his chest as he saw the black shift to translucent. Beneath him, he could see forever. Someone to his left gasped at the sight.

In the next instant, the bottom dropped out of their world and they were in free fall. Or so it seemed. In truth, it was more like a hop off a tree stump, and they landed with a soft thud on the barren wasteland of the Netherworld.

Mars. The whole place looked like the pictures Preston had perused on the internet. As far as the eye could see, there was barren orange terrain with small outcrops of rocks. Logically, he knew it wasn't Mars, or they wouldn't be able to breathe, and they'd all resemble popsicles right about now. But still, he couldn't shake the impression of lifelessness. Nothing beautiful resided here.

A chill swept him. This was where the poor girl would spend her life. Even if the Evil didn't drive her to it, the isolation would drive her crazy. Preston's fist curled, and he mentally railed at the unfairness of it all.

"We all feel the same, agápi mou," Selene telegraphed to him.

He looked at her and saw the compassion in her eyes.

"We don't have much time," Serqet said. "The Guardians will only be able to hold the portal open for fifteen minutes. No more."

"Right." Damian focused his attention on Castor, but mentally projected to their entire group. *"Move to my right. Now!"*

As one, they ran to where Castor stood. The deities formed a semicircle around the remaining group, blocking their escape as the Aether shoved Annabelle behind him and removed the transmutation wand from his long black sleeve.

"Sorry, my friends, but we need you to guard the girl." He didn't sound at all apologetic as he transformed them into four-legged predators resembling wolves. They ranged in size and color, but each was devoid of hair. Their jaws were overly large and took up half their head, giving them a grotesque grinning appearance.

As the screams died off, Preston stood shell-shocked and trembling. He'd no idea this was going to happen, and he feared what came next when Damian faced his family.

"We need you all for this next bit." He gestured for them to come forward.

After a moment's hesitation, Preston gave in to his long-held trust for Damian and Isis. He strode to where the Aether stood in front of the snarling pack of hound-like creatures.

"Go to your counterpart and remove their magic," Set instructed. "Visualize every minuscule bead of power and pull it from their cells. Nothing can be left behind."

Preston approached the animal that had been Delphine. She snapped and growled as she attempted to back away, but her hindquarters hit an invisible barrier, and she yelped her surprise. The only thing resembling the woman he'd known was the terrified amber eyes.

"I didn't know about this, cousin," he told her softly as he walked forward. "I'd not have chosen this for your fate despite the wrongs you heaped on my family. But here we are, and there's no turning back."

She seemed to understand what he was saying, and she bowed her head as he placed his hand between her jagged ears. Keeping his eyes locked with hers in case she decided to attack, Preston began the process of removing her magic. He searched out each bead as Set had instructed, until there was nothing left. Drawing the magic into a ball, he pressed it to his solar plexus and absorbed it completely.

"Be well, Delphine. Know we will continue to watch over Leonie and Armand."

Her solemn eyes met his, and he had no doubt she understood. It was a daring move on his part, but he turned his back to her to face the Aether. He felt Delphine's muzzle nudge his hip as she stepped up beside him. With a nod from Damian, she laid down at Preston's feet and rested her head on her massive front paws.

Selene appeared to have trouble cornering Victor, and he viciously snapped and snarled, but whenever the beast attempted to bite her, it yelped in pain and fell backward.

Spring fared no better as she attempted to corral Zhu Lin.

"Serqet!" Damian's voice rang out like that of Ra. The powerful sound echoed off the orange rock formations around them. "Control them, my queen. We are out of time."

Serqet lifted one hand in Lin's direction and the other in Victor's. As Preston watched, their heads were forced down until their snouts were pressed an inch above the dirt. Selene was tentative in her approach, but Spring appeared more confident and charged Lin.

Everything seemed to be going fine until the words *"Fucking bitch!"* rang out from Castor through their mental connection and captured everyone's focus.

"Katherine practically ripped open my wrist!" he shouted through their link.

With a suddenness that held Preston immobile, chaos broke free.

Victor's head whipped up, and he lunged for Selene's throat.

Preston had no time to call out before the slavering jowls clamped around her neck. Heart in his throat, he charged toward the two, only to stop short when Victor gave a vicious shake of his head.

Blood trickled from the slight puncture wounds where teeth met delicate skin. Salinger could snap her neck, and they all knew it.

A cry off to his right brought Preston's head around. Spring had her foot pressed against Lin's neck and her hands hovered in the air above him as she drew out his power. Tiny sparkling gray lights lifted from the beast and drifted to Spring's palms. Dismissing the scene, Preston faced Victor.

"Damian can halt her death by stopping time. But you? You, I will tear apart limb by limb, Salinger, right before I piss on your corpse."

A low growl from behind him was the only warning Preston received. As he spun around, he saw Katherine's new form launch itself at him. Although he lifted his hands, he wasn't quick enough to conjure the fire to fry her ass.

Help came in the form of Delphine, who tackled Katherine from the side and pinned her to the ground in a stunningly fast maneuver.

Daring to take his gaze from the two animals, Preston gave Castor a visual inspection. Alex's hand dangled from his mangled wrist, and his countenance was deathly pale as he stared back at Preston with pain-filled eyes. "I'm sorry, Thorne," he croaked out. "I thought I had her."

Preston nodded once and sent a mental message to GiGi to use the mending stone to help Alex.

Concentrating all his attention on the one remaining rebellious monster, Preston approached Victor and Selene. "Let her go, Salinger. I won't tell you again."

Victor snarled and clamped down harder. A strangled cry escaped Selene.

Lifting his arms, Preston channeled his elemental magic and conjured a flaming arrow.

"Do you need this one alive, Dethridge?" he silently asked.

"Not at all."

"Good." Using the flame as a visual distraction, Preston floated it until it was a foot away and eye level with Victor.

Selene released another whimper of pain, sending Preston's already galloping pulse into overdrive.

Blade to Victor's heart.

Preston's concealed knife appeared a second before it slid through the beast's ribs, piercing his heart and ending his life.

"Thank you, Alastair," he murmured as he sprinted to catch Selene before she hit the ground.

Blood spurted from the wound in her neck, and her skin lost all color as the shadow of death lurked in her beautiful eyes.

"Don't die, my love. Not here, or your soul will be obliterated." He tried healing magic, but it wouldn't work. "Stay with me, Selene. Please." Applying pressure to the wound, he frantically searched over his shoulder. "Help me! I can't stop the blood flow!"

Damian sent him an anguished look. "I can't, Preston. If I use magic on her, I risk releasing the Evil into her body."

"Let me." Serqet knelt beside Preston. "Move your hand, child. I won't let her die."

He met her honey eyes and saw the honest intent. "It'll gush, and I don't know how much she has left. Be ready."

Placing her hands above his, leaving only a one-inch gap, Serqet gave a small nod, and he jerked his hands away as she pressed hers to Selene's neck. Blinding light escaped through the cracks between her fingers, and he threw a hand up to shield his eyes.

When the glow faded, he lifted his lids to see the skin on Selene's neck knitting together.

With tears in his throat and a gruffness in his voice, he said, "Thank you, my queen."

"Take care of her, Beloved. She's still weak." Serqet touched a hand to his cheek and gracefully rose to her feet.

Preston was never more glad to have been wrong about anyone's intentions in his life than he was at that moment with the Goddess. His gratitude would never allow him to view her in a bad light again.

CHAPTER 35

Inside, Damian could feel the Evil battling to break free from its invisible box. Time was of the essence now, and he looked down at Annabelle.

"You will control them from here on out. They will be your protectors."

"What if they attack me like they did that woman?" Annabelle asked in a shaky, tearful voice.

"They can't. With the transformation, I made it impossible for them to kill you or each other." He touched a hand to her cheek. "I promise you will be safe from them or anything that enters this realm."

She nodded but remained unconvinced.

Only time would allow her to understand the transmutation of their cells and the new makeup of their DNA.

"Come, child." He drew her over to an outcrop of level rocks and ran the wand from one end to the other. The stone shelf turned mattress-soft. "Lie down, Annabelle."

With a tentative look at the others, she did as he ordered. Damian bent over her and met her frightened eyes. He could sense the calming enchantment Preston had gifted Annabelle earlier was fading.

"When I breathe the smoke into your lungs, your instinct will be to fight. Don't, or you'll make it painful." Placing his mouth mere inches above hers, he released the Evil from its prison and blew it into Annabelle.

Valiantly, she lay there, absorbing the thick black smoke as it filled her entire being. The irises of her eyes darkened to charcoal, and for a second, Damian feared they'd misread her mortal status.

The deities joined him at her bedside.

"Is it gone?"

He searched inside himself, unable to detect the intruder. "I believe so."

"Isolde?"

His mother approached and placed her fingertips at his temples. He felt her probe. Felt her magic travel the length of his body and back. After a moment, she released him with a small caress of his cheek and stepped back.

"It's gone," she said.

The five of them joined hands and formed a semicircle around the ledge where Annabelle rested. With a few softly spoken words, Isis drew on the group's magic and sealed the Evil inside Annabelle forever.

Set touched a finger to the girl's third eye. "Sleep, little one. When you wake, the Evil shall be no more."

Annabelle closed her eyes one final time with a breathy sigh.

"It's done," Isolde whispered.

Damian separated from them and strode to where the hounds had gathered. "There's no magic left for you to free yourselves. You won't ever grow old. Never hungry. But know, you'll also never leave the Netherworld." He met the gazes ranging from fearful to enraged. "Your one purpose is to protect that girl. If you attempt to harm her, you'll pay for it with the dissolution of your flesh. Your cells will wither and die, causing you excruciating pain."

The words *"Salinger's residual magic"* caressed Damian's mind. He thanked all that was holy he had the ability to read the others' thoughts, because he never considered the fact Selene had failed to remove Victor's power.

"Sorry to disappoint, Lin, but Selene will be taking care of it shortly. She needs it to teleport back."

Selene was quick to understand and began the magic-removal process from Victor's crumpled body.

The monster previously known as Zhu Lin curled back the skin over his three-inch fangs. Without betraying a thought to his intentions, he lunged toward Spring. The creature was mere inches away from her defenseless throat, and acting on instinct, the Aether raised a hand, twisting his wrist to magically snap its neck.

He'd felt no remorse for killing Lin, but he cursed under his breath at his new dilemma. He needed a fourth—one guard to protect the girl from each direction. It meant someone from their original party needed to be left behind.

Isolde stepped forward. "I'm prepared to take his place. I knew it was a possibility that they wouldn't just accept their fate."

"I'm sorry, Mother." It felt as if his heart were dying as he looked into her tragically beautiful face. "I never intended for you to be a spare," he said raggedly. "I didn't think other than to save Spring."

"It's all right, my darling boy."

They embraced, and all the words he wanted to say, all the apologies for believing the worst of her, lodged into his throat and didn't allow him to speak.

"I know, Damian. I've always known I'd end up here," she whispered into his ear.

He drew back with a frown. "I don't understand."

"I didn't either—at first. The visions of this place drove the Evil insane. It was obsessed with finding more power to prevent this very thing."

The knowledge flooded his brain. "Of course. In fearing its own demise, it brought about the very thing it was trying to prevent."

"Exactly so."

They hugged one more time. "If there were any other way,

Mama…" He trailed off. They both damned well knew there wasn't. All the others had loved ones waiting on them back home, and he could no more destroy their families than he could his own.

"I love you, Damian. I'm exceedingly proud of the man you've become."

"Sabrina gave me a gift," he blurted, hoping to prolong the moment. "She showed me our early years together. What you'd done to save the magical community. How much you loved father and me," he ended on a croak. "I love you, too, Mama."

"We are out of time," Set called.

Damian kissed his mother's temple, and removed the wand from his sleeve. "I'm sorry," he whispered. In the blink of an eye, she transformed into the sleekest of creatures. Gleaming, silky black fur molded to her powerful frame. Her black eyes were the same, though. Love and understanding shone back at him as she bowed her head for him to remove the last of her magic.

As he removed it, he had the stray thought that perhaps by holding her magic close to his heart, she'd be with him forever. When he was done, he bent forward and brushed a hand along her neck. He silently promised himself that if he could save her when they came for Annabelle, he would.

"Goodbye, Mama."

***

Later that evening, after Preston and Selene said the last of their goodbyes to family and thanked the Drakes for their hospitality, they teleported to Thorne Manor. Too exhausted to do more than climb the steps to the porch, they settled into the swing.

Selene curled up in his lap and rested the shell of her ear against the surface of the wide expanse of muscled chest, directly over his heart. The steady beat soothed her and chased away the horrors of the day. "Thank you," she said softly.

"I didn't do it for you, my love." The sound of his deep voice rumbled in his chest.

She lifted her head and frowned in question.

"I did it for me," he said simply. "I couldn't bear your death under regular circumstances, but the idea of your soul obliterated in the Nether?" He shuddered. "I did it for me," Preston repeated.

She smiled her understanding and lightly kissed him before snuggling back in her original position. "My heart aches for the child."

"I know. Mine, too."

Wearily, he urged her up and climbed to his feet. "I have a promise to keep to Annabelle."

"Surely one more day won't matter. What could possibly be so urgent?"

"A boy's life." He told her about the cancer and the family's financial straits. "It's best if I don't delay. I don't know how much time he has left."

"Do you want me to go with you?"

"No, love. You're still weak from the attack." He studied her for a moment. "Are you okay? Mentally and emotionally?"

She toyed with the idea of lying, but decided only honesty should ever exist between them. "I'm not sure the nightmare of having my throat ripped open will ever go away. I think it ranks up there with a gunshot to the head, but I'm okay for you to go do what you must."

His troubled eyes stared back at her. *He saw too much.*

Selene rose on her tiptoes and kissed him again. "Go," she ordered with a light laugh. "I'm fine."

Preston trailed his fingers over her cheekbone, down her face, and finally, touched the tender part of her neck. "This will eventually disappear."

"Serqet said as much. I don't care about scarring. Do you?"

"Not at all. It shows how badass you are." He grinned, but it didn't quite reach his eyes.

"It was terrifying for us both, *agápi mou*. But we're alive, and that's what matters most."

"I know." He drew her close for a longer, more passion-packed kiss. Resting his forehead against hers, he released a tired sigh. "I'm finding it difficult to leave you right now."

"I'll be here when you return."

Preston nodded and touched his finger to the tanzanite ring to activate the telepathy link. Selene was listening in and heard him call his sister. "GiGi, grab your medical bag and meet me in the attic of Thorne Manor."

Other than to express concern, GiGi didn't object, and within minutes, the three of them were gathered around the Thorne family grimoire.

"How do we cure cancer in a human?" Preston asked.

"It's tricky, but it can be done. Spring should have the herbs I need." GiGi shot him a mischievous grin. "The bigger trick is going to be altering the family's memory."

"What do you mean?"

"They can't know witches exist, brother. We'll have to put the parents to sleep, heal the boy, remove his memory, add the suggestion that their daughter is away at school, and then hope they all accept Brandon's miraculous recovery."

"We're going to need a bigger boat," he muttered.

Preston's comment confused Selene, and she feared he was too tired to attempt any of what they'd planned. GiGi quickly explained her brother's nerdy ways and his love of films.

"Jaws," Preston said sheepishly.

Selene laughed at his embarrassment, thrilled to see the fun side of this imposing man.

He touched his ring. "Al. We need you on deck."

Alastair arrived with little fanfare with Rorie by his side. "Fill me in so I can go back to ravishing my beloved."

GiGi fake gagged as Preston said, "Eww. Ex-husband of the beautiful woman and brother of the ravisher here. I don't need to think about these things."

Selene laughed as Aurora drew Alastair's mouth down to hers and kissed him with enough fire to light up the room. He wrapped an arm around her waist and grinned. "Should I tell them to find another sucker to help them, love?"

"No," Rorie said pertly with a tap on his cheek. "That's just a reminder to hurry things along."

Alastair closed his eyes and groaned. "You're such a tease."

"Yes, and that's where the fun is at, darling."

With a snort, he released her. He was turning toward his siblings when he noticed Selene off to the side. His sapphire eyes became serious. "I'm sorry for what Victor did to you today, and I'm glad you pulled through. You complete our family unit, my dear."

Tears burned behind Selene's lids, making his handsome countenance blurry. She blinked rapidly to clear her vision. "Thank you, Alastair."

"Come. Keep my sassy woman company while I assist these two." With a sharp look at Aurora, he said, "She promises to keep her cattiness at bay."

"I made no such promise, darling." Aurora smiled at Selene. "But I have no reason to treat you unkindly. Let's go have a cuppa and see if Winnie has made up more of her delectable cinnamon rolls, shall we?"

Selene purposefully kissed Preston before turning to follow Aurora. She hadn't expected the light swat on her ass, and a meep escaped her lips. Spinning back, she glared, but he only chuckled and said, "We'll be back shortly. If you want to shower and rest, have Winnie show you to my old room."

<hr>

ROUGHLY FOUR HOURS LATER, PRESTON RETURNED TO A SILENT house. He found Aurora downstairs in the kitchen, staring out the window over the farm sink.

"Rorie. Has Selene turned in?"

"Yes."

"Why are you still here? Alastair should've been home long before now."

"I wanted to talk to you, Preston."

"If this is about how you treated Selene yesterday, I'm too tired for excuses."

"No. No excuses. I simply wanted to tell you that I love you, and I wish you every happiness with her." The soft smile made her alabaster skin glow. "She's truly lovely."

"Thank you."

He hugged her for a long moment, thinking about how crazy and off course their lives had gone. In the end, it was all for the best, but he felt a momentary nostalgia for the days when their children were toddlers. With a sigh, he released her. "You'd better head home to my brother, or he'll be back here annoying us soon."

She pointed behind him, and Preston turned to see his brother lounging in the doorway, polishing off the last bite of his cinnamon roll.

"I don't know why I'm surprised," Preston muttered.

"You aren't," Alastair returned with a smirk. He pointed to his chest. "Empath."

"As if any of us could ever forget. Take your woman and get the hell out. I need to sleep."

"Is that any way to treat your favorite sibling?"

Preston laughed, scooped up a plate, and plopped a cinnamon roll on it. "Good night, Al."

"Fine. I'm only giving you three days to hide away with Selene, then I'm coming back to annoy you. This past year has been abysmal."

"For me too, big brother." Knowing it would irritate him, Preston placed a loud, smacking kiss on Alastair's cheek. Then, with an absent wave, he strolled from the room.

"Runt," Alastair called out.

"Jerk," Preston returned.

His brother's laughter made him smile.

As Preston teleported to the hallway outside his old room, he sent a silent thank you to Isis, happy their family was together again and just as it should be. As he opened the door, Selene sat up. Her rumpled, sleepy appearance made him grin. But it was her welcoming smile and the light of love shining from her eyes that truly got to him. He didn't know how he'd gotten so lucky as to win her heart, but he was damned glad he had.

"Come to bed, lover," she called softly, beckoning him with a sultry look. His fatigue disappeared as his joy replaced it. He finally had his own happily ever after, just like Isis had promised.

THANK YOU FOR FOLLOWING THE JOURNEY OF MY THORNE WITCHES series. If you're like me, you don't want to see them go away. Well, they're not. Going away, that is. Some of your favorite characters will be woven into my new series, **The Unlucky Charms**. You can read an excerpt of Piper Thorne and Cian O'Malley's love story, **Pints & Potions**, below. Newsletter: www.tmcromer.com/newsletter

ALSO, IF YOU HAVEN'T ALREADY SUBSCRIBED TO MY **NEWSLETTER** OR joined my **Facebook reader group**, I encourage you to do so. It's the best way for you to stay current on upcoming stories. After I'm done with the O'Malleys, I'll be introducing the next generation of Thornes, and you won't want to miss it. Facebook Reader Group: bit.ly/tmc-readers

---

Chapter One

"YOU NEED TO HURRY UP, PIPER. YOU'RE GOING TO MISS YOUR FLIGHT. Although—"

"Don't say it," she snapped. She was currently lying, belly down, across the top of her overstuffed suitcase in order to make the edges meet. "I think I'm going to be over the weight limit."

"Take everything out but the sexy underwear," advised her

cousin and best friend, Liz Thorne-Xuereb. "Or let me cast a spell to lighten the case."

"I don't have any sexy underwear." Piper willfully ignored the spell comment. She'd be damned if she would use magic for anything she didn't classify as an emergency. To do otherwise would be an abuse of power as far as she was concerned. Of course, her attitude wasn't popular among her family, who used magic with the speed of a ravenous chocoholic consuming bonbons.

Damn, she could really go for some lemon-buttercream chocolates to temper her traveling anxiety right about now.

"*At all?*" Liz screeched, pulling her back into the conversation. Her cousin was clearly appalled that a single woman wouldn't have the basics.

Heat crept up Piper's neck. "Well, I *do*, but not packed. It's *Ireland*, Liz. People dress in layers over there."

"Sure, but eventually they have to strip down—if you know what I mean. And thermal long johns aren't a turn on. What happens when you meet a hot Irishman and take him back to your hotel?"

"It's a B&B, and I won't be bringing any men back to my room. In case you failed to remember, I'm on a dating hiatus for a while. It's called *vacation* for a reason."

"Need I remind you that I found Rafe while on vacation?"

"Rafe found you, and he was in Paris on *business*."

Liz shrugged as she rummaged through Piper's dresser, looking for sexy articles of clothing. "You say tomato, I say tomahto."

"I'm pretty sure you stole that line from him. Regardless, I've sworn off men."

"Irish women are hot, too. Really, anyone with an Irish accent would do."

"You *know* what I mean. And while I'm open to just about anything, it's doubtful I'll switch sides midlife. Seriously, I just need a break from the dating game." Piper snatched the underwear out of Liz's hands as she tried to add it to the suitcase. "Stop, or you really will make me late."

"Let's compromise. Take four matching sets."

"One."

"Three."

"Two and no thongs. I hate those things. They're little more than ass floss."

"Deal." Liz grinned triumphantly. "But if things get hot and heavy, I want a sex tape."

"Okay, *eww*, because you're my damned cousin. You're getting as bad as Mackenzie. Next thing you know, you'll be telling me you're into bondage." When Liz flushed the color of a ripe beet, Piper laughed. "I didn't know you had it in you!"

"It was only handcuffs," Liz retorted.

Piper arched her freshly waxed brows.

"All right, a blindfold, too. But that's all."

"Who was sporting the cuffs and blindfold? You or Rafe?"

"Rafe."

Tickled by the new carefree side of her cousin, Piper hugged Liz. "I'm so glad you found him. You deserved so much better than Franco."

"I still can't believe he stole my magic. Who *does* that?"

"Well, thankfully Rafe discovered his plan in time." She rounded up the last of her toiletries.

Liz cleared her throat, and Piper suspected it still stung her cousin's heart that her now-deceased boyfriend had tried to use her for nefarious purposes. "Enough with all the maudlin BS. Let's get this show on the road. Promise you'll FaceTime me from a local pub while you're sharing a drink with a local hottie."

Struggling against a laugh, Piper said, "I'm telling Rafe that he's not satisfying your urges if you're thinking about my sex life and hot Irishmen."

"Believe me, my woman's urges are completely taken care of—on every level." Rafe's sexy, slightly accented drawl came from the doorway and startled both of them.

Again, Liz flushed, and Piper was positive he spoke the truth. She sighed with the smallest hint of envy. Dark-brown hair, midnight-colored eyes, and six feet of sinewy body, Rafe was every woman's walking fantasy. However, he'd only had eyes for Liz from the day they reconnected a handful of years after their Paris meeting.

Feeling a bit warm herself, Piper returned to the bathroom to retrieve the last of her travel necessities. Once her carry-on was packed, she allowed Rafe to take both cases to the car. When he was out of earshot, she turned to Liz.

"You have to be the luckiest woman on the planet. Promise me I get him in your will should anything happen to you."

"Nope. I have a stipulation that he must mourn me forever. He's not allowed to find comfort with another woman."

"Now you're just being selfish."

They shared a laugh and headed out to join Rafe for the short ride to the airport.

After they arrived at the terminal, Rafe unloaded the cases from the truck and escorted Piper inside. "Remember, no taking candy from strangers. And any guy you're interested in has to provide you with a full name, date of birth, and some form of ID so I can scry and check him out. That way, we can avoid an incident like the last one."

Rafe was referring to Piper's shitty taste in men. Her crappy radar had failed to pick up on the fact her ex-boyfriend—a mortal one at that—was married with a baby on the way.

"Got it," Piper responded with a grin and a hug. "Thanks, Rafe."

"Be safe and call us when you get settled. Liz and I want to know when you arrive, okay? Although, why you don't teleport is beyond me." He glanced around and lowered his voice. "Don't use the name Thorne. Lie if you have to. It isn't safe to bandy about that name when you are on your own, even in this day and age."

"I'll be plain old Piper Kelly. I plan to vacation like a normal person. And I promise to let you both know when I arrive."

Rafe shook his head. "This crazy need of yours to be 'normal' baffles me. We're magical beings. You should embrace your heritage."

It was an old argument between her and her family. It seemed

Rafe had taken their side. No one would ever understand. In a family full of the most powerful witches on the planet, Piper got lost. Not bothering to answer, she kissed his cheek and hugged Liz.

Two and a half hours later, Piper was boarded and on her way to Ireland for her much-needed dream vacation. Two weeks in the Emerald Isle with nothing to do but enjoy the countryside, eat fish and chips, and listen to Irish folk bands play in local pubs. No corporate crap, no IT problems popping up from employees who could barely log into their email accounts. Most importantly, no running into her ex-boyfriend at work or his pregnant wife at their hometown supermarket.

Piper would take the time to lick her wounds and formulate a new plan for a family of her own. Perhaps it was time to rule out a lifelong mate and go with artificial insemination. That way, she would be able to pick a sperm donor based on genetics and brains instead of waiting for Mr. Wrong to come along for what seemed like the millionth time. Goddess willing, by this time next year, she planned to be a mom. It didn't get more normal than that, right?

The idea had a soft smile forming on her lips. The thought of holding her own newborn close and rocking him or her to sleep made Piper's heart ping. All she'd ever wanted was a family to love. At thirty-three, her biological clock wasn't only ticking; it was setting off alarms on an hourly basis.

But first, she'd take one last vacation before her world would be forever altered by a baby. Afterwards, her life wouldn't be her own, and she intended to live it up on this holiday while she still could.

CIAN O'MALLEY DIDN'T MISS MUCH. FROM EARLY ON, HE'D TRAINED himself to gauge the energy of the pub's patrons and work the room. From his position on stage, he noted the stranger among the standard Friday-night crowd. He caught sight of the black-haired beauty the moment she stepped into his pub. Her light honey eyes were bright with excitement, and he immediately recognized that she wasn't from around these parts. Mainly because he knew almost everyone who was. He also recognized the magical glow around her. With such a bright, blinding aura, she had to be a witch —a powerful one at that. If he was mistaken, he'd eat his microphone.

As he picked out a lively tune and sang about a love gone wrong in a way only the Irish could, he tracked her with his eyes. Before this night was out, he intended to not only know her name but also steal a kiss from those glossy, beguiling lips of hers.

His sister Bridget served the stranger a Guinness, and he nearly laughed at the face the woman made upon taking her first sip. A pint of plain wasn't for the faint of heart. But he had to give her credit for trying the dark brew.

The noise of the room abruptly faded away, and her American accent drifted to where he sat. As he transitioned from one song to the next, he watched his new obsession laugh and flirt with some of the other male patrons. Aye, he'd be settling up with those plonkers later for making time with the woman Cian had mentally claimed as his own.

Soon enough, his set was finished, and he made his way through the swell of customers and friends slapping him on the back. When he was less than five feet from her, the dark-haired siren turned her merry eyes upon him. It was as if lightning struck at that moment, and Cian found it impossible to catch his breath. His only consolation was her own dumbstruck expression. She felt the connection as well.

Good to know he wasn't the only fool for love.

"Well, hello, darlin'. I see you've been enjoyin' yerself in me pub." He laid the accent on thick because American women turned to mush after hearing his honeyed Irish tongue.

With sparkling eyes, she asked, "Your pub? So you're *the* O'Malley in Lucky O'Malley's Pub?"

"One of them. Cian O'Malley at your service, darlin'. And whom do I have the pleasure of speakin' with in turn?"

"Piper Kelly."

"Ah, to be sure, you must be a good Irish *cailín* with a name like Kelly."

Her laughter was as golden as her aura. The sound reached in and grabbed him by the nads, making him lose all sense of up or down.

"Does this…" She made a swirling gesture with her hand around his mouth. "…actually work to help you pick up women?"

He placed his palm flat over his heart. "You wound me, darlin'. You surely do."

"Uh-huh." She sounded doubtful, but his soon-to-be woman had a twinkle in her eye, which clearly indicated she liked his suffering.

"Put a man out of his misery and run away with me, why don't ya?"

"I'm sure your wife wouldn't appreciate that." She gestured with her thumb over her shoulder to Bridget, who stood behind the bar, giving him the evil eye.

"Bridget isn't my wife, love. She's my sister. And the look she's gracing us with is because she's vexed I'm passing time with you and not servin' up these louts hangin' about me bar."

"Pull on your wellies, lads," Bridget called out. "It's about to get deep in here because Cian intends to rabbit on in hopes of catching a ride!"

"Ride?" Piper questioned just before taking a sip of her pint.

He mentally debated the merits of honesty when the ginger-haired Seamus, sitting on the stool beside her, spoke up and beat him to the punch. "Shag. Cian's hopin' to shag ye."

Guinness sprayed the air as Piper choked on her drink. Seamus earned a dark glare from Cian as he snatched up a dry bar towel to mop the beer from his face.

"Dry up this mess and don't be annoying me, Seamus, or you'll be finding yourself out on your arse," Cian growled and threw down the damp towel.

"Jaysus, Cian! Don't be hasty," Seamus exclaimed, rushing to comply. "It was Bridget who said it."

"And it was *you* who were repeating it, you feckin' eejit."

"Is this always the way you woo women?" Piper asked.

Her grin was as bright as the morning sun on a clear summer day, and Cian found himself soaking up its warmth.

"If we're being honest, no. I'm much more smooth and charming."

"Good to know you weren't banking on your looks alone."

Although they were in a crowded place, Cian only had eyes for this lone woman. The tilt of her head and the half smile still lingering on her lips fascinated him. She was, without a doubt, flirting in return. Ah, the sight of her sped up his heart. It truly did.

"Love, I have a bet with a few of me mates." He laid it on thick, but he was savvy enough to recognize she was enjoying their exchange. "It's a well-known fact that me boyos look up to me in these parts."

"Uh-huh." She sounded cynical but amused. "So what's this bet?"

"Well, it's more of a tradition, really," he lied. "I'm forced to kiss all the new colleens who stroll into me pub."

"*Forced* to?"

"Aye, and if I can win a kiss from the fairest of women—that be you—I'd be a living legend in these parts."

"Still not seeing where the bet part of this comes in."

"I bet me boyos that you'd take mercy on me and bestow the kiss to end all kisses."

"Interesting. When exactly did you make this bet? Because since I've been here, you've been on stage or here beside me."

Cian could see his sister smirk from the corner of his eye. The pub had grown quiet to watch the interplay between Piper and him.

"She has you there, Cian!" someone hollered.

"It's implied," Cian informed her without missing a beat, ignoring his heckler.

Her left brow practically shot to her hairline, and she bit one corner of the plump lip he was dying to sample.

"One taste, darlin'. That's all I'm hoping for. Then I can die a happy man," he said softly.

"Who am I to stand in the way of tradition?"

He wasn't sure he heard her correctly, but he didn't give her a chance to change her mind. Swooping in, hands cupping her exquisite face, he claimed his prize. When their lips connected, warning bells sounded in his brain. This long-legged dream of a woman was dangerous to his well-being.

Her arms went around his neck, and her fingers wound their way through his hair. Her light caress of his scalp sent desire ricocheting through his entire body. He tightened his hold on her, and had his eyes been open, he'd have closed them in ecstasy. Hoots and catcalls sounded around them, but Cian was damned if he could sever their connection.

Until a cold blast of water from his right side dampened his ardor.

"Bridget, you she-devil!" he swore.

"Stop mauling the customers and get back to strumming. We have a pub to entertain."

"Oh, you can be sure we were entertained, *mo ghrá!*" A male voice called out from a table in the far back reaches of the pub.

"I'm not your love, Ruairí O'Connor. And you'd best be remembering your manners in my pub."

"I'd be your everything if you'd let me, Bridg," Ruairí returned.

"Pfft." She rolled her eyes. "Right. Me and every other woman within a hundred-kilometer radius." Bridget winked in Piper's direction. "Don't believe any of these wankers, girl. They delight in pulling your leg. My brother Cian is the worst of the lot. You're the fifth woman he's hit on this week."

Piper turned disappointed eyes on him but didn't look surprised.

Cian felt a tightening in his chest and scowled his sister from where he stood behind Piper. "Now, don't be spreading tales, Bridget. You'll have my darlin' Piper believing the worst of us." He swept aside the hair from Piper's neck and leaned in to whisper. "Ignore her. She's out to kick a man in the bollocks on her best day. Will you stick around for my next set? I'll dedicate a song to you."

"It's been a long day. Maybe next time," she demurred, apology heavy in her voice.

Although it sounded as if she'd like nothing better than to hang out for another beer and to flirt with him, she also looked like she was on her last leg.

"Are you stayin' local?"

She nodded. "For a few days."

"Good. I'll walk you back to your hotel."

"No need, I'm only right next door at the B&B."

"Humor me."

The steely tone caused her frown and most likely had her wondering where his charming Irish accent had gone. She was clever enough to realize he laid it on a little thicker for the tourists, and Cian surmised it was why she didn't say anything.

"You can trust him to walk you to your room, Piper," Bridget assured her as she built another Guinness at the tap. "He knows if he disappears on me, there'll be the devil to pay." Addressing Cian, Bridget warned, "Five minutes. Any longer, and I'll come for you myself."

Seamus snorted and said, "Five minutes? More than three be one too many for Cian."

Cian shoved him off the barstool.

Seamus had the reflexes of a cat, and the man didn't spill a drop of his beer. "What? I was meaning to get into the gal's—"

Cian clamped a hand over Seamus's mouth. "I ken what you were meaning. You'd do well to shut your pie hole, Seamus McCleary." He released his drunk friend with a second none-too-gentle shove. "He's cut off."

"Ye got a mean streak as wide as—"

"Not another word, Seamus," Cian growled.

"You've wasted two of your five minutes, brother."

"Come on, love. I don't want you to be a witness to murder."

Cian placed his hand on Piper's lower back and guided her toward the door. A current of sorts passed between them, shocking him, and he sent her a sharp glance to see if she'd experienced the same.

She appeared unfazed.

A simple touch had never set him off before. Dry-mouthed, he held his own council and silently walked with her toward the building next door.

"You handled that well," she said as he strolled beside her.

Surprised, he stopped and stared. His laughter, when it started, was deep and boomed out across the night. The sound carried and seemed to echo forever. He reached for her hand and placed a lingering kiss on her fingertips. "Come, let's get you home."

Order Pints & Potions Today!

***

Books in The Thorne Witches Series:
SUMMER MAGIC
AUTUMN MAGIC
WINTER MAGIC
SPRING MAGIC
REKINDLED MAGIC
LONG LOST MAGIC
FOREVER MAGIC
ESSENTIAL MAGIC
MOONLIT MAGIC